METAMORPHOSIS

METAMORPHOSIS

BOOK II: THE COCOON STORY CONTINUES

DAVID SAPERSTEIN

TALOS PRESS

To my Mother and Father

Celia and Louis Saperstein

who taught me to reach for the stars,

and must surely travel among them now.

And to the four women who took my creation, my baby

COCOON, and helped it grow and become...

Susan Schulman

Meg Blackstone

Melinda Jason

Lili Fini Zanuck

Other books by David Saperstein

Cocoon – Book I of The Cocoon Trilogy

Butterfly: Tomorrow's Children – Book III of The Cocoon Trilogy

Fatal Reunion

Red Devil

Dark Again (With George Samerjan)

A Christmas Visitor

A Christmas Passage (With James J. Rush)

A Christmas Gift

Table of Contents

THROUGHOUT THE UNIVERSE WE TRAVEL
LIGHT-YEARS SEPARATE OUR WAKING TIME
SEPARATE OUR WAKING TIME
AND KEEPING TO A COURSE
THAT SEEKS OUT LIVING BEINGS
BRINGING FORTH OUR MESSAGE TO
MANY LIVING THINGS WE DO

TRAVELERS ON THE MILKY WAY
WHO KNOWS WHAT WE'LL FIND TODAY

—"Throughout the Universe"
Written by Joe Messina and David Saperstein, from the musical *Blue Planet, Blue*

FIVE THOUSAND YEARS AGO...

The lost continent we now call Atlantis was colonized by space-faring Antareans as a diplomatic and trading center in this part of our galaxy. When they learned that a comet would destroy the base, a number of Antareans, a diplomatic army, were left behind in sealed "cocoons" under the sea while the rest of the colony was evacuated.

FIVE YEARS AGO...

An Antarean Mothership, parked on the dark side of the moon, sent a Probeship down to Earth with a recovery team to evaluate the status of their cocoons and then begin the rejuvenation process that would restore the sleeping Antarean army.

The human beings on Earth had advanced, and although Antares Quad Three (Atlantis) was gone, a thriving civilization now occupied the land near the hidden cocoons. South Florida had become a gathering place for older humans who, after active and productive lives, moved, sometimes reluctantly, to this warmer climate.

The Antareans set up a processing facility in a partially completed condominium complex that they had purchased. They enlisted the help of a young Earth dweller, Jack Fischer, a fishing charter boat captain, to help transport the daily load of cocoons raised from the ocean floor back to the mainland for processing at night.

Four male retirees, living in condos at the Antares complex, discovered the secret processing room that was not in use during the day. Thinking it a health spa that was part of the facilities of their condo, they used the equipment and thus began an irrevocable metamorphosis that, unbeknownst to the men, prepared them mentally and physically for travel in deep space.

The Antareans discovered that the unforeseen pollution of the air and oceans by human civilization had damaged the cocoons. They were unable to rejuvenate their army properly with the equipment they had brought to earth. At the same time they surprised the four old men who had been using their equipment and found that because of their advanced years the processing had transformed and rejuvenated their bodies and minds, adapting them perfectly for space travel.

A deal was struck. The older Earthmen and their wives located nine hundred thirty-three more old people like themselves who were willing to leave their now unrewarding life on Earth to travel in deep space, replacing the cocooned sleeping Antarean army. Thus the Geriatric Brigade, as the seniors called themselves, was created.

In a wild land and sea chase with the Coral Gables police and United States Coast Guard, the last of the brigade slipped over the side of Jack Fischer's boat, the *Manta III*, and swam to the ocean floor and boarded the secreted Antarean Mothership. The spacecraft departed, leaving Jack and the bewildered group of pursuers behind. As the huge Antarean Mothership soared away into deep space, a silent message was beamed back to the sleeping Antarean cocoons: "We love you…" And then…

FIVE MINUTES AGO...

A heavy rainstorm moved across south central Florida, stalling just east of Miami Beach. All small craft activity along the entire east coast from Key West to West Palm Beach was halted. The storm intensified, closing airports and interrupting all outdoor activity.

Under cover of the storm's thick gray thunderheads and heavy downpour, a small Antarean Probecraft landed and submerged at the mouth of the Red Lake Canal in Coral Gables. Aboard were four Earth humans who had once lived in Florida and one Antarean, the commander of the previous mission that had taken nine hundred forty-one Earth dwellers into deep space.

This small advance group had returned to the Geriatric Brigade's mother planet to prepare the way for some others who had been away from Earth for five years, and to plan the rescue of the hidden cocooned Antarean army.

Their mission, and the decisions they would have to make in the near future, would affect the future of the Earth-human race.

CHAPTER ONE
WHERE'S JACK?

Sheets of rain swept across the lush fairway, sending the last of the diehard golfers scurrying for shelter in their brightly colored personal golf carts. Jack Fischer watched the fleeing hackers with amusement from his vantage point behind the fabled eleventh green of the Boca Raton Golf and Tennis Spa. Most homes in this part of South Florida boasted a Florida room—a swimming pool and patio area totally enclosed, walls and roof, with fine screening that allowed the warm weather in but kept the insect hordes out. Jack had designed his Florida room so that a portion of it was covered by a solid roof section. Thus he was always able to find shade, no matter how sunny the day.

As the rain hammered down and the wind gusted, Jack peered out and grew momentarily concerned about the stability of the plastic bubble that covered his tennis court. He had built the court and then enclosed it in a pressurized air-conditioned bubble so that he could play in comfort, no matter what the weather. It looked like it was withstanding the storm's fury. Sitting back on his chaise, Jack sipped a mimosa and flipped channels on the portable color TV until he found the local news. After watching a story about yet another drug-related killing, followed by hollow, heartening words from the Federal Drug Enforcement Agency that they were "winning the war on drugs in South Florida," Jack perked up because the weather report was next. If it was at all positive, he planned to visit with his friend Phil Doyle, who ran a sport fishing charter boat out of the Boynton Beach Marina. They had made plans to go out that afternoon, but as the

1

weather showed no sign of breaking the fishing would have to wait for another day.

The weatherman began his report. He told the TV audience that it was raining. Then he spent the next five minutes giving weather reports for the entire United States, including, Jack Fischer mused, the temperature in Oregon. The TV meteorologist, who egotistically put "Doctor" in front of his name, again announced that it was raining in South Florida. He gave the current local temperatures in Miami, Fort Lauderdale and West Palm Beach, and told the news anchor that he hoped for a better forecast on the evening program. Jack lifted his glass of orange juice and champagne in a toast. "Now that was one hell of a forecast!" But then again, he mused, they never give a weather forecast in Florida, only a current report that anybody could know by just looking out the window. Perhaps it was against the rules of the Florida Chamber of Commerce. He got up, turned off the TV and stared out at the rain.

Jack had been uneasy all day, attributing it to the depressing weather that had persisted for two days. But there was something more to this feeling than just the weather. At times, during the past five years, after the fabulous adventure he had shared with the Antareans, a sensation of thoughts, voices inside his mind, would come over him. It was as though Amos Bright, the Antarean leader, and some of the old people who had gone off into space as the Geriatric Brigade were calling to him, actually speaking and greeting him from across the vast galactic void. The contacts were always done with love. Although Jack had never quite mastered the art of telepathing his own thoughts, he was able to receive thoughts from others. It was comforting to know, or at least imagine, that his old friends were safe and that from time to time they thought about him.

But today the feeling was different. It was close. Very strong. "Ah, well," he sighed aloud, "they promised to come back for me one day and that ain't anything shabby to look forward to."

Keeping the secret of the Antareans and the Geriatric Brigade had been difficult. He was the first Earth-human to have contact with be-ings from another planet, yet he could say nothing about it. He lifted

2

his glass toward the leaden sky and, draining the sweet orange fluid, thought a silent loving toast to his faraway friends.

At the same time, Ben Green and Joe Finley strolled through the main entrance of the now completed Antares condominium complex. They smiled inside, telepathing to one another rapidly, excitedly.

"I remember it all, Ben."

"Like yesterday. But look how it's changed."

"Yeah. They actually finished the place."

"Can you imagine living here now? Being retired, sitting by the pool, playing gin…"

"Dying of leukemia?" Joe Finley joked, recalling how the Antarean processing cured him. As they walked toward the A Building, passing the pool area, their minds filled with memories of their last days on Earth.

"Pool's filled," Ben remarked, remembering the battle they'd had with the feisty manager, Ralph Shields, when they tricked him into getting the pool filled and operating. Joe Finley glanced over at the B Building.

"It's finished." Ben Green stopped to check out the high-rise condominium that was just a shell when they'd left, partially constructed and sheltering the Antarean processing room that Ben, Joe, Art Perlman and Bernie Lewis had accidentally discovered. It was in that room, using the Antarean equipment they mistook for a health spa, that their own metamorphosis had taken place, forever changing them, expanding their minds and rejuvenating their aging bodies so that they could become the first Earth-human deep-space travelers.

"The place looks good," Joe remarked. "Neat."

"That it does, my friend. But way too small for our purposes this time."

"That, Commander Green, is the understatement of the year!"

The rain began to let up and the sky brightened. Jack tried to telephone Phil Doyle at the Boynton Marina, but the storm had downed telephone lines and he couldn't get through. He wandered into the darkened house with a slight buzz from his fourth mimosa sans food. The air was clammy. As Jack went to kick up the air conditioner he passed his bedroom and heard the sound of running water. The hot tub was being filled. Cathy was still there. He went into the bedroom that he had decorated like a South Sea Island hut. The ceiling was thatched grass. The carpeting, a soft mat covered with faux animal skins. And the furniture was all rattan and bamboo. His king-size waterbed was placed in the center of the room, covered with a false zebra skin duvet and white silk pillows. Underneath, black silk sheets added the final touch of fantasy. Cathy Chung, a Eurasian of exceptional beauty and sexual prowess, sat in the redwood hot tub that was set off to the right side of the bedroom, surrounded by floor-to-ceiling sliding glass doors that looked out onto a secluded Japanese garden. She was nude. Her long, tapered legs stretched across the tub and were barely covered with the foamy water as it rushed in around her. She waved to Jack, beckoning him to join her.

"I thought you went home," he said, slipping out of his flowered shorts. "Want a drink?" He held up his mimosa. She shook her head and arched her back as the water rose. Her breasts, showing their large round, dark aureoles surrounding soft brown nipples seemed to float in the steamy water. "Jesus, you're gorgeous," Jack muttered to himself as he kicked his shorts away, picked up his drink and headed for the tub. At that moment Cathy slipped under the water and her long straight dark hair, more than shoulder length, spread out, floating like a black silk fan. Although they had spent the night together, Jack was aroused by the time he stepped into the hot tub. As he reached for Cathy she grabbed his erection from under the water with both hands, pulling gently. He had no choice but to slip under the water with her as his mimosa's orange liquid blended with the bubbly warm water.

While Jack Fischer played and frolicked, Ben Green and Joe Finley entered the Antares condominium manager's office. A bright young secretary greeted them politely.

"May I help you gentlemen?"

"We'd like to speak to the owner."

"You mean the manager. This is a condo. It's owned by the, ah, occupants. You know, like retired people."

"Okay. Then the manager."

"There are no units available now." She reached for a clipboard with papers attached. "But if you'd like to fill out an application some-one will contact you. We have several other properties and..." Ben cut her short.

"I'm sure you do, sweetheart, but we're interested in talking to the manager."

"He's not here."

"What's his name?" Joe Finley asked.

"Mr. Parker."

"Wally the Wonderful," Ben quipped. Joe laughed, recalling the battles they had fought five long years ago with Shields, the original manager of the condos, and Wally Parker, who was just the mainte-nance director at that time. In the end both men had fought a pitched battle with each other that resulted in Parker being hospitalized and Shields jailed. It had all been a setup to distract them away from the processing room in the B Building.

"I beg your pardon?" the secretary said.

"Just a private joke. What about Mr. Fischer? Jack Fischer?"

"Oh." She smiled. "Now I understand. No. He used to be the own-er, but when all the units were sold—that was even before me—like before I worked here? So he left. It was all like sold."

"Do you know where we might find him?" Ben asked pleasantly.

"No. I'm afraid I don't. He's somewhere up north..."

"New York?"

"No. Not that north. I mean like Lauderdale or Boca."

Ben and Joe thanked her and left. They would have to make an-other contact from the past—the trusted Coral Gables banker, John DePalmer. He had assisted Amos Bright in the original purchase of the Antares condos and had handled all the financial transactions for the visiting Antareans, although he never knew their real identity. When they had left Earth five years ago they signed over the complex to Jack Fischer. Ben and Joe reasoned DePalmer would know where to find Jack. But in order to get that information, Amos Bright would have to make an appearance at the bank himself. They telepathed that message to Amos and their wives, who were waiting for them in the submerged Antarean shuttlecraft. They would all meet at the bank in Coral Gables.

As they walked back through the grounds Ben and Joe glanced over at the pool again and took note of their old table where they had sat, boring day after boring day, playing gin with Bernie Lewis and Art Perlman, watching their lives slowly dwindle down toward the end. Or so they'd thought.

"A lifetime ago," Ben commented softly.

"Well, actually light years," Joe said. And that was true, for in the past five years they had traveled tens of thousands of light years through the galaxy, sampling portions of its wonders, meeting fascinating beings that populated the cosmos. And now they had returned to prepare the way for some of their fellow Earth-human space travelers who were returning to mother planet to act out a ritual that was as old as life itself.

Time was short. They had to find Jack Fischer and gather as much help as they could at the highest levels possible, but at the same time they knew their mission, while of the utmost urgency, had to remain a total secret. Public exposure now could cause a disaster.

CHAPTER TWO
A NEW RACE

When they had left Earth five long years ago, they had done so by choice. Nine hundred forty-one aged human souls chose to adapt their bodies for space travel and leave their home, their Earth, behind, perhaps forever. Some made the difficult choice of leaving families behind: grown children, grandchildren, great-grandchildren, sisters and brothers. They opted for a new and unknown life rather than live out the one they had on Earth with certain boredom and isolation in a society that venerated youth and physical appearance.

It was ironic that American culture attuned itself to physical fitness, diet and exercise in order to, among other things, live a longer and healthier life. When that was accomplished, however, when people did in fact live longer, they were shunted away to areas like Florida, Arizona and Southern California to "retire and live out their golden years."

The decision to leave Earth had to be made quickly by those who were fortunate enough to be approached by the organizers of the Geriatric Brigade, namely, Mary and Ben Green, Rose and Bernie Lewis, Alma and Joe Finley, and Bess and Arthur Perlman. But the secret had to be kept tight and secure. Those with families left letters behind, which Jack Fischer delivered personally. But for most—those who had been deserted, or put away in nursing homes, or left alone in the world to survive on meager pensions, Social Security or handouts, for the largest portion of the group—the decision involved only themselves. They would never be missed.

The Brigade was not an army to be trained for war. Rather it was to be used for education and training on other worlds. The initial mission was to go directly to Parma Quad 2, a large planet near the star we call Sirius the Dog Star.

The Parmans, a crystalline life form, had contacted the Antareans, and the Brigade was sent in answer. The Parmans, who had up to that point avoided contact with extraterrestrials, now wanted to venture into space. They offered a unique exchange: They would serve as navigators on Antarean spacecraft. Because they possessed the ability to draw energy from starlight, no matter how distant, they could lock on to any star and guide a craft to it. But more than that, they could convert the starlight to energy. The closer they drew to the star they focused on, the more energy they could convert, until space and time melded into one. The Antareans realized that with Parman guides on their ships they could finally achieve intergalactic travel.

The deal was struck and treaties entered into. But when the Antareans came to Earth to recover their cocoon army they found it damaged and unusable. It was then that they discovered older Earth dwellers could, because of the nature of the human aging process, be processed and transformed for space travel. Younger people, their bodies still aging and changing, could not take the processing. But nine hundred forty-one older Earth people leaped at the chance to become Earth's first space ambassadors.

As ambassadors they were among the best the Antareans had ever met. On the trip to Parma Quad 2, which would take several months, the Brigade adapted to their new life and newfound energy, while the Antareans aboard the Mothership educated them. The humans were eager and bright students. In particular, the eleven who had chosen to be commanders proved to have an exceptional ability to absorb and process information as rapidly as any Antarean commander might.

They all brought wisdom and an appreciation for life that the Antareans knew was rare in the known universe. Some thought it was a result of the processing itself, while others in the Antarean crew felt that the expanded human brain usage, from slightly more than ten percent of capacity to nearly ninety percent, was the reason for the abilities now exhibited as the Mothership hurtled toward Sirius and the Parman civilization.

The human commanders knew differently. Their race was oriented toward death as a fact of life. It was part of the deal, as Ben Green had told Amos Bright once. We are born and very shortly thereafter we learn we will die. Antareans were born under controlled conditions and died only when they chose to die, or if they were involved in some accident or disaster. An Antarean could live forever. A human certainly numbered his years and valued them. Now that mortality was changed forever.

Now aboard the Mothership was a new race, never before seen in space. And amazingly, with their new immortality, the humans grew in their compassion for others as they learned of distant worlds with very different, but at the same time, very human problems. They asked endless questions of their teachers about the suffering of other life forms in the galaxy.

Amos Bright and the other Antarean commanders aboard the Mothership were certain that their decision to invite these older Earth dwellers to join them had been a proper one. As Amos said to Beam, the female Antarean medical officer on the mission, "These Earth people are quite remarkable. They learn rapidly, but they always want to know more about the beings than the places. They have much love within them, and they want to share that with others."

"Perhaps we have brought them into space for another's purpose."

"You mean for the Master?"

"We all serve the Master. Perhaps He has willed that the time for these Earth people to join the rest of the universe has come. Perhaps they are needed."

"I feel that too. They will grow and come to understand much more than even we about the universe. They are a new race. I think we have been guided to bring them out from their planet to walk among others."

The Brigade had been welcomed by the Parmans. It was as if they knew that those they called integrators, those who would teach them about the known universe, would themselves be new to space travel. The two species got along famously, and the entire Parman orientation took less than two years. During that time several Antarean spaceships were adapted to use Parman guides in their propulsion and navigation systems.

When the orientation and integration process was completed, Parman guides were installed in the Antarean ships and, along with several human crew members, began expanded inter-galactic exploration. Many of the Geriatric Brigade chose to crew with the Antareans who regularly visited planets. Other served aboard Motherships that explored new planetary systems, while some stayed behind as permanent ambassadors to Parma Quad 2.

And so the Geriatric Brigade was scattered throughout our galaxy. Human influence was now and forever to be a part of the universal experience.

CHAPTER THREE
DOWN TO BUSINESS

The shopping center in Kendall was busy as the storm ended and gray skies gave way to patches of blue and sunshine. The mall parking lot showed signs of the rain, with several areas still badly flooded from poor drainage. Shoppers that the rain had kept away, honked and fought for parking spaces near the main mall entrance that was away from the flooded areas.

Ben Green and Joe Finley made their way cautiously through the parking lot toward the blue glass and ceramic tile building that housed the First Bank of Coral Gables. An elderly couple in a 1973 Cadillac Coupe DeVille that had seen better days raced through the lot toward a parking spot that was being vacated by another elderly couple in a new Buick LeSabre. Ben saw the Caddy pick up speed as another car, a 1982 Corvette convertible containing two teenage boys, headed for the same parking spot from the opposite direction. He reached over and pushed Joe Finley back as the Caddy roared into a flood pool of rainwater caused by the drain backup. A wall of spray spewed up into the air on both sides of the car, obscuring it from Ben and Joe's view. The splash was followed by the screeching of brakes as the Corvette tried to avoid the oncoming Cadillac that was now behaving more like a motorboat than an automobile. As the teenagers swerved away, their car, with the top down and the radio blasting irritating, monotonous punk rock, was deluged with warm dirty rainwater from the Caddy's wash. The two boys wound up stalled in the middle of the flood, soaking wet and cursing at the top of their lungs as the couple in the Cadillac slipped into the now empty spot, oblivious to the epithets being hurled at them by the teenagers.

"In some way I really miss Florida," Ben mused, observing the couple as they locked the car, gazed momentarily at the Corvette awash in muddy water above its hubcaps, and strolled toward Burdine's.

"Just some senior citizens asserting their rights out for an afternoon of shopping," Joe said as they approached the bank building, which was sandwiched in between Harvey's, a classy home furnishings store and Loehmann's, a women's discount dress shop.

"Amos must be here," Ben told his friend. "The girls are at it already." Joe Finley looked ahead and saw his wife, Alma, firmly planted in front of the furniture store window, while Ben's wife, Mary, was carefully studying the latest New York fashions in the dress shop window display.

"You can take the woman away from the shopping, but you can't take shopping out of the woman!" Ben laughed as they waved a greeting to their wives.

If John DePalmer was surprised to see Amos Bright, he kept it to himself. Even though five years had passed, he remembered with absolute clarity every transaction he had processed on behalf of Mr. Bright. Of course Mr. DePalmer had no idea that Amos was an extraterrestrial, although he did suspect the man was not your ordinary, run if the mill, entrepreneur.

At their first meeting Amos Bright had asked to speak to then Assistant Manager DePalmer in private. He handed the banker several million dollars worth of diamonds, that DePalmer had then taken to Amsterdam and Tel Aviv and sold for cash and a generous commission. He had also purchased the Antares condominium complex, then an unfinished construction project, for Mr. Bright. And he had staffed it, managed it and eventually sold it on behalf of the last owner, Jack Fischer, to whom Amos Bright had signed over the ownership. Now as his old business associate sat across the table in the bank's private conference room, DePalmer studied Amos and the two elderly couples with him.

"These past five years have treated you well, Mr. Bright. You don't look a day older than when we last met."

"I try to keep in shape. Let me introduce Mr. and Mrs. Green and Mr. and Mrs. Finley. They're good friends of mine. We have some business we'd like you to help us with. I assume that is if you're still able to, shall we say, approach things with perhaps some unorthodox methods."

DePalmer smiled and greeted the two couples. If only Mr. Bright knew how unorthodox things were now in South Florida. The banks were loaded with cash, mostly as a direct result of the drug traffic. But now that the federal government was cracking down on money laundering, the larger operators were moving their cash offshore, using the same "donkeys"—human carriers who brought drugs into the country and took millions of dollars in cash out. Recently twenty employees of a South American airline had been detained with more than seventy million dollars in cash on them collectively. Since the maximum amount allowed out of the country per person is ten thousand dollars, arrests were made and the money was confiscated. With that kind of pressure, DePalmer was sure that the major drug dealers would be seeking the bank's anonymity again in the near future.

In the past, John DePalmer had not been in a position to deal with drug money. Actually, he was not sure he could go through with it now if the opportunity presented itself. He had friends in the banking community who had laundered money for huge fees. They hid their profits in Swiss and Cayman accounts, but deep down they knew they belonged to the ruthless dealers they served. DePalmer was still his own man, but he wondered if he could resist. The interest rates had fallen, the condo market was overbuilt and oversold, depositors had withdrawn huge sums to seek better returns through the stock and bond markets and he had several marginal loans that were now in doubt. Business wasn't great, and his bosses were down on him, pressing for a better bottom line.

As those thoughts raced through DePalmer's mind they were read by Amos and his four companions who were commanders. They silently approved of DePalmer's honesty and agreed to help the man as best they could.

"We have two things we'd like to accomplish today, John," Amos began. "The first is to locate Jack Fischer."

"That's no problem. I speak to him from time to time. Nice young man, although with all his wealth I think he should make more growth investments than he does."

"Living the good life, is he?" Ben Green asked.

"Very much so. Wine, women and song, as the expression goes. Not to tell tales out of school. I like the young man. He just seems so lost…so aimless."

"Well," Alma Finley said, "maybe we've come along at the right time. I think we've got a business proposition for him that he just can't refuse." They all smiled. DePalmer laughed nervously.

"Let me give you his address and phone number. It's unlisted, but I'm sure he'd want Mr. Bright to have it." DePalmer wrote both down on a white pad, tore off the paper and handed it to Amos. "You said two things, Mr. Bright."

Amos reached for the small leather case he'd kept tucked under his arm and placed it on the table. He unzipped it, opened the first compartment and withdrew a thin black Lucite box placing it on the table. He looked up at DePalmer.

"I still like to use the same currency we began our business dealing with," he said as he opened the box, revealing more than fifty Class-D, blue-white, six-carat diamonds, each worth more than fifty thousand dollars on the wholesale market.

"They're beautiful. And perfect as usual?" DePalmer asked.

"Yes. We'd like to sell these, wherever you think best, open a few accounts, obtain some credit cards and the services of a first-rate travel agent."

"I can arrange that," DePalmer said as Amos Bright slid the case of diamonds across the table to him. He looked down at the stones just one more time and then snapped the box shut. "We can open the accounts now and a complete line of credit. My estimate is at least two million, possibly two point five in today's market. Our corporate travel department will handle all your needs."

"Excellent," Amos answered, handing the banker a paper. "Each of us will want an account. These are the names. Divide the money evenly." He stood up as did the others. DePalmer knew the meeting was over.

"If there is anything else you need, Mr. Bright…anything…I am at your disposal. You still have my home number?"

"Yes. We'll be in touch. Thank you, Mr. DePalmer."

They left after the accounts had been opened. Amos returned to the submerged spacecraft to advise those on Antares that the mission was well underway.

Mary Green headed for Miami Airport to catch a flight to New York. It had been more than five years since she had seen her daughter, Patricia Keane, and her three grandchildren. A reunion with them was a joy she had anticipated from the moment they'd left Earth. Her reunion would also be be a test to see how a family might react to a returning space traveler. Their acceptance of her story would affect others who wanted to…who had to return themselves.

Alma Finley hired a car and driver to take her to the Fort Lauderdale airport, where she would get the first flight out to Washington, D.C. She was going to call on an old friend and ex-boss from the days when she was an editor for NBC network television news. Caleb Harris was now the Washington Bureau Chief for the entire NBC news network. Alma hoped that she could convince Caleb that her fantastic story was true, and use his influence to arrange a meeting with the President of the United States.

At the same time Ben Green and Joe Finley, having rented a car, drove north on I-95 toward Boca Raton for their own meeting with an unsuspecting Jack Fischer. Jack was about to be folded back into the world of Antarean visitors from outer space and the Geriatric Brigade he'd helped to organize, process and depart Earth five years ago.

CHAPTER FOUR
TENACIOUS DETECTIVES

While Ben and Joe made their way along the crowded Interstate, Jack Fischer was saying goodbye to Cathy Chung in the driveway. He helped her put down the tattered roof of her bright orange VW Beetle.

"It's gonna clear up," he said, looking at the fleeting rain clouds as they gave way to patches of blue.

"Then you'll be fishing with Doyle, huh?"

"I think so." He opened the door on the driver's side for her. She started to get in, then stopped and gave him a long, tender kiss.

"You're a sweet man, Jack Fischer. Sweet but flighty."

He laughed as she jumped into the car, started the little engine and backed out of his driveway, gears grinding and brakes squealing.

"I'll call you," he shouted after her, knowing his words were lost in the air rushing around her oval face and long black hair as it fluttered in the wind. "Later…" Jack turned and went back into the house to try to reach Phil Doyle again.

A block away, parked under a drooping poinsettia tree, Detective Sergeant Matthew Cummings, serving out his last year with the Dade County sheriff's office before retirement, sat in his Olds Cutlass munching on a half-filled box of Fruit Loops. When the Oriental girl in the orange VW drove past him he slid down in the driver seat to hide. Cathy was concentrating on an old Stones tune and noticed nothing. After she passed Cummings put aside his snack and attentively watched Jack's house.

The ritual of spying on Jack Fischer had been a part of Detective

Cummings's life for nearly four years, ever since all charges against Jack, regarding the strange disappearance of scores of old people from the South Miami area, had been dropped.

The worst part of Cummings's frustration was that he, along with several Coast Guard vessels and helicopters, had chased Jack Fischer's and Phil Doyle's boats, loaded with old people, out toward the open sea in an area known as the Stones. It was obvious that the old people were being tossed into the sea, but when the police and Coast Guard had tried to stop them and make an arrest, their vision had somehow been obscured, the helicopters had malfunctioned and, except for Cummings, no one seemed to have a clear memory of what had happened.

When the area was cleared the old people were gone. Fischer and Doyle were there, outriggers spread with bait in the water as they fished the calm night sea. Above them, unnoticed, an Antarean Mothership loaded with hundreds of volunteer human senior citizens was but a flashing speck in the Florida night sky as the most fantastic human experience ever recorded, travel into deep space, had begun.

Cummings had pressed charges against Fischer and Doyle—kidnapping, transporting illegals, smuggling and even murder. There were people missing, but no evidence they had been on Jack's or Phil's boat. The eyewitnesses, mostly Coast Guard pilots and sailors, could not swear that they had seen these old people aboard. It was all confusing and vague in the pursuers' minds. They had been in sight of two sport-fishing vessels, the *Manta III* and the *Razzamatazz,* and a small helicopter. The weather became foggy and an electrical disturbance caused their instrumentation to go haywire. Divers found no evidence and no one could actually confirm that the fanciful story that Cummings told to the Coral Gables district attorney was true.

Jack Fischer, Phil Doyle and Madman Mazuski, the helicopter pilot who swore he was fish spotting for Jack and Phil, were brought in and questioned. The Antares condominium complex was in Jack Fischer's name, and he was a man of financial means. He hired a top lawyer and things quickly cooled down.

Eventually, in an embarrassing confrontation in the DA's office, Sergeant Cummings testified about old people jumping over the side in an act of mass suicide. His credibility became strained when he went on to talk about a huge underwater craft that emerged from beneath the sea just as a dense fog suddenly appeared. The DA rolled his eyes and looked at Jack's lawyer apologetically. When the Dade County detective insisted that this was a "spaceship that took off into the sky" the DA halted testimony and asked to speak to Cummings alone. A week later the charges were dropped. Cummings was assigned to a desk for a year, along with his partner, Coolridge Betters.

But whenever he could, especially while Jack lived at the Antares complex, Cummings kept an eye on him, convinced that the greatest mass murder in the history of the nation had taken place. He believed that Jack Fischer and his two cohorts were responsible. After the condos were sold and Jack moved to Boca Raton, Cummings would still make the long trip north whenever he could. Someday, he swore to Betters, these killers would make a mistake, and he would be there to nail them.

Something in the air, a tingle down his spine, told Cummings that today might be that day. Moments later, as Ben Green and Joe Finley pulled into Jack's driveway and got out of their car, the disgraced detective knew his vindication was at hand.

"I'll be goddamned," he gasped, sliding down out of sight once again, his balding head and bloodshot brown eyes barely visible above the dashboard. "It's two of those old farts that were on Fischer's boat. They jumped over the side, but they're back. Alive. It's going down again. I can feel it. Okay, you old murdering farts, this time I'm gonna be ready for you!"

Ben and Joe heard Cummings's thoughts. They made a mental note to deal with him later. Right now they had more pressing business with their old friend, Jack Fischer. As they approached the front door, Jack hung up the phone. He had reached Phil and told his friend he'd be at the dock in a half hour. Something turned him around as he walked to his bedroom to dress for fishing. Something pulled him toward the front door; then the doorbell rang. He shuddered and slowly opened the door. Before he saw them, he knew who was there.

Ben Green smiled broadly across his ageless face. "Hello, Jack. How the hell are you?"

"Good to see you again," Joe Finley added quickly, extending his hand in greeting.

"Oh my God!" Jack knew they were there, but he couldn't believe it. "Is it really… are you two who I think you are… who I know you are?"

"In the flesh," Ben answered.

"May we come in?" Joe asked, feeling Cummings's inquisitive eyes burning a hole in his back.

"Sure… sure. Christ, you guys look great!" The two men stepped into the house. Jack closed the door and stared at them. "I never thought I'd see you guys again. Well, not so soon anyway. So, how is everyone? Jesus, you've actually been out there? What's it like? Where did you go? How's Amos and Beam… and…" He stopped abruptly, realizing that he was babbling and the two old men were staring at him with broad grins.

"Let's sit down, Jack," Joe suggested, "and we'll tell you everything."

They went into the living room, and as the two older men sat on a white silk couch Jack went to the bar and poured himself a stiff scotch on the rocks.

"You guys want one?" he asked.

"No thanks," Ben said.

"Maybe a beer?" Joe asked. "It's been a while since I had a cold brew."

"No beer out there, huh? Sounds like a good business to open." Jack reached into the bar refrigerator. "Heineken?"

"Perfect."

He brought the beer over to the couch and settled in an easy chair nearby, taking a slug of his scotch.

"You live alone?" Joe asked, taking a long draw on the frosty green bottle.

"Still a bachelor."

"What about Judy?" Ben asked.

"Judy? Oh, Judy Simmons. Yeah… show biz. She did these commercials and someone in New York saw them and made her a great offer. I haven't talked to her in… God, almost two years. I heard she was in Los Angeles doing TV."

"She was a nice girl. How's your brother?" Ben asked.

"Arnie's fine. He and Sandy moved to Atlanta last year. They have a little girl and another on the way." Jack smiled at the two men, reading their thoughts, knowing what was coming next. "I can hear you guys thinking. I never forgot how to do that, uh, telepathing thing."

Joe put down his beer and fixed his gaze on Jack. "So are you?"

"Lonely? I guess so. Since we finished the B Building and sold it all off there isn't anything for me to do down at the condos. But I keep busy. I fish with Phil on the *Terra Time*. I gave him that boat. I still have the old *Manta III*—can't bring myself to part with the old bucket." Jack had drained his scotch. He stood up to get another. "It's really something…you guys just walking in like this." He reached the bar fully aware that both men were concentrating on him and blocking their thoughts from the Jack's telepathic abilities.

Jack had been a struggling charter boat captain in Coral Gables. The Antareans, disguised as humans, had enlisted his boat and his help in locating, raising and processing their cocoons—special casings containing Antarean soldiers in suspended animation, who were left behind thousands of years before when the continent we call Atlantis was destroyed by a huge passing comet.

The pollution in our oceans had damaged the cocoons and the Antarean rescue party was unable to revive them. It was at that time that Ben, Joe and two of their friends, Art Perlman and Bernie Lewis, discovered the Antarean processing room. Thinking it was a health spa and part of their condo's facilities, the four men used the equipment that changed them, their wives and the course of human history.

The Antarean cocoon-processing equipment, though deadly to young earth bodies, worked wonders on the aging humans. They were cleansed, strengthened and transformed into perfect specimens for deep-space travel. These four men became the core of the Geriatric Brigade—941 seniors, processed to replace the cocooned Antarean army.

Before their departure, the Antarean leader, Amos Bright, signed over the ownership of the Antares condominiums to Jack and promised to return for him one day when his body had aged sufficiently to be processed.

Now, five years later, as Jack sat with Ben Green and Joe Finley, he knew that although he had abused his body somewhat, it still was only thirty-five and decades away from using Antarean deep-space processing as his gateway to space travel and a long life.

"So you guys here for a visit? Vacation? Maybe pick up some back Social Security checks?"

"No," Ben began, "we're an advance party. Joe and I came with our wives and Amos Bright on a Probecraft. The others, well, some of the others are following on an Antarean Watership."

Joe Finley stood up and walked to the large picture window that faced out onto the golf course. Two elderly couples were playing the eleventh hole. Joe watched the ponderous, creaky golf swing of the man closest to the window. He was well into his seventies. The man's wife sat in their golf cart shouting words of encouragement and praise as his golf ball skittered along the plush fairway and stopped fifty yards ahead. Finley also noticed Detective Cummings hiding behind a hedge of newly planted brush bottle pines that bordered the fairway.

"Does that cop hang around here much?" he remarked as he turned back to Jack and Ben.

"Cop?"

"Cummings. From Coral Gables."

"The one who chased us that last night," Ben chimed in.

"Oh, that cop. Is he out there?"

"He's spying on us," Joe said.

"Yeah, well, he comes around now and then. He was a mess after you guys left. They arrested us, you know. Phil and me and the Madman. But they couldn't make anything stick. The Coast Guard guys were totally confused and then when old Cummings and his partner—what was his name?"

"Betters," Joe said quickly.

"Yeah, Coolridge Betters. Well, they both started yapping about kidnapping and mass murder. For a while it was a little sticky but DePalmer got me a first-class lawyer. Eventually old Cummings began to rant about you guys and the all the old folks going over the side and the Antareans and the Mothership, and well…"

"They certified him and dropped it all?" Ben said, smiling.

"Not certified. Just moved the poor guy to the back burner. He's over the hill. Retires soon, I think…" Jack then realized he was sitting in a room with two men, once over the hill retirees, who were considerably older than Cummings. He blushed. "Sorry about that, guys."

"That's okay. We've come to realize that over the hill is an earthly term. It's all relative." Joe smiled kindly at Jack.

"I can dig that. You guys look like you're gonna live forever."

"In a manner of speaking that might well be true," Ben remarked. "And if you recall, Amos promised to come back for you when your time came."

"I think about it every day."

"Good," Ben continued, "because now we need your help once again."

"If you guys want to use the condos again, that's a problem. They're all sold."

"No, Jack," Joe Finley said, sitting down next to the ex-charter captain, "the condo complex is way too small for our needs this time."

"This time we're going to need more than a few charter boats and a processing room," Ben added as he sat down on the other side of the young man, clapping his arm around Jack's shoulder. "And now I'm going to tell you the most wonderful story you ever heard."

Jack took just a moment out from listening to Ben and Joe to call Phil Doyle and say he would be by later with a big surprise. He then sat down between the two visitors and listened. When they finished, Jack sat silently for a long, reflective moment. Then a wide grin turned into laughter. He let out a joyful "whoopee" and danced around the room. "Guys! This is absolutely great! Fantastic! I'm with you all the way. When do we begin?"

Joe and Ben relaxed and smiled. "We already have," they said in unison.

CHAPTER FIVE
OH, MOTHER!

Mary Green's flight to New York's La Guardia Airport had been uneventful. There was a moment, however, shortly after takeoff from Miami International, when she realized that it had been years since she had put her life in the hands of beings other than the Antareans or the Parman guides. She sat, feeling the DC-10's powerful engines propel them forward, knowing that a human being was flying the airplane with a rather primitive technology compared to the transportation she had used for the past five years. The idea that she might lose her life in an earthly plane crash, no matter how remote the chance, drove home the adaptation she had made to life in deep space. She loved her life more now than she had ever imagined. Being back on Earth, in the relatively frail human aircraft, gave her a sense of mortality that she had not experienced for a long time.

At the same time Alma Finley was preparing to depart on her flight to Washington, D.C. from the Fort Lauderdale airport. The women communicated with one another, sending comforting thoughts about flying in the Earth's atmosphere. They had a good laugh about it. Still, each of the women monitored the cockpits on their flights, chiding one another for doing so, but feeling more at ease listening in on trouble-free communications from takeoff to landing.

By mid-afternoon, with the late spring sun nearly overhead, Mary Green walked along the peaceful, tree-lined street two blocks from her daughter's home in Scarsdale, New York. She had asked the taxi driver to drop her off a distance from the house so that she might approach it unnoticed.

23

Birds sang. A black squirrel chased a gray one across the street and up a ponderous oak. The only car that passed was a Mercedes station wagon carrying two preschool kids, a yellow Labrador retriever and a harried, young, affluent suburban mother. Mary's thoughts drifted back to another such tree-lined street where she and Ben Green had once lived in Westport, Connecticut, before they retired to Florida. It had been a good life, she mused. But then, in a very real sense, she had been reborn, and in these past five years she had walked down some very strange other-worldly streets tens of thousands of light years from here.

But this was her home planet—Mother Earth. It was May, warm and blooming—azaleas, rhododendron, the last of the tulips and the first of the marigolds. She breathed deeply of the sweet spring air whose perfume filled her expanded and enhanced brain with awakenings long forgotten. Her unabashed joy at being alive quickened her pace, moving her along quickly, until she was only a few short steps away from the home of her daughter, Patricia.

Mary hesitated, unsure of how it would be to suddenly appear after so many years, after such an abrupt departure. Ben had written the letter they had left behind for the immediate family. Jack Fischer had delivered it, as he had delivered all the other letters left behind by the members of the Geriatric Brigade who had families on Earth they cared about. So many had no one. So many had been abandoned or sent off to South Florida to live on inadequate Social Security or, in the worst cases, welfare. During their travels in space, as the members of the Brigade got to know one another, horror stories were related by many rejuvenated elderly space travelers of degrading treatment, neglect, and, for some, physical abuse.

But in the case of the Green family, things had been different. Theirs was a solid, loving family that supported one another. Mary was sure that after the initial shock of seeing her mother alive, Patricia Green Keane would welcome her with open arms.

In their letter to the family, Mary and Ben had written of their love for their children and grandchildren. They explained the great adventure they had been offered by the Antareans, the chance to live a long, full and useful life. Without knowing what really faced them in outer space, they had speculated on being among the first humans to meet beings from other planets in our galaxy, and how honored they felt to be chosen to walk among the stars. The letter was filled with love and kindness and a hope that the family would understand and be happy for Mary and Ben.

As Mary approached the large Tudor, set back from the street with the driveway hidden beyond a row of hedges, she noticed the front door of the house was open. She stopped and looked beyond the hedge to see her daughter unloading groceries from the rear of a new Volvo station wagon. The woman, a forty-year-old clone of her attractive seventy-two-year-old mother, lifted two packages and walked through an opening in the hedges toward the front door. Mary Green stood still.

For a moment, Patricia was frozen in her tracks, unwilling and unable to believe her eyes. Mary reached out to her daughter telepathically with comfort and love. "Yes," she thought, "it's me. I've come home." Pat dropped the groceries and flew across the neat, freshly cut lawn, weeping tears of joy, thrilled to overflowing that her mother was home.

The women embraced as Pat sobbed and laughed and cried, unable to let go, afraid that Mary was just an apparition that might vanish if she loosened her grip.

"Darling," Mary said after nearly a minute had passed. "I've come across our galaxy, over sixteen light years, to see you and you're squeezing the breath out of me."

"Oh… oh Mother," Pat said as she loosened her hold and stepped back, keeping her hands on Mary's shoulders. "It is you? Oh God, how we all missed you. Dad? Where's Dad? Is he okay?"

"He's just fine. He's in Florida. You'll see him soon. He sends his love."

"Mom! Oh God…" Pat could not contain her emotions. She embraced Mary again. Tears streamed down her tanned cheeks. A moment later, after Pat realized they were standing out in the street, both women walked hand in hand to retrieve the scattered groceries and then disappeared into the house to catch up on five years of separation.

Ben Green, riding in Jack Fischer's car toward the marina at Boynton Beach, felt all of his wife's emotions telepathically, as did all of the commanders. They knew the Green family could be a test case—a measurement of how the other families might react to the sudden reappearance of the geriatric space travelers.

CHAPTER SIX
EX-BOSS AND OLD LOVER

Alma Finley's flight to Washington, D.C. had been delayed. When she finally landed at National Airport it was four P.M. The rush of business people trying to get out of the nation's capital, as well as those arriving to do business the next day or returning from forays out among the population, turned the small terminal on the Potomac into a madhouse of briefcase and garment bag toting humanity. She had called Caleb Harris from Florida and advised him that she would be late. They agreed to meet in a small watering hole that the media frequented. It took Alma the better part of an hour to locate a taxi and get clear of the airport traffic.

Although it was May, the temperature was close to eighty degrees Fahrenheit and D.C. humid. The taxi was not air conditioned. *How far this is*, she thought, from the advanced technology she was accustomed to on Parma Quad 2 and Antarean Motherships. Even the diminutive Probeship was luxury class compared to her transport during the short journey from Florida to Washington today.

"Now you sure you want the NBC on Michigan? 'Cause we got that NBC place over on Kentucky too," the cab driver asked.

"Yes, I'm sure."

"There's those executive folks over there. I know 'cause my sister, she works there, and they go home pretty early. About five for sure, and with this traffic and all, we won't get there till maybe five-thirty, ma'am." The man was honestly concerned.

"I know," Alma answered softly. "But they expect me. I called ahead."

"That's smart of you. You must know D.C." Alma nodded and mused to herself—*A world long ago and far away...* as he turned up the ramp leading from the parkway onto the 14th Street Bridge.

Off to the left, Alma gazed at the Jefferson Memorial and felt a twinge of homesickness. She had been a reporter on a local New York television news program. It was there that she met Caleb Harris. He was a senior editor for NBC. They'd met at a New York Emmy Awards dinner long ago, just after her divorce and before she'd met Joe Finley. Harris and she had a brief love affair until she realized it was just part of her loneliness and that she didn't love him. The affair ended, but they remained friends. Caleb Harris offered her a network reporting job after he became NBC's New York network anchor. Now he was Washington Bureau Chief for NBC and a senior vice president of the network. He had become a trusted "grand old man" of broadcast political commentary.

When she first called from Florida, he'd been coy on the telephone. "So you want to come up to seduce me again after all these years?"

"Now how could an old woman like me seduce a famous TV personality like you? You must have your pick of the intern pool these days."

"There's never been anyone like my Alma." He laughed.

"You're damned right," she'd said. "Now let's make a date so I can get on with this seduction."

"Are you okay, Alma?" he asked, genuinely concerned. "I mean calling me out of the blue after all these years."

"I'm fine, Caleb. Perfect. And I promise you an evening you'll never forget."

"Now you're talking, sweetheart. Bring it on..."

They sipped gin and tonics and munched on a mixture of peanuts and pretzels at a tiny corner table. The bar, a gathering spot for network news people, was busy. Once in a while one of them threw a curious glance in Caleb's direction. If their eyes happened to meet, Caleb's icy gaze exorcised the intrusion immediately. He enjoyed the power, especially when Alma noticed it.

"You are beautiful beyond belief," he told her and then quickly followed with, "Jesus that sounds like the worst cliché... but I swear you don't look a day older than when I last saw you. What is it, fifteen years?"

"Twenty, sweetheart, and you're very kind."

"I'm being honest. That Florida climate must agree with you, Alma."

"Well, let me be honest too. I've been away from Florida for a while."

"Traveling?"

"Yes." She smiled. "You would definitely call what I've been up to traveling. Could I...?" She pointed to her empty glass. He signaled to the attentive waiter for another round. Alma then slipped a thought into Caleb's mind. The newsman frowned, turned, and in a loud voice called to the waiter. "No limes this time, Jimmy." He turned back to Alma, an expression of disorientation on his face. "You did say no limes, didn't you?"

"No, but I thought it."

"What's that supposed to mean?"

"You asked me what I've been up to? I need you to just listen. Don't get up, don't humor me and whatever you do, don't make a scene. What I'm about to tell you is the news story of the century, perhaps of all time. And before I begin, you have to promise me you will keep it completely confidential, except to those I designate."

"Wow. Now that sounds heavy." Caleb mulled over the idea that Alma Finley might be a bit senile. He recalled his own mother's bout with an illness late in her life that today had a name. Alzheimer's.

"There's nothing wrong with me," Alma said, reading his thoughts.

"Who said anything about that?" The waiter arrived with their drinks, cleared the empty glasses and quickly departed.

"You thought Alzheimer's."

"How the hell do you know that?"

"You thought about your mother too."

Caleb leaned across the table. "Jesus, Alma... what's going on here?"

"Like I said, Caleb. A wonderful story." She took a sip from her drink. "For the past five years I've been on four different planets in our galaxy."

"Oh Christ!" But before Caleb Harris could go any further, Alma began to transfer images of Parma Quad 2, Antares, Subax-Rigel Quad 3 and Hillet in the Alphard Galaxy into his cerebral cortex. After the initial shock of feeling Alma in control of his mind, he began to enjoy the trip. It was, as Caleb later described to the President, a multimedia light and sound show that filled all the senses.

Fifteen minutes later he was huddled in the narrow hallway next to the men's room, a pile of quarters stacked on the scarred shelf of the pay phone, using every ounce of clout he possessed to arrange a meeting with the President of the United States immediately.

He returned to the table smiling like the Cheshire Cat. "Fifteen minutes. Margo McNeil said she'd go out on a limb for you, not me. We get fifteen minutes. Seven-thirty tomorrow morning. Then he's off to Camp David."

"Is that Honey McNeil?"

"She's Press Secretary now."

"She remembered me?"

"Quite clearly. She said you were one of the few people who took time to talk to her when she first came to the network from Chicago."

"She's very bright. Didn't she have a thing for Malcolm Teller once?"

"People gossip. Who's to say?" Caleb shrugged and smiled.

"So you still take care of your own, huh?"

"I never approved of digging into personal lives as long as it didn't affect the job."

"And us?" Alma asked softly.

"We were discreet, weren't we?" he said, reaching across the table to take her hand.

"Yes," she answered. "And now how about we grab a quiet dinner someplace private. There is another part of this story that needs telling before tomorrow's meeting. It's critical that we convince President Teller to help us."

"Well, all you have to do is get inside his head the way you did mine and convince him…"

"No," she said, interrupting. "I can't do that. It's not allowed. Only in an emergency."

"It seems to me that whatever you need of him, is important. Critical, you said." He signaled for the check.

"But if I let him know what I can do... well, eventually it will frighten him and those around him. Imagine having these powers in a negotiation or at a summit?"

"It would be invaluable," he agreed. "Overwhelming. Yes, I understand." The waiter brought their bill and Caleb signed it.

They walked out the front door into the warm spring night. "Is that little Lebanese place still open over on 17th Street?" Alma asked.

"Still there, pillows and all." He hailed a taxi, but before they got in Caleb Harris held Alma with both hands, firmly grasping her elbows. "Thank you for coming to me. For trusting me."

She smiled and touched his weathered, handsome face. She said nothing as she stepped into the cab, but her friendship swelled deep inside his sometimes cynical heart.

Scores of light years away, in the system surrounding the star called Scorpius on the ice planet Antares, an enormous Antarean Watership, crewed with a full complement of crystalline Parman guides, specialized Antarean medical and flight teams, forty-two humans and four off-planet humanoids, catapulted up from the planet's core and cleared its gravitational pull. One of the Parman guides locked on to a tiny speck in the firmament: Earth's sun. The Watership began to accelerate. The rite of return had begun for its special human passengers, taking them on a journey that many Antareans were beginning to believe had been decreed by the Master eons before humankind ever appeared on planet Earth.

CHAPTER SEVEN
UNDER SURVEILLANCE

When Jack Fischer and Ben Green took off for Boynton Beach in Jack's car, while Joe Finley drove his rental car back down to Red Lake, Detective Sergeant Cummings was forced to make a quick decision. He chose to follow Jack and Ben, and while he noted the make, model and license plate of Finley's car, he couldn't help but feel frustrated in not knowing where that old man was headed.

The Boynton Marina is just south of the Boynton Inlet—a cut of water that connects the inland waterway with the Atlantic Ocean. Boynton Beach, a retirement community along Florida's eastern Gold Coast, has its share of affluent homes and high-rise condominiums. With the phenomenal growth of South Florida, towns such as Boynton Beach, Delray Beach, Lantana, Boca Raton and West Palm Beach have blended into one long, heavily populated retirement/resort town, each with a marina, condo developments, sandy beaches, shopping centers and a variety of restaurants ranging from expensive French chic to Pizza Hut and McDonald's.

Cummings kept his distance behind Jack's silver Lincoln Town Car. His pulse quickened as he saw the car turn east off the main highway US 1 and then turn left into the marina. As he jockeyed for position to make the same turns, his radio crackled alive with the voice of his long-time partner, Detective Coolridge Betters.

"Car fifty-eight. You out there, Matt?"

"Dr. Betters, I presume?" Cummings answered after quickly snatching the radio mike off its mount.

"What's up, Sarge? I got a message to get back to you pronto."

"Go to our channel."

"On my way." They both switched their radios over to a little-used frequency that they used to talk privately.

"Take this down, then grab an unmarked and see if you can pick up the trail," Cummings said as he swung his Olds Cutlass into the marina parking lot. The sight that filled his eyes caused his heart to noticeably skip a few beats. "Jesus Christ," he muttered.

"You want me to look for Jesus Christ?"

"What? No. They're here, Coolridge. By God they're here!"

"Hey Matt, what's 'here'?"

"Fischer—"

"Not that again. Look man, you've got ten months to retirement and..."

"Listen to me, partner," he interrupted. "They came back today. The old guys came back."

"What old guys?" Betters's voice got serious.

"The old guys that were on the boat that ran you off the canal and made me the laughing stock of Dade County. Only now they're here, and they've contacted Fischer and he's taken them to the marina."

"In Boynton?"

"Bingo, Sherlock. I'm looking at Fischer, Doyle and one of the geezers. The big one who went over the side last."

"What's goin' on?"

"Another snatch I'll bet. Okay. Another one of them is headed your way. Maybe to the Gables—to that Antares condo place they used last time. He's driving a new dark blue Electra. A rental. Florida plate is ARM-335782. He left Boca about twenty minutes ago so if you stake it out on I-95 in North Miami, maybe Ives Dairy Road, you should pick him up in another twenty."

"You want me to grab him?"

"Hell no. Just shadow... see where he lives and who he sleeps with."

"You okay, Matt?"

"I haven't been this okay in five years, partner. We're gonna get them this time and shove it right up that DA's pie-hole."

"Yeah, well, just take it easy and don't jump the gun."

"I'm cool. This time I'm gonna have the proof and nail these mothers. Now go, and give me a shout when you pick up the trail."

"You got it, Matt. I'm outa here!" The radio clicked off. Cummings knew their conversation could have been monitored, maybe recorded. He only hoped that friendly ears hadn't made much of it and would let their lack of formal police radio talk without the mandatory "roger," "over" and "out" pass as just two over-the-hill, about-to-retire cops chatting about the good old days.

Ben Green had also monitored the police conversation while Jack looked for Phil Doyle aboard the sleek forty-eight-foot Hatteras *Terra Time.* He sent the information along to Joe Finley, who exited from I-95 and drove south along Route 1 to his rendezvous with Amos Bright at the submerged Probeship. Detective Betters would have a long, unfruitful wait on the Interstate.

"Well, I'll be damned," Phil Doyle exclaimed as he came out onto the fantail of the *Terra Time* and saw Ben Green standing on the marina dock. "Jack said he had a surprise, but I never expected…"

"Keep it down," Jack whispered to Phil. "We don't want the world tuned in to this."

"Sure. So come aboard, Mr. Uh…" Doyle had forgotten Ben's name.

"Ben. Ben Green." The old man jumped spryly aboard the luxurious fishing boat.

"Yeah. Ben. Right," Phil said. "You want a drink?"

The weather had become sunshine and fair skies. The marina was fairly quiet. By May most of the boats that winter in Florida have left for their summer homes in the northern waters of Chesapeake Bay, Cape Cod and Long Island Sound. One fishing boat, the *Downtime,* which moored next to Doyle's boat, had just returned to dock. The catch consisted of one large barracuda, two good-size dorado and a thirty-pound snow grouper. The mate, a shaggy young man with a red beard and bare chest that was covered with fish scales, glanced up from his fish-cleaning chores to watch Ben come aboard his neighbor's boat. Doyle took notice of the mate's curiosity.

"That's a hefty snow grouper you got there, Billy."

"He goes over thirty."

"Where'd you get him?" Doyle asked as Ben and Jack entered the main cabin behind him.

"On the second reef north of the inlet."

"You sure you didn't drop a hook down on the six-hundred-foot wreck?"

Billy looked away. He was embarrassed. The regulars who fished these waters knew certain spots that would always produce big fish such as the snow grouper now being butchered on the dock next to Phil Doyle. It was an unspoken code that those spots were left alone as much as possible so that when charter customers, paying as much as five hundred dollars a day to fish these waters, had bad luck, the charter captains could go to the special spots and pick up a good fish or two. This insured return business and good word of mouth which was the life blood of the dwindling charter fishing-boat business. In this instance, Doyle was certain that the young mate had dropped a heavy line down to the wreck at six hundred feet just off the inlet. It was one of the few places that snow grouper still inhabited in these waters. The fish would bring five or six dollars a pound, maybe more if Billy could sell it in small chunks to the old people who came down to the dock to buy fresh fish. If not, he would take the grouper steaks and sell them to a local restaurant.

"Well," Phil called over to Billy, satisfied that he had distracted the nosy young man from speculating about who Ben Green might be, "I'm sure glad to hear that. Maybe a good sign that the fishing's coming back."

"Maybe," Billy answered, knowing he'd been let off the hook and grateful to Doyle for that gesture.

Below deck, Jack sipped a cold beer and lounged on one of the two sofas that lined the main cabin wall. Ben, momentarily in telepathic contact with Mary in Scarsdale, enjoyed a frosty Pepsi in the spacious galley.

"That kid is a royal pain in the ass," Phil remarked as he entered the posh carpeted cabin. He smiled at Ben Green and sat down next to Jack.

"It's nice to see you again, Phil," Ben said as he enjoyed the emotions Mary sent him while she was reunited with their family seventeen hundred miles to the north.

"So what's up?" Phil asked, looking from Ben to Jack and back to Ben. "I mean the last time I saw you, Mr. Green, you and a bunch of your buddies were cutting one hell of a trail into the wild blue yonder."

"They're back on a mission, Phil. We're gonna help them."

"Doin' what?" He squinted and narrowed his focus at Ben. "We gonna gather up some more old folks for you?"

Ben laughed at Doyle's description of their last meeting. "No. Something quite different this time."

"Yeah." Jack grinned. "This time the flow is in the other direction."

As Ben and Jack related their plans to Phil Doyle, Detective Cummings waited patiently in his car, watching the *Terra Time* and waiting for his partner to pick up Joe Finley's trail. The late afternoon sun would set, and night gather upon the sleepy marina, before Cummings realized no one was on the boat.

What he didn't see was the submerged Antarean Probeship arrive after dark with Amos Bright and Joe Finley aboard. It parked silently underneath the *Terra Time*, picked up Ben, Jack and Phil as they quietly slipped over the side and boarded the Probeship through an open hatch. It then headed to the marina in Boca Raton where Jack had docked his old charter fishing boat, the *Manta III*. They had a full night's work ahead to prepare the equipment so that Amos might examine the cocooned Antarean army left behind on their last visit when they were unable to process them. If things could be arranged, the Watership speeding toward this part of the Milky Way Galaxy might fill its fluid storage compartments with the Antareans army that had been asleep for five thousand years.

CHAPTER EIGHT
GRANDMA'S BACK

Mary had hours to spend alone with her daughter Patricia before two of her grandchildren, Pat's daughters Cori and Beth, returned home from school. They sat in the breakfast nook of the spacious modern kitchen, sipping coffee, holding hands and trying to catch up on five years of separation. Pat, the proud mother, went on for twenty minutes about her daughters. Cori was the youngest, a student who had wanted to be a doctor for as long as anyone in the family could remember. Beth, on the other hand, lived in an adolescent dream world in which school was a bore and a waste. Tall, slender and quite beautiful, Beth bore a remarkable resemblance to Mary in her younger days. The oldest daughter, Cynthia, was just completing her third year at Emerson College as a communications major.

Mary felt a void in her life, having missed so much of grandmotherhood. Ben tried to sooth her from a distance, but also felt regrets.

"And how is Richard doing?" Mary asked after Pat paused to get more coffee.

"Just great. He'll be a full partner in a few years. The market is booming."

"Market? What about the law?"

"He's specializing in corporate mergers, so he spends a great deal of time with underwriters and bond people. It's all very complicated."

"Is he happy?"

"He loves his work."

"And you, darling?"

"Me? I'm fine, Mom. I've been thinking of going back to work or maybe school…" Pat brought the coffee carafe to the table. "You know, Mom," she said as she filled their mugs, "when you had gone we were told there had been some kind of accident. They said that several people had drowned and were missing," she said sarcastically. "Until that Mr. Fischer brought us your letter we didn't know what…" Pat paused. Her tone grew angry. "Why in the name of God did you do it? How could you just go off like that and not say anything?" Then Pat's eyes filled with tears as she recalled their grief when they'd thought Mary and Ben had died.

"I'm sorry, dear. There was no other way. It had to be a secret."

"For a month? The letter was almost worse. You were out there," Pat gestured toward the window. "We couldn't talk… we couldn't anything… when would we ever see you again?"

"I'm here now."

"But it wasn't fair. Not to me or Melanie."

"Yes. I understand. How is your sister?" Mary asked. She had not had a good relationship with her other daughter.

"Off on another of her expeditions. The Great Barrier Reef this time. She's a Ph.D. now. Marine biology. Something to do with sea mammal viruses."

"Anyone special in her life?"

"Every day it's someone special. One man? Not my sister."

"Pat, darling… I'm sorry we left that way." Mary stood up and walked to the sunny window. She paused there for a moment and then turned. "No. That's not exactly true. I guess you could say we made a selfish decision about our own lives and we hoped that you would understand." Pat went to her mother's side.

"Of course we read the letter over and over. But it was, in a way, as though you and dad were… were dead—gone out of our lives. Then when Mr. Fischer explained all the details about the cocoons and the Antareans, we were happy for you but it was hard to imagine we would never see you again. Can you understand how frustrating that was? To know you and Dad were out there someplace and we couldn't know…" Mary took her daughter's hands and held them to her breast. She telepathed calming love to Pat.

"Do you feel our love for you?"

"Yes, Mother. It's wonderful."

"Have you felt that during the past five years?"

Pat looked at her with surprise. "Why, yes. How did you know? Many times. It was as though you and Dad were here with us. The girls, especially Beth, often said, out of the blue, 'I have this feeling that Grandma and Grandpa are still with us and that they love us.'"

"We do. And those feelings, the way you feel my love now, is what we send to you from across the galaxy. We are with you, my dear Patricia. We will be with you always." The two women embraced. It was then that Pat noticed the enlargement near the base of her mother's skull.

"What's this?" Pat asked, gently touching the rounded ridge that ran along Mary's spine and up onto the top of her head. Most of it was hidden by Mary's hair.

"An implant," Mary answered, stepping back from Pat and turning so her daughter might get a better view of the enlarged brain.

"They did this to you?"

"I volunteered. It had to be done to those who wished to command."

"Why? What is it, this implant?"

"There are some things that we are not allowed to tell. If you can wait until the girls and Michael come home I'll tell you as much as I can. What happens here, with my family, with you... well, you see a great deal depends on how you react to our new lives; to the things we've seen and done and must now do."

For the first time Patricia Keane realized that her mother, once a quiet, even at times subservient wife, mother and homemaker, was now vitally alive, strong and in control of the situation. The past five years had changed Mary Green in ways Patricia didn't understand. For a fleeting moment the word *alien* passed through her mind.

Yes, my child, Mary thought to herself. *We are home on our mother planet and at the same time we are aliens among our own kind. We are a new race. But where do we really belong?*

Later that evening, after Cori, Beth and Michael Keane got over the initial shock of seeing Mary, they enjoyed a family dinner seated around the mahogany dining table that had been a gift from Ben and Mary to the Keanes when they had moved to Florida. Mary explained that their words and thoughts could be sent across vast distances, and that she and Ben had always sent them love. That was what they'd felt. She told them of their decision to become commanders. Cori, the fifteen-year-old, examined the cerebral implant carefully.

"And this expands your brain function to full capacity?" the teenager asked.

"Even beyond that. We can combine our thoughts, our wills and energy. We are eleven commanders, but when we join telepathically, even across light years, we become one hundred times more powerful."

"Can you speak to Dad now?" Michael Keane asked.

"I am! He sends his love and is glad to see you are all looking so well and grown up. He can't wait to give you all a big hug."

"He can see us?" Beth asked incredulously.

"And hear you, and if I touch you then he feels that too."

"Then here's a kiss, Grandpa," Cori said as she got up and kissed her grandmother. Everyone laughed until Cori, suddenly startled, gasped. "Oh. It can't be. But I just felt someone kiss me back."

"Grandpa did that," Mary told her youngest granddaughter. "And this is for all of you." One by one, each at the table had the sensation of Ben Green gently kissing them on the forehead. Michael touched his balding pate as his father-in-law sent him a greeting.

"The others?" Pat asked. "Your friends from the condo. Where are they?"

"Alma and Joe Finley are here with us. The other seven are on a mission."

Something was gnawing at Pat. "Mom?" she asked. "You and Dad wrote in the letter that you would be gone, well, perhaps forever. You said you would live a long, fruitful life out there. Mr. Fischer said the Antareans seem to live forever. So why did you come back? I mean now… so soon?"

Mary looked around at her family, knowing the moment had come for her to make a decision. On the Probecraft they had discussed it over and over. It was a judgment call that depended on how the family responded to Mary's return. She wanted desperately to tell her family about their mission, but she feared the knowledge she would impart might be an impossible burden for them to carry in secret for as long as they lived on the Earth.

"Before I answer you, and I promise I will, let me tell you a little about our adventures 'out there' as you call it; about some of the worlds we have seen and the beings we have met. Afterwards, if you insist, I will tell you why we have come home to our Earth."

Commander Ruth Charnofsky, formerly of lower Collins Avenue and now in her ninety-first year of life, stood alongside Commander Frank Hankinson on the Watership flight deck. Hank had been a newspaper publisher in St. Louis, and although he had opted for commander status, his wife Andrea had not. The Watership was approaching light speed as Ruth and Frank watched the Parman guides change shift and lock on to the Earth's sun, a tiny dot in the cosmos that was their beacon home.

"They are taking us home," Ruth said.

"That was or is?" Frank asked.

"An interesting concept," she mused as her thoughts went far out to the great red giant star Rigel and the planet Subax-Rigel Quad 3 that had been her home for the past three years. Beyond the planet and its great red sun, her thoughts were of her new husband, mate and friend Panatoy, the tall humanoid from that world with whom she now shared her life in that inhospitable world. Ruth loved Panatoy as dearly as she had her Earth-human husband who had died decades ago. Dear Panatoy who now slept below deck, suspended in his special atmospheric chamber, awaiting the Watership's arrival on Earth and the revelation of the awesome secret they carried on board. She could picture his strong, graceful body, glowing with the bluish pigmentation of his people that had come to seem so beautiful, so *right* to her.

CHAPTER NINE
ARE THEY SAFE?

Jack kept the *Manta III* in good shape. With the sale of the Antares condo complex, he had enough money to buy any yacht his heart desired, but the old charter boat was his love. It was docked along the Inter-coastal in Boca Raton, just south of Yamato Road.

During the night while Detective Cummings kept his vigil near *Terra Time*, the Antarean Probeship slipped out of the Boynton Beach Marina and headed south, submerged near the bottom of the Inter-coastal Waterway, to Jack's dock in Boca Raton. They moored the Probeship directly underneath the broad-beamed *Manta III* and proceeded with their preparations for diving at the Stones tomorrow morning.

It wasn't until well after midnight that Cummings suspected he had been duped. Interior and running lights had been left on aboard *Terra Time*. Now they clicked off simultaneously. A timer? Cummings speculated. He got out of his car and cautiously approached the luxury Hatteras yacht. There was no sign of life. Only the gentle lapping of water against the sturdy dock pilings and fiberglass hull broke the eerie stillness of the moonless tropical night.

The detective boarded, flashlight in hand, his badge conspicuously pinned to his crumpled tan sports jacket. The last thing he needed was to be taken for an intruder. Charter captains had the reputation of being very touchy about strangers aboard their boats. The door leading to the main cabin was open. Cummings turned on his flashlight and played the beam around inside.

"Hello. Anybody home?" he called in a friendly voice. No answer. He moved into the cabin and strained to hear sounds of people sleeping below. Silence. The *Terra Time* was empty. Somehow, Fisher, Doyle and that old man had slipped away.

Earlier that evening Coolridge Betters had radioed to inform his partner that the rental car and elderly driver, as described, had never made it to Ives Dairy Road on I-95. Both cops agreed that Betters should head down to the Antares condo complex in case it was being used as a base again. Cummings had not heard from Betters after that.

Instead of trying to raise his partner on their prearranged radio frequency, Cummings found a pay telephone on the deserted dock and called his partner's home. The aging detective answered on the fifth ring.

"Hello?"

"It's Matt."

"Oh. Hey man, listen, I'm sorry about not getting back to you, but my radio went down right after I got to the Antares condos."

"You see the old guy?"

"I did. Well, not exactly the guy, but I found that rental down on the Red Lake Canal, just below the condos. Damned near the place they tossed me out onto that lawn five years ago."

"But you didn't see the guy?"

"I saw nobody. You want to stake out the car?"

"Not now. It's just you and me. We can't be spreading things too thin."

"How'd you make out, Matt?"

"They gave me the slip."

"They took the boat out?"

"No. But somehow they got off without my seeing them."

"Maybe they went to Fischer's boat."

"He still has that old tub?"

"He keeps it up in Boca somewhere. I can't remember the name..."

"*Manta III*," Cummings blurted out. "I'll never forget it and the sight of those old people going over the sides. It still makes me sick."

"I can get on the horn in the morning with the Boca Coast Guard station and see where it's registered."

43

"Do that first thing. I'm gonna get me a motel in Boca for the night. I'll call you at seven."

"You want to meet up there?"

"Keep an eye on that condo. After I check out the *Manta III* we can talk."

"Okay, Matt. Get some rest."

"Not till those creeps are in the lockup."

Betters heard from Cummings precisely at seven A.M. He had already spoken to the Coast Guard, who confirmed that Jack Fischer kept a thirty-eight-foot fishing boat, *Manta III*, docked near the U.S. Army Corps of Engineers facility on the Inter-coastal Waterway.

"I'm on my way," Cummings said. "I'll radio when I get an eyeball on the boat."

A half hour later, a disappointed Cummings reported to Betters that the *Manta III* was not in its slip. When he'd asked around, the fuel barge attendant recalled seeing the *Manta III* leave just before dawn. The attendant, a grizzled, toothless old Greek who smoked a crooked, foul-smelling DiNoble cigar, chuckled when Cummings flashed his badge and asked for more information. "Do you have a more precise time that they left?"

"Coupla hours. The sun no for to come yet."

"Did you see who was on the boat?"

"Dark. Hey, it's night before the sun she come up."

"Which way did they go?"

"To the ocean. Through the inlet up to the bridge." And then as an afterthought he added, "He take that old tub out pretty fast. I guess he for to have trouble keeping up with submarine."

"Submarine?" Cummings repeated. "There are no submarines in the Inter-coastal."

"Maybe." The old Greek chuckled again. "Maybe I just make imagination."

Cummings knew he had lost Fischer and the old man for the time being. He radioed Betters to go up to Boynton Beach and keep an eye on Doyle's *Terra Time*. "I'll hang here until the return." They had to come back to one of the boats, Cummings reasoned, unless they had a submarine like the old barge guy had claimed. But that was ridiculous and Cummings dismissed the thought.

The *Manta III* was on site over the Stones. While Jack and Phil stayed above, keeping an eye out for intruders, Amos Bright, Ben and Joe detached the Probeship from the *Manta III*'s hull and guided it beneath the calm, crystal-clear water that allowed sunlight to penetrate and illuminate the reef below. The Antarean and his two human commanders left the Probeship through the pressurized hatch and swam freely toward the reef. They located the doorway to the secreted chambers and carefully uncovered the seals that protected this section of the sleeping Antarean cocoon army. The seals were intact and undisturbed—exactly as they had been left five years ago. Amos located the chamber locking marker and, slipping an oblong metal device from the leg pouch on his wet suit, inserted the sharp end into the marker and activated the mechanism. The chamber door slowly slid open, hardly stirring the sandy nearby.

The chamber was undisturbed. Hundreds of cocoons, snugly nestled against one another on racks, glowed with a faint red light at the tip of each. Each rack held fifty cocoons, and in this chamber there were three racks. Ben, Joe and Amos entered the chamber, each swimming down along a rack, checking to see that all of the cocoons were viable. Satisfied, the men paused for a moment and thought a prayer for their sleeping companions. They then resealed that chamber and went on to check out the three remaining chambers. Everything was in order. Later that evening, after they returned to the dock and had hidden the Probeship, Amos Bright would send a message to the Antarean Watership, now only weeks away from its earthly destination.

"Our brothers and sisters are well and asleep. They await your arrival and the great day of awakening. We send you love."

Back at the dock in Boca Raton, a restless, unshaven Matthew Cummings was buoyed when he caught sight of the *Manta III* chugging up the Inter-coastal toward its marina. This time, in the light of day, Jack kept the broad-beamed fishing boat down to four knots. This allowed the Probeship, attached to the *Manta's* hull, to ride low in the water and therefore out of sight. Cummings backed away from the dock, crouching in the shadows cast by a copse of palm trees. The old Greek watched the detective hide. Then he saw the *Manta III* approaching. Chewing on the cigar stub, he muttered to himself, "That submarine is under the boat. I can see. Well, if Jack stops to get gas, I tell him. If not, I just watch what the cop does."

But Ben, Joe and Amos didn't have to be told that Cummings was there. They had already tuned in on his presence. Their problem was not how to confront the Coral Gables cop, but when.

CHAPTER TEN
A SACRED MISSION

Amos Bright's message to the Watership was joyfully received by all who were awake and functioning, including the six human commanders who were gathered for a conference. Bess and Arthur Perlman, Bess's sister Betty Franklin, Bernie and Rose Lewis, Ruth Charnofsky and Frank Hankinson sat around the oval obsidian table that contained a data screen. They studied detailed, three dimensional maps of the western coastline of South Florida and the ocean floor offshore. The huge Antarean Watership groaned slightly as the Parman guide farthest forward adjusted its crystalline alignment to compensate for a momentary change in the far distant Sun's ultraviolet radiation caused by the release of a huge solar prominence.

Antarean Waterships had been named for their primary function to carry liquids, usually under extreme pressure, to planets and Antarean colonies in the galaxy. Huge storage tanks, each capable of holding hundreds of millions of gallons of pressurized fluids, were the prominent feature of the vessel. The tanks, attached by service walkways to one another, trailed out behind the flight deck and crew quarters, which they dwarfed.

Mostly, these vessels carried water to arid planets. At other times the modular tanks were filled with liquid oxygen, hydrogen and nitrogen, and transported to planets or colonies without natural atmospheres of their own. The Antareans were gifted in their ability to create and maintain entire atmospheres around smaller planets or under specially constructed domes. Many diverse living beings depended upon Antarean technology and integrity. Failure of either could mean a disaster of major proportions. The Antareans, respected and ancient travelers, held the trust of the water users. Many of the Antarean's customers were dependent upon Waterships for survival

This particular Watership had three tanks. Two of the huge containers were filled with exotic mixtures of life-support gasses from four diverse planets. The center tank was filled with liquid oxygen for ballast. It had been recalled from the Rigel Quad 3 system, where it was replenishing an atmosphere to Subax, an ice planet near the red giant star Rigel.

Ruth Charnofsky, who lived on Subax, studied topographic details of the undersea area near the Stones. "The closest place to park the Watership, as far as I can see, is here," she said, pointing her remarkably smooth, tapered finger, once bent, wrinkled and locked by age and crippling arthritis, at a spot on the ocean floor nearly three miles from the site of the cocoon chambers secreted in the reef called the Stones.

Bernie Lewis leaned in to see the location. "That's the old wreck off Boynton Beach. It'll mean moving the cocoons a long way underwater."

"We have the flight crew and the Probeship," Bess Perlman said.

"At that distance, it could take weeks to move all those cocoons," Art Perlman chimed in, "and some of us won't all be able to help."

"And I'm sure Ben and Joe will get Jack and his friends to help again."

"We'll make do," Ruth Charnofsky said with finality in her voice, indicating that she had come to a decision. Her keen, concise manner of taking action when discussion had to be concluded made her the natural leader among the Earth-human commanders. "How we proceed will depend on where Amos, the Greens and the Finleys find the facility we need," Ruth continued.

"That will be the key," Bess Perlman agreed, shifting in her chair uncomfortably. She was not feeling well. Everyone in the room sensed her discomfort.

The problems they faced were indeed unique and unexpected. Five years ago, when the elderly Earth-humans who chose to travel with the Antareans underwent the physical transformation required for off-planet life, no one had anticipated or completely understood all the effects of Antarean space/body/mind processing on them. As it turned out, halting the aging process was only the beginning. The complete cleansing of blood and bone marrow, organs, and the lymphatic and respiratory systems removed all disease and damaged tissue. This process was dangerous to younger humans, which is why those who chose to leave the planet had to be seniors of at least sixty-five to seventy years of age. The Earth-human reaction was unique in Antarean experience in that the aging process not only stopped, but slowly, at first imperceptibly, was reversed.

Beyond physical cleansing, repair and reconstruction, an expansion of the human brain's capacity to near full potential was also begun in the processing room. The commanders had consciously undergone additional mental enhancement with cerebral transplants, a device that brought their mental capacities up to Antarean commander level. But the expansion of functioning brain capacity, thought to be perhaps ten percent in most Earth-humans, increased to nearly ninety percent for those who did not become commanders. The commanders capacity went beyond that to nearly one hundred percent; potentially equal to Antarean commanders.

All of the Earth-human space travelers had weathered the journey to Parma Quad 2 well. They spent two years living within the Parman society, teaching and being taught, acting as ambassadors for the Antareans, and generally integrating themselves and the Parmans into the galaxy which contained a seeming endless multitude of life forms, societies and civilizations.

It took another two years of many intra-galactic trips before it was evident that one special aspect of the processing was unique to the Earth-human race. Reproductive systems that had ceased functioning twenty to forty years before had slowly awakened and begun to work again. All of the space travelers, male and female, could become sexually active if they chose to do so. Not long after that, another unique effect became evident. Fertility!

As the Watership hurtled toward Earth, twenty-eight of the women aboard were pregnant. Married couples, who already had great-grandchildren, were about to become parents again. And many new couples had been formed by widows and widowers.

Four of the expectant mothers on board had taken off-planet mates. Rather than separate these couples, those who required special environments had been put into a state of suspended animation and sealed in cocoons engineered by the Antareans. Each contained the required gasses, light spectrum and nourishment for each particular race of humanoids. Much like the Antarean cocoons now resting on Earth's ocean floor, the containers could function indefinitely, preserving the precious life within.

Precious life were the key operative words throughout the galaxy. It was, in fact, the primary reason why this Watership now raced toward Earth. The birth law, like most laws advanced and enlightened living beings adhered to, was sacrosanct:

"All new life to come is a gift. Whenever possible, the birth of new ones is to be accomplished upon the home planet of the mother, or the egg bearer, or the divider. The highest priority of passage is to be given to any and all travelers who ask to be taken to home planet for the purpose of giving birth. This right shall be denied to no life form."

This Watership, along with members of the Geriatric Brigade, was now on that sacred mission.

CHAPTER ELEVEN
THE OVAL OFFICE

The President of the United States sipped his black coffee and smiled cordially at the attractive woman now seated across from him. She was relaxed and comfortable, settled in the pale blue armchair. Her forest-green dress blended perfectly with the chair's fabric and dark blue carpet, both emblazoned with the presidential seal. They had been introduced by Caleb Harris and Margo McNeil, the President's Press Secretary. After the introductions they both had left the Oval Office, leaving the President alone with Alma Finley. He quietly admired her good looks as he mused to himself, "They say this woman is almost twenty years older than me and she's just about the sexiest female I've laid eyes on in weeks."

President Malcolm Teller, a Democrat from the Deep South, was sixty-three and the first president to be divorced while in office. His wife had waited until his first term was over, and the official party announcement made that Teller would seek a second term, before she filed for divorce. Her grounds were adultery. She made the proof a public campaign issue. To the chagrin of the Republicans, now controlled by the Evangelical Right, and Teller's enemies in his own party, the public that always liked the underdog perceived the President as a wronged man. Since it had been widely rumored that both Teller and his wife led separate private lives, his wife's denunciation came as no surprise to the Washington press corps and the knowledgeable public. He was a man caught by a wife whose own sexual activities and proclivities would not stand the scrutiny of a public investigation either. This was not fair play. As Margaret Simpson Teller wrung her hands and bemoaned her role as the betrayed wife, the voters chuckled to themselves. The spokesmen for the white Christian Right and their Evangelical television preachers were as voices in the wilderness. The media didn't buy it. Mainstream television didn't bite. Only the sensationalistic rags and Teller's enemies in the media picked up on the story, much to the chagrin of the Grand Old Party who counted on public rejection of a "sinner" and saw only understanding instead.

Malcolm Teller was reelected in a close, hotly contested race. With his place as a two-term president secure, he openly dated, inviting some as not so secret overnight house guests in the White House. Many of the nearly seventy million baby boomers, born after the end of WWII in 1945 and the engine of the turbulent 1960's, almost regarded their President's open dating and sexual activities as patriotic. Telling stories about the sexual appetites of past presidents, long kept secret by a protective and elite Washington press corps, was now a popular parlor game.

"Women are my friends," Teller proclaimed when questioned about his rumored affair with the attractive fifty-three-year-old shapely blonde, blue-eyed Prime Minister of Sweden. "And when they are as brilliant and attractive as Prime Minister Johanssen, then," he announced, "I say let the courses of nature and national interest converge and go forward together!"

He was comfortable with women and secure with himself. But there was something unnerving about Alma Finley.

"I think you're attractive too, Mr. President," Alma said softly a moment after Margo McNeil had closed the Oval Office door behind her.

"I beg your pardon?" he said, wondering if his carnal thoughts about this woman were somehow showing on his handsome, suntanned face. "Did I say something I didn't hear?"

"No, Mr. President," she laughed gently, "you didn't say a word. But you thought it, didn't you?"

"Thought what?" he asked, growing uneasy. Margo McNeil had asked that he see this Mrs. Finley as a personal favor. The Press Secretary and he were supposed to spend the weekend alone at Camp David. He knew Margo was looking forward to it, so it surprised him when she asked that they delay their departure. He was sure this had originally been a fifteen-minute appointment, but when the Press Secretary introduced Mrs. Finley she inexplicably remarked that she and Caleb Harris would be back in thirty minutes.

"You were thinking I'm a sexually attractive woman, and you were surprised you felt that way because of my age."

"How in the name of… are you a… one of those mediums?"

"No." He stiffened.

"Well, I guess my press notices proceed me. Good guess." Alma put down her coffee cup and settled back in the comfortable antique armchair. As she did, the President, seated on a matching divan across from her, leaned forward, his dark brown eyes focusing on her calm, intelligent face. He concentrated his attention. "Exactly what can I do for you, Mrs. Finley?"

"You can just listen for fifteen minutes, Mr. President. I'm going to tell you the very best story you've ever heard."

And she did.

The weekend at Camp David was cancelled, as were most of the presidential appointments for the next few days. The Secretary of Defense, Gideon Mersky, one of Malcolm Teller's oldest friends and closest advisors, was summoned to the White House. He arrived to find Caleb, Margo, Alma and the President huddled in a meeting in the Oval Office. Alma, in the interest of saving time, tuned into the Secretary's mind and quickly brought him up to speed. The process so amazed him that, convinced she was telling the truth, he immediately became enthusiastic and excited.

"Mal," he began, addressing the President in familiar terms, "do you realize what this means to the country? Imagine having a woman, no… what did you say, four people?… right, four Americans capable of listening in on our enemies' most secret thoughts… of telepathing information securely all around the world… of having the experience of… what shall I call it… alien technology. It boggles the mind, Mal. It's absolutely sensational."

"No, Mr. Secretary. We will not to be involved that way." Alma was firm. She allowed her annoyance to permeate the minds of the others in the room. With the exception of Gideon Mersky, the others understood Alma's concerns. But the tough Defense Secretary shrugged off Alma's objection.

"Mrs. Finley," he said in a matter-of-fact tone of voice, "I understand you are under certain… restrictions, shall we say? I can, uh, live with that. I can live with the fact that you have made promises; sworn allegiances to other planets, governments, whatever. But unfortunately, or perhaps fortunately, you are now back on, as you put it, home planet, the land of your birth. You are an American citizen under American law. It may well be that you will have to decide your loyalties either to America or to these aliens. Antareans you call them, who I might point out, although welcome, are still in this country illegally."

Nervous silence filled the room. Alma blocked her thoughts and reached out to Ben, Joe and Mary. In an instant they communicated, discussed and concurred.

"Then we have nothing more to discuss, Mr. President. Thank you for your time. Thank you, Caleb and Margo. I'll be going now."

"Just a moment, Mrs. Finley," the President said. He turned his attention toward the Defense Secretary. "Perhaps you haven't grasped the total situation here, Gideon."

"I've grasped it, Mal. This woman and her people want us to help them. Fine. All I've said is that we could use their help as well."

Caleb Harris couldn't contain himself anymore. "You're an idiot, Mersky."

"What you think of me personally is of little consequence, Caleb. I'm here speaking as the Secretary of Defense; as an advisor to the President; as the person with the mission to keep this country free and strong; and as an American."

"Did it ever occur to you that this situation might go beyond those rather parochial boundaries?" Caleb responded.

"There's nothing parochial about being an American…"

"Let's stop this nonsense immediately!" Interrupting, the President was on his feet. "I apologize for this, Mrs. Finley. Gideon here means well, but he's a bit of a zealot. I don't think he's quite grasped the enormity of the situation, or its importance in the context of human history."

"I understand Mr. Mersky's position," Alma said calmly. It's all very natural. Very human. In fact, one of the most interesting conversations, or rather confrontations I should say, that we Earth-humans had during our orientation and training was regarding our ideas about nationalism. The Antareans, who have been space travelers for thousand of years, have carried the code, the unwritten laws, to many parts of our galaxy. When we few humans, who had lived on this little speck of a blue planet, first stepped out into the cosmos, one of the first attachments we lost, and oddly clung to at the same time, was our citizenship of Earth. The dichotomy of that fact was driven home as we watched our home-planet dwindle and finally disappear into the black void. The strange thing was that none of us ever referred to ourselves as Americans again. We were of Earth, or bipedal, human, humanoid or warm-blooded mammal dweller from Quad 3. But never American. I suppose it would be like someone at a world conference of nations proclaiming he was from Yonkers or Keokuc or Sacramento. Too provincial or parochial. In deep space we don't talk of such things. We know the scope of our vast galaxy; the variety of life, society and civilization out there. It would be futile, and honestly quite arrogant, to ever hold nationalism as more important than the preservation of life, one single life, no matter what its origins or physical appearance. We simply don't live in caves anymore, Mr. President, and though I don't wish to appear superior to you in any way, almost everyone on this planet still does. I think we made a mistake coming to you. I think we may have made a mistake trying to bear our young on our home-planet." Alma stood and prepared to leave. "It is not too late to intercept the Watership and have it return to Antares. The cocoons are well hidden, safe and viable. The Antareans can come for them another time."

"Please, Mrs. Finley." The President reached out and took Alma's hand gently in his own. "Please. A moment. I want you to stay. I want to help you. There will be no strings attached." He glared at the smug Defense Secretary. "I will personally vouch for the safety and secrecy of your mission. The government of the United States and the powers of this office are at the disposal of you and your friends. Please, stay."

Alma knew the President was sincere. She reached to obtain a sense of Mersky's mind. She stared at him. He returned her stare. He was a tall, gaunt man with a shock of dark curly hair that cascaded unruly, blending with heavy eyebrows and a salt and pepper beard. Dark penetrating eyes were his most dominant feature. They burned with laser intensity. Then he was in her mind. "I don't know if you can hear me, Mrs. Finley. I am not sorry about what I said, but I will apologize if the President asks me to. However, I want you to understand that I will do whatever he asks or orders me to do. And I will do that with all my strength and energy. That I pledge to you!"

The corners of Alma's mouth curved upward slightly. Her gaze softened. "Thank you, Mr. President," she said aloud, still staring at Gideon Mersky. "And thank you, Mr. Secretary. I am sure you will be a tremendous asset to our mission."

The tension in the room abated. They all sat down again, relaxed and eager to begin planning. A secure conference room on the fourth floor of the Executive Office Building adjacent to the White House was to be temporary headquarters where plans could be made for the Watership's arrival and the events and actions that would follow as the mothers-to-be of the Geriatric Brigade neared term.

CHAPTER TWELVE
TO TELL OR NOT TO TELL

Before dinner Patricia Keane called her oldest daughter, Cynthia, a junior at Emerson College in Boston, and told her to come home and why. Cynthia rushed by taxi to Logan Airport and caught the last Pan Am shuttle to La Guardia Airport. Being the first-born, she had a special relationship with her grandmother. When she arrived home she leaped out of her father's car and ran to the house. Mary Green was in the kitchen helping Patricia clean the dinner dishes. Cynthia rushed in and hugged her grandmother, tears flowing, squealing for joy.

"Oh Grandma! Oh God, how I missed you. I love you. Oh!" She squealed. "I am soooo happy!".

Mary stroked her first-born grandchild's hair and held her tightly to her bosom. Cynthia had been a girl of fifteen when she last saw her. Now she was a woman of twenty. The measurement of time passed, of family missed, was most apparent in the changes she saw in Cynthia.

With everyone gathered, they settled comfortably in the screened porch that served as a family room in summer. It was a warm May evening. Where to begin?

"Let me begin by telling you about the night we left this planet. So much was happening around us. The others, most of the members of our Geriatric Brigade, were being shuttled out to the submerged Antarean Mothership. Eleven of us remained behind in the processing room because we had chosen to become commanders. Our bodies had already been processed. What was then required was a surgical procedure, a cerebral implant." At that point she once again showed them the bump on her skull.

"Did it hurt?" Lisa asked.

"Not at all. But we had to remain fairly quite for about an hour so that the implant could root itself to our cerebral cortex. While that happened we began to learn how to combine our minds and think and act as one. The power of it was awesome. And then, we could wait no longer. The police were coming because they thought someone had kidnapped a bunch of old people and were torturing them, or worse. We boarded two boats that the Antareans had and made our way out to the Mothership. The Coast Guard was all around, helicopters, cutters, speedboats, police boats… it was chaos. The Antareans kept our pursuers confused and at bay while we slipped over the side into the ocean."

"You jumped into the ocean at night?" Cori interrupted. "Weren't you afraid of sharks?"

"No my dear. We were afraid of nothing. The Mothership was far below, more than four hundred feet, glowing brightly to welcome us. We swam toward it without breathing."

"Not breathing?" Michael asked. "How did you…?"

"Air just wasn't necessary. It seemed but a few strokes and we were there. A round portal opened below us and we swam to it. It was a wonderful substance, like a membrane that allowed us through but kept out the sea. My first impression of the Mothership was that it was bright and warm and above all, safe. The others—the old people we had gathered from all over the country from the abject poverty of Collins Avenue, from degrading nursing homes, from our old friends who hadn't moved to Florida—were all there. We eleven were their leaders. Everyone was in awe, smiling and excited. Alive!"

The Keane family sat enthralled by Mary's story. She continued, describing the takeoff, the journey away from their Mother planet, the long weeks of learning, teaching, training for their new lives. And finally, their arrival on Parma Quad 2. Mary then spoke about that planet where they'd spent nearly two years, and other places that she and Ben had visited as commanders and teachers on the Antarean Mothership.

From time to time, when she wanted to make a point or clarify a location, they stepped outside the porch into the backyard to gaze up at a star-filled sky. Mary identified certain stars as systems she had visited with Ben and the Antarean Mothership after leaving Parma Quad 2. There was unbelievable wonder, even in the eyes of her cynical Wall-Street–hardened son-in-law when casually, she pointed out a star and said, "We were there just about seven months ago on a survey measuring the rate of expansion of the Talican planetary system. Then we returned to Parma Quad 2, over there." Her finger swept across the midnight sky to the Dog Star, Sirius.

"I'm not an astronomer, but that seems like quite a distance, Mom," Michael remarked, tracking the vast expanse of cosmos between the two stars.

"From here it is," Mary answered. "Up there it's a little closer. Of course, with the Parman guides we travel pretty fast. It depends on their star fix and the rate of ultraviolet absorption they set."

"The speed of light?" Cori said. She was a straight A student, quite the opposite of her sister Lisa, whose one dream was to live in Beverly Hills and be a movie star.

"Of course," Lisa answered unexpectedly. "They have to travel that fast or they wouldn't be here."

"It means," Michael Keane interjected, "that we are looking at stars as they were before Grandma was there because it takes the light from those stars years to reach us here."

"Then how did Grandma get here before that light if she traveled at the speed of light?" Cori asked. No one answered. Mary chuckled and turned to all of them.

"I said we travel fast, dear hearts, but I never said at the speed of light. No, light speed would take way too long. The Antareans, with their Parman guides, can displace space. In effect, they bend it. Something like using the shortest distance between two points by moving those points closer together and then traveling along the new distance created."

"Like making your own short cut," Cynthia suggested.

"Something like that. A short cut that they build and then use. Not one that existed before. Light moves in a relatively straight line, and for some trips light speed is adequate. But the Parman guides take light, a certain part of starlight that is, and absorb it. In effect they pull light in. The closer we get to our destination, the more they pull or absorb and the more accelerate until the route is bent beyond light speed."

"Does it hurt?" Cori asked.

"Does what hurt, darling?"

"To travel that way?"

"No. But without the processing we had back in Florida five years ago, it would be impossible for us to travel in space at all. And more interesting than that is the fact that the Antarean processing only will work on older Earth humans." She gestured up toward the starry night sky. "You young people will have to wait until your body ages if you want to go out there with us."

"Wow," Lisa said. "There are so many stars, so many places to go and see. Will you see them all, Grandma?"

"Maybe not all, but your grandpa and I plan to keep on traveling for as long as we can. There is talk about beginning to travel to other galaxies."

They walked back to the porch filled with awe of Mary Green's adventures. Patricia was exhausted from the strain of the day's events. The girls wanted to hear more about the planets Mary had seen and the beings she had met. They kept their grandmother up for several hours after Pat and her husband had gone to asleep.

Cori and Lisa Keane had hardly slept. They awoke with more questions for their grandmother about the beings she had met: how they lived, did they have music, how they dressed, what their schools were like, what they thought about humans. Were there other humans like us? Or were they different? How? They pleaded with their mother to let them cut school the next day. Patricia Keane had no choice but to agree. For the first time since joining his law firm, Michael Keane called in sick so he could stay home with the rest of the family to hear more about Mary and Ben Green's adventures

It was another sunny spring day. They gathered around the breakfast table, a wrought-iron glass-top affair with matching upright chairs that were as uncomfortable as they looked. Patricia so loved that set and no one dared complain. The sun poured into the large kitchen. Mary tried to help with breakfast but the girls insisted on serving her. She was the guest of honor.

"You're an ambassador, Grandma," Cori announced as she served grapefruit halves topped with maraschino cherries. With a flourish she placed a grapefruit in front of Mary and began to hum, "Hail to the Chief."

"That's for the President, dummy," Lisa chided her younger sister.

"Well, maybe Grandma will be president of a planet one day," she answered, giving Mary Green a kiss. "I love you, Grandma."

"I love you too, darling. I love all of you very much." Mary sat back in the hard metal chair and observed her family. How had she missed them? After five years, what did they really think about her return? It was part of her mission to explore her family's feelings so as to help the others who were one their way to Earth make decisions regarding contacting their own families. Last night she had talked about some of her adventures in the broadest terms to them.

There was no way of knowing how detailed she should be. It bothered her to reach into their minds from time to time to see what effect her stories and her presence had on them. There was love and genuine happiness for her return. They were relieved that she and Ben were alive and well. But underneath those very human feelings there lurked another thought. Grandma was different. Grandma knew so much, had seen so much and was in some undefined sense, superior. She had not physically aged. She was strong and healthy and nearly eighty years old. But she looked much younger than they remembered. There was an undefined separation between them. It frightened Patricia. And deep within his mind an emerging idea gnawed at Michael Keane's id. Alien, he thought. Mary is an alien. She is no longer of this world. She calls herself Earth-human. She speaks of other worlds as though they were her home, and of other beings as though they were what? Human too? Or something else? What has she become? Who is she? Mary listened silently to these thoughts and was concerned.

A large plate of toast, Lisa's chore, was the last item to be brought to the table. It was dark; nearly burned.

"The toast is burned," Cynthia complained as she passed the scrambled eggs to her father. Lisa grinned impishly.

"It's good for your teeth that way," the seventeen-year-old actress-to-be retorted.

"You sound like a commercial," Cynthia shot back sarcastically.

"You think so? You really think so?" Lisa was suddenly serious. "I'm going to see an agent in New York next week. She's Leslie Blackman's agent and she gets her lots of work."

"Leslie Blackman is beautiful." Cynthia fired back, but Lisa ignored the remark.

"Maybe… but I've got character. Right, Grandma?"

"You were always a character, dear. A wonderful character!"

"See!" Lisa then took a piece of toast and scraped off the charred top until the piece was half its original size. Everyone at the table burst into laughter. Lisa played it to the hilt, slowly buttering the toast, taking a large bite and then rolling her eyes in delight.

Mary caught herself laughing, filling up with old feelings: pride in her family, love for her grandchildren, the sense of being an older generation observing and enjoying the renewal of life. But she and Ben were, in many ways, alien. She felt guilty. Perhaps they should have stayed behind five years ago. The grandchildren had grown, matured into wonderful young women. Her other daughter, Melanie, was halfway around the world in Australia, a marine biologist… a stranger. How much had she and Ben missed? Was it really worth leaving?

At that moment Ben Green reached her mind and quelled her doubts. "Yes, my darling, it was, and is worth everything. What we do is very important." And then their thoughts melded as they recalled their son Scott, a casualty of Viet Nam, a name, along with fifty-thousand other human beings, engraved on a long, dark, brooding strip of black marble in Washington, D.C. With that thought, and the potential for starting a new family that Ben and Mary knew they now had, the decision was taken.

Mary would not reveal the entire reason for their return to Earth. She told her family it was to bring the cocoons back to Antares, but mentioned nothing of the pregnancies aboard the Watership. And the fact that she was now absolutely certain she was going to have a baby too.

CHAPTER THIRTEEN
A TEAM GATHERS

There were 1,158 satellites and space hardware of one sort or another circling the Earth in a wide variety of orbits and distances. Their purposes were as varied as science could devise and execute. Of all these Earth-human extraterrestrial hardware, only thirty-seven had the capability of noting the entrance of the Antarean Probeship that carried the Greens, Finleys and Amos Bright into the atmosphere. Only seventeen of those had the capability of instantaneously relaying information on the intruder back to their Earth stations. Six belonged to the United States, five to the Soviet Union, two to Japan and one each to India, England and Israel. The Probeship entry was so fast that by the time these satellites locked in on it the Probeship had blended into an active thunder storm weather system and appeared as just an electrical anomaly. However, because it was initially classified as an extraordinary event, what little data gathered was studied by these governments. Since the occurrence had terminated over American soil the highly secret Defense Intelligence Agency, DIA, had the task of deciphering the event. Heavy weather eliminated the possibilities of visual sightings and most of the local Florida airports were closed down, making radar contacts few and inconclusive. Within two days the final DIA report stated the anomaly as Electrical Atmospheric Disturbance—EAD/close file.

An Antarean Probeship is a relatively small, fast craft, about the size of a railroad car and highly maneuverable. On the other hand, a Watership is a large visible craft, more so if it has three huge high-pressure storage tanks in tow. To bring that to Earth undetected was a far more complex matter than finding a weather system for cover.

With the President and Defense Secretary on board, the first order of business was to identify and recruit a small and highly specialized group of people who would share Alma Finley's secret on a need-to-know basis. With sleeves rolled up, President Teller and Margo McNeil worked on a list of trusted people who would be part of the inner circle. Caleb Harris and Alma Finley plotted out a schedule of events based on updates Alma received from her husband Joe, the Greens and Amos Bright. This data, from the approaching Watership, continually flowed back and forth through the commanders' minds.

Landing the Watership secretly was the first problem to be solved. Gideon Mersky took charge of that aspect of the operation. He would put together a small team of his brightest logisticians and give them a hypothetical problem without revealing its veracity.

The president chose his newly appointed Undersecretary of Health, Dr. Mohammad Khawaja, a board-certified neurosurgeon of Pakistani heritage, to oversee the medical aspect of the operation. The doctor was a deliberate man, known for this eclectic approach to problems. It was for this reason that he was chosen. No one could imagine what complications these pregnancies might hold. The women were, although processed to travel in space, old. Could their bodies take the strain of childbirth? And with all the space travel they'd done, being exposed to a variety of atmospheres, gravities and exotic foods, what effect might that have on the babies? When he was informed of the four interplanetary matings with humanoids from other planets, Dr. Khawaja sat down and thought for a long moment before he finally spoke. "So to be clear, Mr. President, you are tasking me to design an obstetric and pediatric facility for patients that by all rights should be under the care of a geriatrician. And then to prepare for circumstances we, I, cannot begin to fathom." He smiled slyly. "But, you know, it is quite an interesting challenge. We must anticipate all eventualities. Therefore, I will require a large facility, perhaps many. There will be housing for the couples, prenatal care, and of course a complete obstetric department. Then I will want pediatric intensive care units ready with delivery and operating rooms, a surgical staff—

both gynecological and geriatric... at least until we can establish the health of the mothers and the viability if the babies in their wombs." He chuckled. "That, Mr. President, is a specialty I can assure you is quite rare—gynecological geriatrician." Everyone in the room joined in his amusement. "Then the nursery. That will require a specialized staff as well..."

"I think you're going to need engineers and chemists too," Caleb suddenly said. "Those four mixed marriages..."

"Matings," Alma corrected him.

"Yes, well, from what we've heard it's possible that the babies might be... I don't know. I mean I hate to say it, but not human... at least human as we know it. They might need special environments."

"The Watership is bringing atmospheres," Alma said.

"Yes," Doctor Khawaja stated, "but Mr. Harris is correct. We will have to design and build environments, not only for the babies but for the non-human, I mean non-Earth-human parents. And these special babies might have requirements different from either parent. Yes, engineers, chemists, biologists... I believe many experts will be required."

"Can it be done?" President Teller asked.

"I believe so, Mr. President," the Undersecretary answered. "The problem will be to keep this a secret. You know many of the best scientific minds in this country, and frankly I think we should settle for nothing but the best... well, some of those people have a different point of view from us about government, or at least about your administration."

"I don't think that's a problem," Gideon Mersky said. "When those folks, and I don't care what their politics are, find out that they're going to have the opportunity to work on some real live extraterrestrials, I think they'll go along with whatever we ask."

"And afterward?" Caleb questioned.

"After what?"

"After the babies are born and well... safe. After we don't need many of these uh, people anymore. What then?" Everyone in the room looked at Alma.

"Well, we'll just have to cross that bridge when we come to it," she said wistfully. "The problem at hand is to find the best people and the best facility. Secrecy and the welfare of the mothers and the babies are our principal mission's criteria."

"I agree," President Teller said. "We'll just have to educate those folks."

Dr. Khawaja turned his attention to Alma Finley. "Can you tell me anything about the changes you experienced while these Antareans processed you?"

"After the processing here on Earth we all experienced euphoria. I never felt so well, so healthy. Clean is the word that comes to mind. We were disease free. My husband's leukemia was completely cured. People that came to us crippled with arthritis, palsy, heart disease— they were all made well and whole. My friend Bess had, has, a sister, Betty. She was a stroke victim, confined to a bed in a miserable nursing home. With my own eyes I saw her transform and become completely functional." Everyone in the room had stopped their work as they listened to Alma relate her story. "We eleven, the commanders, had to make an additional adjustment to the implants. But the real change was within here..." She paused and gently tapped her chest. "Within our psyche. It took nearly four months Earth time to reach Parma Quad 2. That was a period of adjustment and learning. We all believed that we had done the right thing, leaving Earth, that is. And physically we were well prepared for the rigors of space travel. But as we pulled away from our planet, as it grew smaller, a profound silence swept through the whole group, nine hundred forty-one strong. In what seemed like a few moments we felt the Mothership slow down. There, outside the membrane we had entered through, we saw Saturn. It was the only planet in our path out of the solar system. It was glorious—a huge orange ball whirling within a kaleidoscope of rocks and debris of all manner and shape and color."

"Our Voyager took some great pictures of Saturn," Mersky remarked.

"Yes, of course, Mr. Secretary, but to see it in person... It's enormous. Or at least we thought so until we visited some other planets.

And the Antareans say that they have observed moons the size of Saturn in the Hydra Galaxy."

"And to think it cost us five hundred million dollars to look at photos of what this woman casually observed," the President mused.

"Not so casually," Alma continued. "The reality of what we had done... being this far away from... well, from home, gave many on board second thoughts. Had leaving Earth really been the right thing to do? It was an uneasy moment. The Mothership picked up speed again and we settled into our quarters. It was also unsettling that such a huge vessel had a very small crew. There were only five Antareans on the flight deck plus the seven that had been on Earth. Of course there were three pairs of Parman guides, but they remained in quarters or outside on the hull for most of the trip. Only toward the end, when we were approaching Parma Quad 2 and had learned the rudiments of their language, did we understand how intelligent and advanced the Parman were."

"So you were in school on the ship?" Caleb asked.

"Yes. It was difficult, but fascinating. Then, oh maybe two weeks out, we slowed again and actually came to a stop. You can imagine our excitement when we looked out and saw three other spaceships. Zeridian science vessels from the area of our galaxy we call Pleiades. Amos Bright, the Antarean leader, invited some of the Zeridians aboard to meet us. They were bipedal mammals from a water planet. By our standards they were short, three to four feet. They greeted us by touch. Very soothing and warm. It was a wonderful time for everyone. And by that time everyone had become so familiar with the Antareans that the Zeridians didn't seem, well... alien to us. Meeting them brought that into focus for everyone in the Brigade. It was as if we had stepped through Alice's looking glass into a totally new dimension, a startling new way of seeing others and ourselves. Even though we were millions of miles from Earth, for the first time, to everyone Earth-human on board, we understood that we were changed forever. We were part of something far beyond our earthly experience in a place that accepted us as belonging."

"Did this apply everywhere you went?" Margo McNeil asked.

"Yes." Alma answered, "Everywhere the Antareans have been in our galaxy."

"That is very interesting," Dr. Khawaja said, "but what I am really driving at is to understand what physical changes you have experienced. Changes that might give me some clue as these unusual pregnancies and how that might affect a fetus."

"I don't know," Alma answered.

"You've had no physical examination?"

"Never."

"Then we will have to explore every eventuality we can imagine until we can examine the uh, the patients."

The phone rang. Dr. Caroline Macklow from NOAA, the National Oceanic and Atmospheric Administration, was in the outer office. Margo McNeil went out to get her. Dr. Macklow, a Ph.D. specializing in oceanic pollution, was fifty years old with wispy gray-brown hair, a face that appeared too small for her owlish green eyes and a smile that was disarming. She was tall, nearly six feet, and carried her large frame upright. She entered the room and immediately paid her respects to the President. After she had met everyone, she was sworn to secrecy and brought up to date on the historical events that were about to happen. Dr. Macklow's expertise would be valuable in the salvaging of the cocoons.

As the day wore on, the team grew. Two of Gideon Mersky's whiz kids, as he called them; Phillip Margolin, a military analyst he recruited from the Rand Corporation, and Alicia Sanchez, a project supervisor at NASA, were assigned to work on the problem of masking the Watership's arrival and landing.

Dr. Michelangelo Yee, the President's science advisor, was brought in to coordinate and vet the personnel Dr. Khawaja, whose background and contacts were mostly outside government in the scientific community, gathered for the project.

The chief of the White House Secret Service detail, Benton Fuller, who had been with President Teller for his first term, was briefed and instructed to hand-pick three other trusted agents who would remain loyal and keep their mouths shut.

Caleb Harris and Margo McNeil schemed of ways to keep the inquisitive press at bay.

The Undersecretary of the Navy, Captain Thomas Walkly, one of the highest-ranking African-American navy officers on active duty, was brought in to coordinate the naval activity in the area of the Stones before, during and after the arrival of the Watership.

By the end of the day the White House group had grown considerably, defined the mission and potential problems, and had made some firm decisions.

The Watership had to be screened as it approached Earth because its size and configuration made it easily detectable, even by unsophisticated radar.

A medical facility that already existed was required for the returning mothers and fathers-to-be. After some discussion it was agreed the recently completed wing at the NASA Space Medicine Center in Houston, Texas, could be effectively sealed off without attracting attention.

Everyone concurred that approaching private industry would be risky and difficult to control. Dr. Khawaja would discreetly contact some of his colleagues in the academic world. He had good friends at the Albert Einstein Hospital in New York, the Massachusetts Institute of Technology, the University of North Carolina in the Research Triangle and Stanford University in California.

The logistics after landing would be handled by the Navy under the command of Captain Walkly. The returning Brigade members and a few Antareans would be taken by a guided missile frigate to Elliot Key, a small uninhabited and inconspicuous island south of Miami. From there speedboats would ferry them to the Florida mainland, landing approximately twenty miles east of Homestead Air Force Base. From that unmarked vehicles would transport them to the base where a C-5A MATS cargo plane would be waiting to complete the final leg of their journey to the Houston Space Center.

By three A.M. everyone was beat, but they had made progress. Alma thanked them all. She would remain in Washington to coordinate their activities with her fellow commanders. Caleb offered her his bed for the night; he would sleep on the sofa. The President suggested she be a guest in the White House. Alma declined both offers, stating she preferred the privacy of her hotel.

After they had all left, Malcolm Teller and his Press Secretary had a drink alone in the White House's Red Room, a baroque sitting room with a deep red carpet, plush red velvet Louis XIV chairs, black marble cocktail tables. The walls were covered with red flocked wallpaper and mundane oil landscapes by artists of the late eighteenth century. They discussed and marveled at the events of the day as they sipped twenty-year-old Chivas Regal Scotch.

Neither was tired. The stimulation of the historic day and the scotch eventually led them to the President's bedroom, where they made love in the Abraham Lincoln bed.

CHAPTER FOURTEEN
RACING TOWARD MOTHER-PLANET

A week later the Antarean Watership entered Quad 3, Earth's quadrant of our Milky Way Galaxy. In a few days the Parman guides would change over to light speed and, keeping the planets and moons of our solar system between them and Earth, make their final approach.

The idea to use the Watership had come from Chief Commander Ruth Charnofsky. After learning of the human pregnancies she circumvented the normal chain of command on Subax, a planet steeped in military tradition and strict obedience to unwritten common law, and contacted Amos Bright directly through the other commanders. It might have taken weeks had she gone through the proper channels. Her mate Panatoy, the Subaxian chemist, concurred with her decision.

The plan was to contact all the pregnant Brigade women and gather them on Antares. Then, using the Watership, initiate a round-trip mission that would bring the humans home for birth on the Motherplanet and return the cocoons secreted undersea to Antares where they could be processed and reanimated. She convinced Amos Bright that it was foolhardy to leave the cocoons on Earth any longer than absolutely necessary. "There is an unstable, primitive political environment there," she argued, "that could erupt into nuclear holocaust at any time, endangering the cocoons by poisoning the oceans with radioactivity."

The destruction of those nine hundred twenty earthbound Antareans would be a great loss to their race which, uniquely, was able to inhabit planets that could not support life on their surfaces.

Antareans are underground dwellers who capture the heat and energy from their planet's core. All food and water is artificially created without benefit of natural sunlight or atmosphere. Millennia ago, this thriving civilization made the decision to apply their energies and efforts to the exploration of space. Now they are known throughout the galaxy to more than one thousand races and civilizations. They revere and cherish life, having progressed genetically to the point where their life span is indefinite. They are a limiting society, which means that new life will not be created unless an old life dies. Each death has to be confirmed and the body, or any remains, returned to Antares. From that inert tissue material the Antarean gene-splicers and in-vitro scientists extract and manipulate genetic matter that, in effect, recreates the dead Antarean. It is a clone, a replicate of the deceased, and a valued member of Antarean society, but has no memory of previous life.

More than five hundred Earth years pass before a new Antarean reaches adulthood. During that time it is educated, trained and permitted to work in the Motherplanet, far beneath the barren, forbidding surface. After this apprenticeship, the new adult is allowed to begin space travel and exploration on one of the eighteen hundred Antarean space vessels now in operation throughout the galaxy. At the time that the Brigade arrived there were two hundred thirty-six thousand Antareans alive. At any given time more than fifty thousand of them are either traveling in space or serving on distant planets or Antares.

Ruth Charnofsky's idea was accepted and a grateful Antarean high council granted her citizenship on Antares—a high honor for an off-planet being.

The expectant Brigade parents had gathered as planned and as they began the final leg of their journey home, Ruth, swelling with her Subax–Earth human baby in her womb, pondered just what this child might be, or become.

Ruth was ninety-one years old and until five years ago, had barely survived on her meager Social Security checks. Now she was a strong commander and citizen of Subax, Antares and Earth. She had traveled among the stars, witnessing sights and wonders only dreamed about by her fellow Earth-humans. She contemplated this embryo growing inside her. What was this baby? Her mate Panatoy might be called an animal by the bigoted cretins on Earth. She knew him to be a kind, thoughtful and loving humanoid male—as good and tender as her late husband, whom she had buried more than thirty years ago. What would their baby be? Earth-human? Subax? And what might the three other mixed matings onboard produce? For that matter, what would the fully Earth-human babies, about to be born to elderly parents, look and be like? What genetic changes had the processing for space travel wrought? This was all new ground, reaching into the unknown. But wasn't that what she had seen and heard throughout her travels in the galaxy? Blending and mixing; evolving and changing. For unlike the Antareans, who opted for controlled genetic reproduction via cloning, most of the known life forms in the galaxy reproduced by means of DNA exchange. The blending of genetic material was possible among uncountable species resulting in great diversification. And yet, so much of it was similar. Humanoid was the predominant species—warm-blooded, mammalian, bi-pedal, gas breathing, with a relatively similar brain size and nervous system configuration. There were myriad variations arrived at by natural selection, environmental and climate change and solar spectrum. In other advanced civilizations genetic manipulation had flourished, producing incredible adaptations and varieties of humanoid life.

The animal and plant kingdoms stretched across the galaxy as well with millions of species and varieties that were also constantly changing... blending... becoming.

And beyond that, civilized intelligent life forms of crystalline design and non-carbon base thrived in gaseous vapor clouds and on planets with seemingly barren landscapes void of atmosphere.

It was also theorized, but not yet confirmed by the Antarean astrophysicists and astronomers, that another life form existed within the electrically charged solar winds and nebulae from which new galaxies and solar systems were formed as others aged and disintegrated into the void. A myriad of life spread across our vast galaxy and, it was believed, to that unending expanse called Universe.

Yet, if you opened your heart and mind to this endless dwelling place, as Ruth Charnofsky had when she fell in love with her blue Subaxian chemist, it was hard not to see that some grand plan was at work here. What appeared haphazard and evolving in swirling masses of gas and matter was, in fact, of brilliant design. New galaxies were created... new stars... new planets... and within it all, life becoming, blending, growing, changing and evolving while producing an endless variety of existence built by stardust.

Hurtling along at inexplicable speed toward her Motherplanet, Ruth Charnofsky contemplated the new life form growing within her body. She had but one desire—to give birth and nurture her child. This was, she believed, the ultimate Universal purpose.

CHAPTER FIFTEEN
A LANDING PROGRAM

Nobody would ever suspect that the modest log cabin set deep in a grove of tall Norway Pines on the rise above the Beaverkill River was, in fact, the think tank for Operation Earthmother, as the project to aid the returning elderly space travelers had been named by the Secretary of Defense. Upon close inspection, a trained eye might notice that aside from the usual white satellite dish sported by all the recreation homes in this area, this cabin had an additional black mesh dish hidden one hundred yards to the north of the cabin among thorny blackberry bushes. Its purpose was to receive and transmit high-speed encoded data from the DOD's space computer main-frame facility at the Pentagon.

The misty rain that had begun at dawn continued to midday. Alicia Sanchez, a tall, thirty-two-year-old NASA project manager who had a Master's from The Massachusetts Institute of Technology in astrophysics and a Ph.D. in quantum mechanics earned at Stanford University in California, parted the kitchen curtains and peeked up at the low, moisture-laden clouds. They showed no sign of clearing. Her gaze then traveled down to the river where, at the edge of a deep pool on the far side, her partner and cohort for the past eight days, Phillip Margolin, cast a fly to trout rising along the riverbank. On the third cast a two-pound brown trout rose for his perfectly cast fly and within ten minutes Phillip had netted the sleek spotted fish. Alicia watched from behind the curtain as Margolin carefully removed the fly from the trout's lip and gently returned the fish to the crystal-clear river. She experienced a mild rush of adrenaline, which told her she liked him even more upon witnessing that gentle act from the outwardly tough computer expert.

Smiling to herself, she turned from the window, walked out of the kitchen and sat down at the computer terminal in her work area. Her two assistants, Martin LoCasio and Oscar Berlin, both assigned to her from NASA headquarters in Houston, had gone into Roscoe, the closest town in this upstate New York community, to get the New York Times and to buy groceries.

It was hard to believe that only eight days had passed since Alicia had been secretly flown to Washington, introduced to Secretary of Defense Mersky and Phillip Margolin, an aide to the Secretary and a Ph.D. himself in chemistry, rocket sciences and computer analysis. Eventually she met President Teller when a briefing regarding Operation Earthmother was held in the Oval Office. It was there that she'd also met Alma Finley and heard the fantastic story of the Antareans, the cocoons and the pregnant women from the Geriatric Brigade on their way home to Earth.

Alicia brought up the latest computer reentry model on her screen. It had been refined last night. She began to run it against the parameters Joe Finley had supplied earlier this morning. *He's a really nice old man*, she thought to herself as she leaned back, craning her neck to look into the screened-in porch where he bunked. He was still sleeping on the daybed they had set up in there for him. Phillip and she had spent hours pumping Finley about his travels in deep space. As they listened to his tales of planets and civilizations, it became apparent their education was inadequate to grasp the idea of this galaxy, perhaps the entire universe, teeming with life. Finley was kind and quickly put the matter in perspective, reminding them that not too many years ago he was a taxi driver in Boston, struggling to get a fading acting career on track.

"We've spent pretty much our entire existence on this planet under the assumption that we were alone in the cosmos. Our assumed self-importance and self-centeredness has closed our minds, most of us that is, to the idea that we might be just one little populated planet in a universe of living beings on millions, maybe billions of planets. Give the idea some time and you'll eventually understand how wonderful it is to be part of a living universe. And of course now we are witnesses to how foolish it was to hold that belief. Then again, seeing is believing, I suppose. If the people of Earth ever knew what dwells beyond their myopic vision it would change just about every narrow belief they hold."

"But they don't know," Phillip had responded.

"Will you tell them?" Alicia asked.

"I cannot. A primary rule of the Antareans that we have promised to keep. No interference with civilizations until they are ready."

"And we are not?" Phillip asked.

"Not by a long shot. But someday, if Earth gets its act together," Joe had told them, smiling, "I'll be the first to bring the word."

Philip offered Joe his room, but he insisted on sleeping on the porch even though it was damp and chilly. When Alicia protested, he told her about the weather conditions on Parma Quad 2, where the temperature differential was a full ninety degrees hourly and the humidity a constant state of super-saturation. "It was like living inside a steam bath that froze every hour on the hour, then thawed out for a while, then froze again. This porch is a delight for me."

Satisfied that Finley was still asleep, Alicia went back to running the model against her own program which tracked the moon's position relative to South Florida on the day projected for the Watership's arrival. The initial results looked promising, but the rapidly approaching deadline worried her. According to Finley, the Watership could be in position on the moon's far side in less than two weeks and they were scheduled to present a viable plan to the Secretary and President in two days.

A half an hour later, Phillip Margolin came through the back door into the kitchen on the run. He still wore his wet hip boots, tracking mud and sand across the cabin floor. The door slammed behind him, startling Alicia. She looked up from the computer's monitor. The noise also awakened Joe Finley, who cocked one eye curiously open toward an animated Phillip Margolin.

"We missed a key element last night," he announced as he carefully placed his bamboo fly rod against the wall behind Alicia's computer terminal. He tossed his hat, a dirty plaid affair covered with trout flies, onto the nearby Early American knotty-pine sofa. Without further comment he slid a chair over next to Alicia's and proceeded to clear the work she was doing off her TV screen, pecking furiously at the computer keyboard.

"Never completely accept all givens as immovables."

"I beg your pardon!" she said, grabbing his wrist firmly. "I happen to be in the middle of something." She was three inches taller than him, and a karate black belt.

"Just give me a second, okay? I think I know how we can do it!" He made no attempt to either free his wrist or fight her grasp. He allowed his piercing dark brown eyes to speak for him. She understood the passion and intelligence that lurked behind that gaze and eased her grip. He slid his hand out of her grasp and proceeded to enter and move data rapidly. Joe Finley, now fully awake, came into the room and watched Margolin as he furiously and precisely restructured the reentry model.

"What's up?"

"Phil's on to something more exciting than a trout... so he claims." There was mild sarcasm in her voice.

"That looks like you've got something going here," Joe remarked as he moved closer to the terminal.

"Not something, Joe. Everything. It's *the* answer," Margolin stated firmly. "But it's going to mean parking two of the Watership's tanks, probably the ones with the atmospheres, on the far side of the moon. Then we have them configure the third tank this way." He keyed in the program and a three-dimensional model of the Watership with one of her storage tanks nestled close up and crosswise against her stern came onto the screen. Phil Margolin keyed in another command and the model began to rotate, rising above what appeared now to be the moon's surface. The Earth was far off in the background. "With this configuration we can mask the entry all the way from the moon and create the shadow we need with the reentry of the new shuttle *Remembrance*."

"What about the atmospheres?" Alicia asked. "They'll need them in Houston sooner or later."

"I'm hoping they can manufacture what we need there. The three tank configuration is too large for what we have available for masking now. Or maybe the Probeship can shuttle down whatever gasses are necessary a bit at a time. What do you think, Joe?"

Finley studied the video screen. He understood what Margolin had in mind, but it would require conferencing with the others. His wife, Alma, was still in Washington coordinating the arrival of the Watership with the efforts now underway by a special Navy Seal team under the command of Undersecretary Walkly as they prepared to clear and secure an undersea area near the Stones.

After studying the plan for a moment more, Joe Finley concurred. "This way we are sure to bring the Watership down totally undetected. Doctor Khawaja will have to deal with the atmospheres."

Mary Green had ended her family visit in Scarsdale and returned to Florida. Shortly thereafter she and her husband Ben flew to Houston where they met with Dr. Khawaja to help prepare the hospital facility.

Amos Bright, Jack Fischer, Phil Doyle and their chopper pilot buddy, Madman Mazuski, worked out of Boca Raton aboard the *Manta III*, preparing the cocoons in their chambers for transport to the Watership after it had been safely landed and hidden beneath the South Florida seas.

"It will mean bringing in more new people," Alicia said. "For the atmospheres."

"That's possible," Phillip answered. "But this can bring everyone in undetected in one shot."

Joe left the room to have privacy while he contacted Amos Bright, Alma and the Greens. Margolin watched the old man carefully. After Finley was out of sight he looked at Alicia, who was standing beside him now.

"They do it telepathically, you know."

"I know," she answered.

"All across the galaxy."

"Yes."

"I'd love to know how to do it. How about you?"

"Are you kidding? I'd give my right arm to know." Their eyes met and Margolin, a tough, dynamic scientist, who had been all business since they'd arrived at this mountain retreat, smiled warmly at his attractive Latina partner.

"Keep the arm. It suits you," he said softly as he touched her right arm.

"Huh?" She blushed. *Did he know she'd been attracted to him the moment they'd met in Washington?*

"Your arm." He squeezed it gently.

"Not that arm," she said causally. "I meant the other one." She smiled at him. Her eyes went to the screen. "We still won't have a final deployment configuration for the first screen until we fix a firm point of entry." He released her arm but continued to hold his gaze.

"That won't be determined until the last minute, for both screens I imagine."

"Is something wrong?" she asked.

"Wrong? What could be wrong? The fishing is great and we've licked the problem. Quite the opposite."

"You're staring at me."

"You're beautiful, so I'm staring at you."

She blushed. "We've been together for eight days. How come I suddenly got beautiful?"

"The work's almost done here."

"So that's how it is? Business before…" She didn't finish the sentence because he immediately stood and moved very close to her.

"Pleasure?" He smiled. She eased back.

"You make me uncomfortable, Phillip. We're working here… Mr. Finley is…"

Margolin's demeanor changed abruptly. He was all business again. "Of course. You're right. I'm sorry."

"That's not necessary."

He sat down and began to work. She sat next to him and watched as he refined the model and began making printouts of the proposed trajectory for the Watership's trip from the moon to rendezvous with the space shuttle *Remembrance*.

"Thank you," she said softly.

"For what?"

"For saying I was beautiful."

"You are. It's a fact." He kept a matter-of-fact edge to his voice. She leaned over and gently kissed him on his cheek.

"So are you, hotshot," she whispered. A flush of red appeared on the nape of his exposed neck, but he said nothing.

A few moments later Joe Finley returned to say that the atmospheric tanks could be secured on the moon's far side and that the burgeoning group now firmly ensconced in the new wing of the Space Medicine Center would add physicists with expertese in the physiological and thermodynamic properties of exotic gasses.

He had also received sad news about one of the passengers aboard the Watership, but he kept that to himself.

CHAPTER SIXTEEN
NEW LIFE IN SPACE

It was Commander Ruth Charnofsky who gave Joe Finlay the bad news. The first woman to become pregnant had miscarried. The fetus was badly deformed. The parents were Commanders Bess and Arthur Perlman.

The Perlman's had requested that the other commanders not be told of the tragic event. Bess blocked her emotions and withdrew into her own private world. The six other commanders aboard, including her husband, could not enter her mind to comfort her. She was distraught, at times weeping uncontrollably. Nevertheless, rumors of what had happened spread through the Watership to the other expectant parents. A wave of fear permeated the journey. All of the pregnant women began to wonder if their babies would be carried to term.

Art Perlman knew he had to somehow break down the barrier that Bess had created. Physically she recuperated from her ordeal. Her body mended quickly. But after four days her mind still remained shielded, keeping out the others—keeping the pain of her loss to herself. Ben wondered if that might be nature's way to work out the loss. He rejected the idea and doubled his efforts to console his wife.

They had conceived the baby on Prima Maugur, a giant moon in the Pasadian System near the blue dwarf star known to us as Mira in the constellation Canis Major. This is a system where everything was huge—moons, planets, comets and asteroid materials were all of a grand scale. Gravity, even on Prima Maugur, colonized by Antareans, was enormous compared to Earth. Perhaps that had caused the fetus to be aborted. But the child was deformed, and that raised questions in everyone's mind about the viability of pregnancies in Earth-human women of their age, even with processing. It was true that their reproductive systems had been rejuvenated, but were they functioning normally?

Art Perlman was suspicious that the miscarriage had something to do with their being commanders. Somehow the genetic change, or perhaps the cerebral implant, or both, made normal reproduction impossible for them. Beam, the Antarean medical officer who had been on the last mission to Earth and who was now aboard the Watership, assured Art that was not the case. If anything, she maintained that the changes they experienced as commanders probably made them fertile before the other men and women in the Geriatric Brigade. It was true that Bess was the first to become pregnant. Ruth Charnofsky was second, and she too was a commander. But all signs showed that Ruth's pregnancy was proceeding normally even though her mate, Panatoy, was not Earth-human.

After spending time alone with Bess, holding her hand and speaking softly to her in their dimly illuminated cabin, Art Perlman finally grasped the deeper reason for Bess's behavior. During their marriage on Earth they had no children. That had been a deliberate decision that Bess made after she discovered her husband's involvement with organized crime. He had been a high-level, but outside, accountant and lawyer for the mob. He was never indicted, arrested or prosecuted. But his name was always in the newspapers and on radio and television. He had been called to testify at every congressional crime hearing, beginning with the Kefauver Committee in the early 1950s. Bess, whose father had been a renowned judge in Brooklyn, refused to have children, as she put it, "To give her husband and his kind an heir to train to continue in their dirty work." She never knew that her father, the Judge, was also on the mob payroll, and Arthur never told her.

With an inheritance of her own, and a full-time job as a saleswoman in a high-priced dress shop in downtown Brooklyn, she never accepted what she called "blood money" from her husband. Even when her widowed sister, Betty Franklin, was confined to a nursing home after having a stroke, Bess paid for her care, never bending to accept her husband's money even though they had retired to Florida years before. Betty was now also a commander. She knew her brother-in-law's past. She also knew about her father's involvement. Once she had been taken from the nursing home and processed by the Antareans, Arthur Perlman asked her to keep the secret from Bess. She agreed.

After the Perlmans spent that bitter childless life together and were confronted with the opportunity to leave the Earth with the Antareans, Bess chose to believe that they were embarking on a new life; a new beginning. She convinced herself that her God, the One the Antareans called Master, had given Art and her a second chance. The pregnancy was confirmation of that belief. She was convinced it was a sign that Arthur had finally been forgiven for his earthly sins and life of evil. But after the miscarriage, when she withdrew into a shell, she felt this loss was a punishment for her husband's crimes—retribution from an angry God.

Bess was sleeping when, after knocking, Beam walked quietly into the cabin. It was a spacious room decorated with a mixture of artifacts collected from Parma Quad 2, Antares, Prima Maugur, Hillet, a planet in the Alphard system, and a few keepsakes the Perlman's took with them when they left Earth five years ago. Bess lay on the bed, her back toward her husband and the Antarean visitor. Beam wore her human skin covering—that of an attractive thirty-year-old blonde, blue-eyed Caucasian. Now that they were approaching Earth, where she would have to wear it almost constantly among the staff being assembled in Houston, she wore it often aboard the Watership so as to stretch out any creases and make sure it molded to her body perfectly.

So many years had passed since he had seen Beam's covering Art almost didn't recognize her when she entered the room.

"Hello, Commander Arthur. How is Commander Bess?"

He stood up. "She's resting. Do I know you?" Then he reached to her mind. "It's you, Beam! I'd forgotten. Forgive me. I never think of you this way anymore, only as Antarean."

"But do I still make an attractive Earth-human?"

"Of course. Those young doctors in Houston are going to be stunned by you."

"Well, we'll see about that. Anyway, this time my human skin is thicker."

Bess, who had awakened when Beam came in, listened to the conversation. She and Beam were old friends... good friends. She had been one of the first to discuss what being an Antarean female was like with the bright medical officer. In a society that cloned their kind, Beam still admitted there was a deep inner force within many female Antareans that harbored an urge to bear young directly—to be a mother.

Beam walked to the side of the bed and reached out to Bess, gently stroking the older woman's long hair. Beam recalled when Bess had begun her processing five years ago at the Antares condominium in Coral Gables. Her hair had been white then. As the rejuvenation process progressed, Bess's hair became darker and darker until it took on a sheen and chestnut color that was now spread out on the pillow. Bess responded to her gentle touch and allowed Beam to feel her pain for an instant.

"I am so sorry, Bess," the young Antarean whispered. "I am here to share your grief. To help if you will allow it." Bess did not respond. Art, sensing that the women wanted privacy, left the room. "Bess? Will you speak to me?" No response. "Then will you at least listen? We cannot find your mind and so we cannot find a way to tell you what has happened. Please. Will you listen?"

"Yes. For you Beam, dear friend." Bess whispered.

"Thank you." Beam paused, choosing her words carefully. "We are all so sorry for what happened. The baby was not right. At times, that is the Master's way. Even with our methods... well... there are some who are just not right. But we have so many aboard who are soon to be mothers. They have heard what has happened. They are worried. Deeply concerned. This is not good for them and for the babies that are coming." Bess turned slowly, her tear-filled eyes swollen from crying, and looked at Beam.

"I can't do anything about the babies that are coming."

"Yes, my friend, you can. You can help Commander Charnofsky and your own sister Betty. You can help me. We must calm the women and their mates. We must assure them that everything will be good… that this event… this journey to Motherplanet is right. That this is the Master's work."

"Losing my baby was the Master's work."

"Perhaps. Who is to say? I believe that these babies coming to us are a new race. An important race. All Antareans believe that their birth was preordained eons ago. It is our mission to do all we can to insure they survive and thrive."

"Mine didn't," Bess answered bitterly. She sat up, reached for tissue from the nearby night table and blew her nose.

"I know. I am sorry. It was not right. The next will…"

"There will be no next!"

"Perhaps. Who is to say? Would you have believed it possible at all five years ago? Have you not traveled among the stars and looked upon the Master's great work?" Beam was a religious Antarean, trained that way because as a medical officer she would be close to many Antareans when they died. It was part of her duties to certify an Antarean death so a replacement might be created. And sometimes death, which could be voluntary, had to be administered by a medical officer. It was the sovereign right of an adult Antarean to request his or her own demise. For a race that revered life, and for whom there was no limit to the time they had to live, they also respected the decision to end life as a rational and personal right of every adult Antarean. They did not look upon death as a finality, but rather moving on to another level of existence. Their bodies, their flesh, were renewable. The proof was that the clone that replaced the dead Antarean looked exactly like the one that preceded it, but the life force within, the spark that they said came from the Master, that which Earth-humans call soul, was unique unto each individual. That was what moved on to another level of life, or existence within the Master's grand plan.

Bess wiped her eyes and accepted Beam's words. Her Antarean friend was correct. The time for self-pity and recrimination was over. The births to come were important and had to be nurtured.

"I'm sorry," Bess said. "I've been selfish." She opened her mind and heart. Immediately the consciousnesses of the other commanders, some from across the galaxy, rushed into her brain and brought comfort and strength. Strongest of these was her husband, Art. She silently called to him. He entered their room and crossed over to the bed. Beam stood and backed away as Art and Bess embraced. As Beam closed the door behind her, allowing the Perlman's their privacy, so did the other commanders disengage their minds from Bess, leaving her alone with her husband to mourn their loss together for the first time.

Later that night two of the women went into premature labor within an hour of each other. They were friends—both originally from St. Louis. They had been recruited by Andrea and Frank Hankinson who were the first people recruited by Ben Green, Joe Finley, Art Perlman and Bernie Lewis in Florida five years ago.

After Parma Quad 2, Frank Hankinson, who was a commander, led a group of his friends to live and work in the Alphard system which is located in the constellation Hydra. It is a six-planet system with the dwarf Alphard as solar source. Two of the planets, Betch and Hillet, are populated. A humanoid life form evolved on Betch, which is a seasonal water planet about twice the size of Earth. The Antareans established relations with the Betch civilization thousands of years ago and because the Betch were not space travelers, helped them colonize Hillet, a less hospitable planet devoid of humanoid life or civilization. Over the millennia the Antareans changed the atmosphere and weather conditions on Hillet, warming the surface and increasing the rainfall, thus causing agriculture to flourish. With a stable food supply the population increased. Today, although the Betch and Hillet histories record the colonization, the Hilletines consider themselves a race apart from their Motherplanet Betch and have their own language, technology, religions and governmental forms. The relations between the two planets are cordial, but neither are races that chose to travel in deep space. The Antareans provide the only transport between the planets.

It was on Hillet that Frank Hankinson, his wife and three other couples, all from St. Louis, settled and worked as teachers and ambassadors. And it was there that these two women became pregnant.

Arthur Perlman watched his wife administer to the two women in labor. His heart went out to her, but she was strong, using her telepathic abilities to soothe the anxious mothers-to-be. Frank entered the labor room, which had been hastily prepared by Beam's Antarean medical team, woefully inexperienced in the matter of human birth. Although they were not expecting, the Hankinsons had come along on the trip because he was a commander. She was not. During the trip they had discussed the idea of trying to have a baby, but after seeing Bess miscarriage, they decided to wait until there was more data regarding birth among the Brigade Earth-human women.

"I'd hoped we could have made it to Earth before this," Frank told Art.

"I guess even at Parman guide speed, nature will have her way," he answered wryly. "Babies will be born in their own time, no matter how many light years traveled."

Bess and her sister Betty were with one of the women, Julia Messina, a stout, dark-eyed woman with short black hair that offset an oval, olive-complexioned face that reflected her Sardinian heritage. Julia's husband, Vincent, a fireplug of a man whose leathery skin bore witness to his years in the construction trades, hovered nearby, his brow furrowed with concern. Both sisters concentrated on the couple, keeping their minds relaxed and positive as Julia's labor intensified.

The other couple, Lillian and Abe Erhardt, were calmer and fatalistic about their baby's birth. Ruth Charnofsky, herself five months pregnant, and Rose Lewis, also a commander, were present to care for Lillian, who as a younger woman forty-five years ago had given birth to twin boys in the back seat of a taxi. Her husband, then a young Marine corporal fighting against the Japanese in World War II, was ten thousand miles away across the Pacific on a tiny rock of an island called Iwo Jima. Now, they held hands and offered their appreciation to Ruth and Rose, whose telepathic powers helped to ease Lillian's labor.

"Looks like it's going well," Art said to Frank. He smiled at Bess. "I think we serve no purpose here."

"Women's work, huh?" Frank commented, understanding Art's desire to leave.

"I guess. It's certainly not ours anyway." He was nervous himself.

"They've got things under control." Frank waved to his St. Louis friends, the Messinas and Erhardts, and left the delivery room with Art.

The babies were born within seven minutes of each other. The Messinas had a girl, the Erhardts twin boys once again. The first Earth-humans born aboard an Antarean spaceship—any spaceship for that matter. They were perfectly normal and healthy, if a little premature. But they didn't appear premature. They looked full term, fully developed, strong, alert and hungry. All aboard the Watership greeted the babies with cheers and love. Their arrival and condition gave everyone a tremendous emotional lift and quashed the fears of the remaining expectant parents. The two Earth-human mothers, both close to eighty but looking much younger, nursed their infants—a sight never before seen in the galaxy.

The cries of the newborns echoed throughout the Watership as it now sped past Jupiter, slowing imperceptibly again as the Parman guides slowed down their solar ultra-violet absorption rate. Their arrival on the far side of Earth's single moon would take place within the week.

CHAPTER SEVENTEEN
FEDS AND COPS

I think it's time we reeled in those two fish," Secret Service Agent Benton Fuller remarked as he adjusted his chaise to catch a more direct exposure to the late afternoon sun.

"I hear you," Gary McGill, FBI Special Agent from the Miami office, agreed. His job was to coordinate security clearances for presidential visits to the southeastern United States. He was a personal friend of Benton Fuller, which is why the Chief of the White House detachment had requested that McGill be brought into Operation Earthmother. "The last thing we want is a couple of loaded pistolas floating around out there just waiting to go off."

The federal agents were discussing the status of Detective Sergeant Matthew Cummings and his partner, Detective Coolridge Betters. The Antarean Watership was scheduled to arrive within five to six days, and the two Coral Gables cops were going to be in the way. They were at McGill's home—a modest pastel-pink stucco house located adjacent to a canal that ran west out of Perine. The local claims to fame were the Parrot Jungle and Monkey Jungle, tourist attractions that brought mobs of visitors twice a year when the schools up north closed for winter and spring vacations. But these days, Perine was just a sleepy South Florida town, the perfect location for the headquarters of Operation Earthmother. The house next to McGill's had been taken over by Navy Undersecretary Captain Thomas Walkly and his staff of three. They were coordinating naval operations with the special maneuvers to ostensibly increase the interdiction of drug traffic in the waters between the Bahamas and Florida's east coast.

"I'm amazed they've kept this investigation of theirs to themselves," McGill said. He wore a bright-flowered Hawaiian bathing suit and sipped on a Bloody Mary diluted from melting ice. Both men were in their late forties, tall and trim. They worked hard at keeping in shape as their jobs demanded. In South Florida, with the burgeoning drug trade claiming the lives of all manner of law enforcement people as well as traffickers, Special Agent McGill knew the value of having his muscles and reflexes toned and sharp.

Likewise, given the responsibility of protecting the president in a country where there were more privately held arms than there were citizens, and a world teeming with radical, religious and politically motivated terrorists intent on becoming martyrs for their causes, Secret Service Agent Fuller kept also himself in top shape, although these days as he neared fifty the task became more and more difficult. He turned over onto his back and reached for his own drink, a gin and tonic.

"Those two cops have an agenda all their own. I checked out their files. They were involved with our uh, shall we say 'visitors' the last time they were here. In the end there was a DA who made them look like jerks. I think they're motivated to set the record straight."

"Yeah," McGill interjected, "I checked that out myself. They've been onto that Fischer guy and his buddies like flypaper."

"Mr. Bright is concerned. He adamant about keeping those cocoons out there safe."

"I hear that. So, how do you want to do it?"

"I'm not sure yet. One think I do know is I don't want the Coral Gables Sheriff involved. The last thing we need is a local yokel knowing what we know."

"That would be a circus. You want another?" McGill asked, motioning toward Fuller's empty glass.

"No thanks. Anyway, here's where I 'm heading. I think maybe the best way is to involve the two detectives in the pickup."

"The Navy cover exercise?"

"I'll have to check it out with Walkly."

"He seems to be wound a little tight."

"He's okay. Just military. He doesn't want his end screwing up."

"Assuming he says okay, when do you want to move on them?"

Agent Fuller thought for a moment, considering the few secret service agents he had. In the end, after pressure from the Secretary of Defense, he had been authorized to brief only three of his most trusted people, two men and a woman, on the extraordinary events that were unfolding. They were now spread around—one man was with the President, another with Mary and Ben Green in Houston, and the female agent assigned to Alma Finley who would soon arrives with her husband, Joe. But for now, it was up to McGill and Fuller to handle the two snooping detectives.

"I think ASAP." Fuller looked up at the sun turning orange-gold as it sank lower in the western sky. No more sunning himself today. "As a matter of fact," he said, getting out of the comfortable chaise, "there's no time like the present. Let's get cleaned up and pay the good Captain Walkly a visit."

The same setting sun turned the waters of the Inland Waterway into a rich golden liquid that reflected onto the crisp white hull of the *Manta III* as it rocked slightly in its Boca Raton slip. Jack Fischer, Phil Doyle and Madman Mazuski lounged on the fantail, sipping beers in full sight of Detectives Cummings and Betters.

Below the waterline of Jack's broad-beamed vessel, the Antarean Probeship was alive with activity. Amos Bright finished transmitting new data regarding the cocoon chambers to the Watership. He then coordinated a telepathed conference between Alma Finley in Washington, Joe Finley in Roscoe and the Green's in Houston. He related how Secretary Mersky's people, Margolin and Sanchez, had presented Joe Finley with a viable solution for bringing the Watership and its passengers to Earth. Amos agreed with Joe's assessment and had forwarded the plan to the Watership's flight crew as well as the Brigade commanders on board. Joe Finley and Mersky's team would pack up and leave the Catskill cabin. They would return to Washington and join Alma to make a presentation to the President.

The Greens reported progress with the NASA Space Hospital facility and medical teams that were carefully being assembled.

The problem of manufacturing four different atmospheres for the off-planet fathers was under study. The engineers were having a problem in keeping Panatoy's atmosphere stable under the pressure and temperature conditions required. They needed a precise molecular and subatomic breakdown of the inert gasses for the Subaxian chamber. Amos had passed their request to the Watership. It would take a few hours for the reply.

Operation Earthmother seemed to be progressing well. All involved were aware that some of their movements in Florida were being monitored by the two aging detectives, Cummings and Betters. Benton Fuller and the FBI were on the case but Amos Bright had not heard from the Secret Service agent for a while and was acutely aware that the two Miami detectives were lurking nearby.

"We finished preparation of all the cocoons today," Amos said. "Jack and his friends have been invaluable."

"And you're sure those two cops are no problem?" Ben Green asked.

"We're watching them," Amos said.

"Persistent, aren't they?" Alma remarked.

"Obsessed is more like it," Amos answered. "The Secret Service and FBI are watching."

"Have they followed you out to sea?" Mary Green asked.

"Once last week. They rented a helicopter."

"Rented?" Ben questioned.

"One of those that take people for rides out in the Everglades, I think. But they had some, uh, let's say engine trouble and had to turn back."

"That was convenient," Joe said, laughing. He understood that Amos had caused it.

"I take it that's a sign they haven't said anything to their superiors," Alma said. "Otherwise they'd have used a police aircraft." The others agreed.

They were right. But barely. Matthew Cummings and Coolridge Betters had not shared their suspicions with their fellow police officers or the District Attorney. They had, however, hired an old friend who was an ex-underwater cameraman, now the owner of a small engineering company that manufactured underwater housings and lights for professional motion picture cameras. The man, Hans Leiter, had hidden underwater near the Boca Raton outlet to the ocean late one afternoon. He used a special underwater camera and high-speed film to photograph the *Manta III* below her waterline. Hans Leiter gave the undeveloped film to the two detectives he mentioned that here seemed to something lashed to the hull of the *Manta III*, But the Inter-coastal water was murky and he couldn't see what it was. He suspected it had something to do with drug smuggling, and knew that when you lived in Miami, the less you knew about those things the safer you were.

That afternoon, Cummings had the film developed. Although both detectives had no idea what the Probeship actually was, they concluded that it must be a submarine for smuggling drugs. They discussed the possibility that it was perhaps time to bring in help.

Jack, Phil and Madman Mazuski were made aware that the detectives from the Coral Gables sheriff's office were watching them. The white one, Cummings, was in his car at the corner of the marina parking lot. The black cop, Betters, was across the waterway on a houseboat moored at the private dock of a high-rise condominium.

"Like living in a fishbowl," Jack remarked after he spotted Betters watching them through binoculars.

Mazuski gulped diligently on his fourth beer and grunted. "Mr. Bright should have fixed that chopper to ditch. That would have discouraged them."

"And brought an investigation down all around us," Phil said. He had ceased taking out the *Terra Time* each day as a ploy to keep one of the detectives occupied. "Betters is a smart old cop. He caught on that my boat was just a diversion after the second day. Even if Cummings always took what happened five years ago personally, we're not sure they haven't left some information about us around somewhere... you know... in case something happens to them."

"Jesus, Phil," Mazuski said. "You've been watching too much *Miami Vice,* on TV."

"Phil's right," Jack said. "And Mr. Bright agrees. We can't take any chances. That's why he just gave their chopper a small problem. But I wonder how long those two are going to be satisfied just watching us."

"Why don't the old guys and Amos go into their heads and scramble their brains?" Mazuski suggested, chuckling.

"Because it's not their way," Jack responded. "But they'd better do something soon. The Finleys are due back soon, and I don't think Cummings will hold much longer when they show up."

At that moment a blue Ford Taurus pulled into the parking lot and stopped in the spot next to Cummings's Olds. The detective paid little attention as the driver got out, locked the door and then went to his trunk. Probably a boat owner, Cummings surmised, checking the man's casual clothes. Had he seen the similar car parking in the condo lot across the waterway, with a similar-looking, similarly dressed man getting out and approaching Betters on the houseboat, he might have been suspicious. As he refocused his attention on the fantail of the *Manta III* the passenger door of his car opened and the man leaned in and flashed his United States Treasury Department ID that identified him as Secret Service Special Agent Benton Fuller. Across the Inter-coastal at the same moment, Detective Betters was staring at ID belonging to FBI Special Agent Gary McGill.

CHAPTER EIGHTEEN
THE STRIP CLUB DEAL

Cummings had chosen the "quiet" place where they could talk without attracting attention. He'd radioed over to Betters, who by that time had been briefed by McGill, to meet at Marty's Cozy Nest on Biscayne Boulevard in North Miami Beach. It was a twenty-four-hour club featuring pole dance strippers and a steady clientele ranging from truck drivers to businessmen in suits to horny retirees.

Cummings and Fuller took I-95 and arrived twenty minutes ahead of Betters and McGill. "You call this quiet?" Fuller asked, amazed at Cummings's choice of a meeting place.

"You wanted a place to talk privately, right? We won't be disturbed here. I know the owner. He's a retired fruit and vegetable man from Philly." Cummings pointed Fuller to the rear of the dark, smoke-filled strip joint. They settled into a booth. He gestured for Fuller to be seated across the blue marbleized Formica table. A tall, glassy-eyed, bleached-blonde girl with bare silicone-filled breasts approached. She wore nothing but a checkered apron and a sequined G-string.

"Hiya, Sarge. I ain't seen you in a coon's age."

"How's it going, Midge?"

"It's goin'... It's comin'. Where's your cute black buddy?"

"He'll be along. Gimmie a Coors." He turned to Fuller. "You want something?" he asked.

"Coke."

"In a glass or on a glass?" Midge asked. Fuller looked confused. Cummings laughed.

"He wants a Coca-Cola."

"Then he should say so," she muttered, doing an about-face so that her ample buttocks, still wet with perspiration from her performance on the runway, brushed against Benton Fuller. Cummings enjoyed the federal agent's discomfort. It was why he'd chosen to come to this place. Like many local Florida policemen he wasn't impressed with the federal law enforcement people. They were supposed to come into Florida to close down the drug traffic, but they kept their information and operations to themselves, placing little trust in local police departments. The fed's theory was that the drug kingpins had the local police on their payrolls. In some cases that was probably true, but it gave a bad name to all the police. The honest cops resented it. Deep down, when Cummings had suspected the old men and Fischer were in the drug business, he dreamed about a major bust without the feds. Now that they had shown up he was sure he would lose the collar and they would take the glory.

"Is there a telephone here?" Fuller asked.

"Next to the toilet in back."

"I've got to call someone to meet us. Does it really have to be here?"

"You wanted quiet and safe, right?"

"He's a naval officer."

"Tell him to leave his sailor suit home. Hey, maybe he's a customer."

Fuller got up and went to the phone. There were just a few patrons in the club, and they were gathered at the wide bar that served as runway for the strippers. As Fuller walked away, one of the girls, a dark Cuban named Carla, was doing her act. Marta, one of the other Cuban girls, watched Fuller walk toward the back of the club. She got up from her bar stool and threw a questioning glance at Cummings. The cop smiled and nodded for Marta to follow the man. She did, thinking she was about to make a few extra dollars on a slow afternoon.

While Fuller was making his call, and, Cummings hoped, having difficulty with a Cuban hooker who wasn't used to taking no for an answer, the drinks arrived along with Betters and McGill. Midge set the drinks down and gave a warm welcome to Betters.

"You want a bourbon, Hon?"

"Neat. Some branch water on the side. How about you, McGill?"

"Coca-Cola. Ice."

"At least this dick's local," Midge said, moving her act away toward the bar. Betters and McGill sat down opposite one another.

"Where's Fuller?" McGill asked.

"On the phone. He said he had to call a sailor."

Betters looked at his partner questioningly. On the ride down neither detective had learned what was going down. All they had been told was that Jack Fischer, his friends and the old people were now under federal surveillance and that the cooperation of the two Coral Gables cops was required.

There was a sudden ruckus from the rear, excited raised voices and then the distinct sound of a man's voice saying, "Get your hands off me and back off!." A moment later Marta came stomping past the booth, her bare breasts bouncing with each angry strut. She stopped across from the table and glared at Cummings.

"That ain't no John. That's a *maricone*. He don't want no woman." She continued her angry march until she disappeared behind the bar into the backstage dressing area. Benton Fuller returned to the table.

"Trouble?" Cummings asked innocently. Betters fought to keep a straight face.

"Goddamned hooker tried to grab me back there. Right in the middle of a phone call."

"To Walkly?" McGill asked.

"Yeah. I told him to meet us here."

"And how to dress, I hope," Cummings interjected.

Fuller glared at Cummings. "He'll be up in forty minutes."

"Alone?"

"Yes."

Midge returned with the rest of the drinks. She placed them gently on the table. "Now darlin's, will that be it for y'all?" she asked with a sudden, sweet Southern voice.

"I've got this," Fuller offered, reaching into his pants pocket. Betters, who was sitting next to The Secret Service agent tried to stop him, but it was too late. "Holy shit!" the Fuller exclaimed, "my money's gone!"

Cummings grabbed Midge's wrist. "Move your butt on the double and tell Marta I want the wallet NOW!" He spun her with one swift movement and slapped her rear end hard. "And everything that was in it!" He turned to Fuller. "Not to worry. It'll be back in a moment."

It was returned with apologies.

By the time Captain Walkly had arrived, dressed in jeans, a Grateful Dead T-shirt and torn dirty sneakers, Cummings and Betters had been filled in on most of the operation. It was big, bigger than they had imagined. The old people were "world-class" drug kingpins from Hong Kong. Jack and his friends were involved in the largest narcotic shipment the Federal Drug Enforcement Agency had ever tapped into. It was going down within the next week. From this point on the movements of the old people, Jack, his friends and the submarine operator would be monitored by the feds and the United States Navy. That was where Captain Walkly figured in the operation, which, they were told, was code-named Earthmother. He arrived in time to tell his part of the story.

"We were worried about you two," he began, after Midge had brought him a Coors Light and a round of drinks on the house for the others. She began to apologize for Marta again, but Betters told her to forget it and to get lost.

Walkly continued, "Because the key to the operation is that submarine attached to the bottom of the *Manta III.*" As he spoke he examined the photos of the Probeship that Cummings and Betters had obtained. "To think that they might have seen the diver who shot these…"

"They didn't. He's the best," Cummings said proudly. *He must be*, Walkly thought to himself. *Amos Bright hadn't picked him up telepathically.*

"Well, in any case, from here on in we can't take any chances. You two will stay with us until the operation goes down. I've cleared that with your boss."

"I don't know about that…" Betters started to object.

"That's it!" Walkly was firm. "I've got several ships moving into the area with nearly eight hundred men, choppers, sea sleds and a nuclear submarine. Nothing is going to screw this up. Nothing!"

"Besides," McGill added, "we need you boys. You're familiar with both their boats and that chopper pilot of theirs."

"Mazuski," Cummings muttered. "He's a drunk and a menace."

"Well," Fuller said softly, "after we nail their asses the only thing he'll be flying is a steel prison cot. Isn't that right, Captain?" Walkly's eyes had drifted over to the runway where Marta was now performing.

"Huh? Oh, sure," Walkly answered, turning his attention back to the group huddled in the booth. "That's for damned sure. I need you two aboard the chase boats to make positive ID on that *Manta III* and the *Terra Time*. As a matter of fact, I want you men to make the arrests when the time comes."

"You really mean that?" Cummings asked. Betters rolled his eyes. He was wary.

"You guys were on to these rats five years ago, and they slipped out of it." Fuller sounded sincere. "We know how much heat you took for that mess. You guys deserve this part of the collar. We'll have our part of it too, as will the Navy."

"There's plenty to go around," Captain Walkly said as he watched Midge's pendulous breasts sway and slide to the music. "Plenty..."

Amos Bright came up through the galley of the *Manta III* and joined Jack, Doyle and Mazuski as they watched the final rays of the sun disappear in the pink and blue cloud-streaked western sky.

"The cops left and didn't come back," Jack told him.

"I know. Our people from Washington are with them now."

"Does that mean they're out of the picture?" Phil Doyle asked.

"In a manner of speaking," Amos answered. "Let's just say that the next time we see them it will be under new and different circumstances."

CHAPTER NINETEEN
THE FACILITY

Everything appeared normal at the Lyndon B. Johnson Space Center, NASA's sprawling headquarters and training facility thirty miles southeast of downtown Houston. Since the terrible accident that destroyed the space shuttle *Challenger* and with it the lives of seven heroic American astronauts, NASA had a tough struggle to regain the confidence and support of Americans in the space program. New safety programs were initiated and the Johnson Center was now a beehive of activity. It was not uncommon for two or three missions to be in various stages of preparation at one time. The launch schedule of shuttles had reached almost one per month.

There had always been a space medicine center in Houston. In the mid-1980s a specialized facility had been opened in San Antonio, Texas, with the specific mission of applying the knowledge and experience gained in space medicine to benefit more Earthbound humans. Then, as America prepared to begin manned flights to planets within our solar system, the Johnson Space Medicine Facility was reactivated and expanded. It was in the recently renovated hospital wing of Building 11 that Dr. Khawaja had set up the Operation Earthmother facility designed to accommodate the expectant parents of the Geriatric Brigade.

Several days before the extraterrestrial guests were scheduled to arrive, the chaos that the twenty-one doctors representing seven specialties, eighteen engineers of various talents, twelve chemists, ten physicists and scores of support people, ranging from hardhat sheet metal and foundry laborers to surgical pediatric nurses could cause as they interacted suddenly calmed.

Mary and Ben Green had arrived and met with the entire staff in a secure auditorium next to Mission Control. They were the first "aliens" the staff had seen. Everyone was curious. Many of the top scientists and doctors who had been wooed by Dr. Khawaja, Dr. Yee and the President had serious doubts that this operation was what they had been told. Some were convinced there were secret military reasons. For others, the details of Operation Earthmother seemed too fantastic to be true. There were also grumblings of covert political activities being the real reason for the secrecy and security surrounding the project. This undercurrent became acute when four atmospheric temperature-controlled chambers were ordered on a crash basis. Overnight several new engineers, chemists and physicists arrived, taking over most of the second and third floors that had previously been set aside for staff living quarters. No one was told what the new arrival's mission was, and so rumors persisted.

But as they listened to the Greens explain the operation in detail, including the history and travels of the Brigade, the entire group understood they were about to become an extremely privileged group of humans.

"It was a natural thought, and many of us, scattered across this galaxy had it simultaneously. When we learned that birth on Motherplanet was an important part of the galactic unwritten laws, we experienced oneness with life as we had never felt before. Mary and I are here as witness to the wonderful news that we, Earth-humans are not alone in this galaxy—perhaps the entire universe. We are all part of something wondrous, something alive and ongoing." Ben Green had captured the audience's attention. Not one person stirred. They hardly breathed.

"Earth is our Motherplanet," Mary told the audience, "and we are coming home to have our young. You have all done a magnificent job. Some months ago, as we all gathered on Antares awaiting the Watership, some of us had serious doubts about how much help we might get upon our return. It was the Antarean leader, Amos Bright, who settled our doubts. He pointed out that we, the Geriatric Brigade, had responded and aided his race without reservation on their voyage to Earth five years ago. He saw no reason why our fellow human beings would not respond in kind and aid us. He was correct. While you do your work here, he is tasked with the responsibility of recovering the cocoons so they may be returned to Antares and reanimated. Many Earth-humans are aiding in that endeavor too."

"That which you have done and will do in the weeks and months ahead will be recorded as one of humanity's finest moments," Ben said. "You are hosts to Earth's first visitors from our galaxy. We are deeply grateful to all of you and we bless you."

The Greens then telepathed to all the other commanders, who in turn singly and collectively reached out to each individual in the audience with thanks. The resultant swell of goodwill and love passed from the commanders to the expectant parents aboard the Watership and beyond, throughout the galaxy, to all the other members of the Geriatric Brigade.

And then it was time to get back to work with new purpose.

The overall plan for the facility was the cooperative brainchild of Dr. Khawaja and the eccentric Sino-American obstetrician-pediatrician Dr. Michelangelo Yee. Dr. Yee, whose seventy-six-year-old arthritic hands were no longer able to perform the delicate fetal surgery he had pioneered, was still the incontestable leader in the exciting new field. He was, as Dr. Khawaja stated, "beyond the leading edge of fetal medicine."

The hospital wing for Operation Earthmother was three stories high. Each floor could be sealed off, and sections on each floor could also be isolated by impenetrable, sterile shielding. It contained the most up-to-date medical and environmental technology available.

Everything was designed to be centered on the moment of birth. The top floor contained examination rooms, including ultrasonic machines and amniocentesis facilities. Dominating the floor were the operating-delivery rooms. They were built in groups of three in the center of which was a pediatric intensive care unit capable of servicing nine infants at a time. Three state-of-the-art incubators, complete with life-support systems and isolation chambers, were available in each pediatric intensive care room. At the completion of delivery the obstetricians would immediately pass the infant into intensive care where it would be tended by a complete medical team. This would free the staff in the delivery room to care for the mother. A geriatrician was attached to the obstetric staff. On the surgical floor there was also an adult intensive care unit with a dozen beds and a complete staff.

The infant would remain in intensive care while it was tested and evaluated. Blood and other fluid workups would be done in laboratories attached to the unit. Chromosome evaluations would also begin. After a period of stability, and if there were no apparent problems, the infant would be moved to a transitional nursery, where, assuming there were no complications with the mother, the newborn would be joined by its parents. There were three complete units with this configuration on the top floor.

At the south end of the floor the engineers had broken through to the floor below. They had constructed four atmospheric chambers, each divided in half, much like a duplex apartment. The top portion of the chamber would be prepared to accept the newborn from each of the four mixed matings. The lower portion of the chamber would serve as housing for the non Earth-human parent.

If the newborn had dominant characteristics of the father, it would be immediately transferred, along with its own pediatric team, to the chamber. The chambers contained breathing apparatus and protective suits for the medical teams. Data regarding gaseous mixtures, temperature, pressure and humidity for the chambers had been supplied by Beam from the Watership. But the engineers and scientists knew that they had to be prepared to adjust these environments once the off-planet fathers arrived. Then more crucial adjustments would have to be made for the newborn if it was unable to survive under normal Earth conditions. Once the infant was born, the doctors and scientists might have only moments to analyze the situation before they made the decision to move the infant to a suitable environment for survival.

The second, or middle floor, contained the lower portion of the duplex chambers at one end. Then there were four completely staffed nurseries with a capacity to care for fifty babies. An additional pediatric intensive care unit and several laboratories were on this floor, just in case an emergency arose in the regular nurseries. The rest of the floor was devoted to examination rooms and housing for the Brigade fathers.

The lower, first floor contained staff living quarters, the kitchen, housing for security people and a special apartment set aside for the President, complete with the communication equipment required to run the country should he decide to make an extended visit.

The top floor was painted green, the second floor blue and the bottom floor yellow. The special sterile seals, hidden in the walls and controlled by the chief of security, a Secret Service agent assigned by Benton Fuller, were bright red.

There was one other facility tucked away in the basement of the large hospital wing. Everyone prayed it would never be used. It was the pathology lab.

CHAPTER TWENTY
THE PLAN

They gathered in from Houston, Miami, Roscoe and Washington. Operation Earthmother's first phase was drawing to a close, perhaps more to a climax that would bring the Watership in safely and undetected to Earth, and the expectant parents to the special facility being prepared at the Johnson Space Center.

The meeting was scheduled to take place at the Omega Conference Center eleven floors below ground at the huge five-sided edifice of American military power, the Pentagon. This top-secret conference and command facility had been originally constructed after the Cuban missile crisis during the administration of John F. Kennedy. It was initially planned as a nerve center and communication switching complex for the President's military staff and political advisors who might remain in the nation's capital after a nuclear attack. As time passed, many Secretaries of Defense paraded through the Pentagon, coming and going with administrations, often fading rapidly when their military adventures failed. However, each secretary became enthralled with the Omega Center concept, many of them thinking that perhaps in the event of nuclear war they might be the one high-ranking official remaining to lead the country to victory. And so each somehow managed to appropriate funds to update and improve the center until it now, when it boasted more computer and communication capability than the fabled War Room deep underground at SAC headquarters in Omaha, Nebraska.

Phillip Margolin and Alicia Sanchez arrived the day before yesterday along with Martin LoCasio and Oscar Berlin, their two NASA staffers. They spent their time setting up the presentation they would make in the Omega Center to the other key members of the Operation Earthmother group.

The hot, humid early June morning was a harbinger of the typical Washington, D.C. summer that would soon arrive. It was fast approaching that time when the nation's capital emptied of government functionaries, bureaucrats, legislators and administration staffers and filled proportionately with tourists from the four corners of America and the world who came to observe this fabled seat of power. What they found were monuments, cool empty marble halls, a plethora of statuary ranging from the great to the pitifully insignificant, expensive museums, enormous buildings stuffed with mountains of paper—the flotsam and jetsam of bureaucracy tuned to a fine art, and of course the brutal heat and humidity, the hallmark of a Potomac Basin summer.

Alma and Joe Finley settled back in the limousine that Secretary Mersky had sent to their hotel to bring them to the meeting. The traffic across the Key Bridge, stretching from the massive Lincoln Monument to the entrance to Arlington National Cemetery, flowed equally—inward toward Washington and outward to Virginia. Above the bridge, high on a bluff in the cemetery, the monument, grave and eternal flame of the slain John F. Kennedy was visible to the two Brigade Commanders.

"How long ago was it that we visited Kennedy's grave?" Alma asked.

"1970... No '71," Joe recalled.

"I'm still sad about that. It was a terrible time." She leaned back into the soft seat and found Joe's arm waiting there for her.

"I suppose we wanted... we expected so much from him."

"A magical time," she said, rubbing her cheek against his caressing hand.

"Camelot." He looked at her and stroked her cheek. "I love you dearly Alma, but I can't do it. Not yet anyway."

After dinner with Caleb Harris, Alma and Joe had returned to the Mayflower Hotel. They stopped for a nightcap in the oak-paneled bar. The conversation came around to Mary Green's pregnancy.

They'd talked for most of the night about it. All the commanders now knew of the normal births on the Watership and were relieved. Alma wanted a baby—the baby she'd never had. She had spent her young life building her career, with no time for marriage or children. Joe had been her first marriage. It was his second. Somewhere he had an ex-wife and two daughters who'd been alienated from him for decades. His experience with children was distasteful. They had talked about it, but Joe remained noncommittal. Until now.

"Do you want to tell me why?" she asked, leaving her cheek against his now immobile hand.

"I'm not sure I can. It goes deep. There are emotions I thought I'd never have to confront again. Darling, I'm sorry. The idea of children... of being able to have children now... I mean, I'm just not sure I want that."

"But I do, Joe. I want it very much."

"I know. I have to ask you to wait. Please. We have time." He smiled and looked at her. "Perhaps forever. And there's so much to do and we're not so sure that..."

"You mean why Bess miscarried?"

"Well, yes. It may have something to do with being commanders. We just don't know. I want to be sure. I don't want you to be hurt the way Bess was." She took his hand in hers.

"Does that mean you want to have children someday?"

"If we can. If they will be normal, then, well... yes. With you, for you, yes." He kissed her hand and then her lips as the limousine exited the parkway and headed toward the Pentagon.

Mary and Ben Green and Dr. Khawaja landed at Dulles International Airport at nine that morning. They were met by two other limousines; one from the Department of Defense with instructions to take the Greens directly to the Pentagon, and the other the Undersecretary's private car that would first take him to his office at the newly revamped Department of Public Health and Welfare, and then across to Virginia and the meeting in the Omega room. Since he'd been in Houston for the better part of three weeks, his desk was piled high with documents that required his attention.

They parted company. As Mary and Ben began their journey to the Pentagon they reached out to communicate with Alma and Joe, but found their fellow commanders were blocking.

"They are near," Ben commented.

"We'll see them soon," Mary answered. She was tired and a little nauseous. She closed her eyes and breathed deeply.

"You okay, honey?" Ben asked, putting his cool hand on her slightly damp forehead.

"Just the old morning ills. You'd think that with all that physical processing I had morning sickness would have been fixed."

Ben laughed. "I guess the Antareans never have that problem. As far as I know there's not any nausea in a petri dish."

"Very funny," she answered, smiling weakly. "I'm not sure that isn't a politically incorrect remark." She then transferred some of her discomfort to Ben, whose stomach became queasy too.

"Thanks," he said. "You're all heart, mother." Mary then cut off the discomfort, satisfied she had distracted him sufficiently. She had wanted to change the subject because when they had tried to contact the Finleys moments ago, Mary had sensed something underneath Alma's block. Something private. Something she understood. Fear—the very fear that Mary, who was also a commander, had about the baby growing inside of her. Would it be a baby like Bess Perlman's? She also wondered if the three healthy babies, born aboard the Watership to Brigade parents, were different from those whose parents were processed as commanders.

"What is it?" Ben looked at his wife, feeling her block.

"Just a private woman's moment."

"Why don't you lie back and take a nap? We've got at least a half-hour before we arrive."

Amos had left Jack and his friends to watch over the Antarean Probeship, since a Navy or police presence might be cause for suspicion. Jack would sleep aboard the *Manta III*; and now that Detectives Cummings and Betters had been removed from their surveillance, Phil Doyle brought the *Terra Time* down to Boca Raton, mooring it alongside the *Manta III*, thus affording even more protection to the submerged Probeship. Only the old Greek on the fuel barge watched these comings and goings with any interest. No one suspected he was aware of the Probeship's existence.

The Navy Skyhawk Raider, piloted by Captain Thomas Walkly, banked for final approach into the Naval air station at Annapolis. They came in low from the north over Chesapeake Bay. Amos Bright thoroughly enjoyed the ride.

"You'd make an excellent Probeship pilot, Captain," Amos remarked as they skimmed above the marshes and wetlands.

"Thank you, sir," Walkly answered. "I'd sure like to take a crack at that aircraft of yours someday." He touched down gently on the blacktop runway.

"Just get older, Captain Walkly, and we'll see what we can arrange." A few moments later Amos and the Navy Undersecretary were in a Navy jet helicopter on their way to the Pentagon.

The President had come to the Pentagon earlier that morning, ostensibly to be briefed on the new DOD weapons procurement budget. That is what the White House press corps had been told. It aroused little interest. In fact there had been little press interest in the activities of the people in the Earthmother group. The only close call had come when Sam Bixby, a veteran White House reporter for the Gannett Newspapers, noticed Alma Finley enter the White House press entrance with Caleb Harris. He'd come over to say hello to Alma, whom he remembered from her days as a news editor in New York. She was older than Sam, a pleasant aging woman, he recalled, with a nice word for everyone.

When he saw her, she appeared not to have aged. In fact she looked younger and quite beautiful. He'd said hello. She'd been cordial. When he was about to ask her what she was doing in the White House, Caleb Harris, who was not on Bixby's A-list, whisked Alma away with a weak explanation that "they were late for an appointment." Bixby's curiosity had been tweaked and he followed the couple, expecting them to exit the White House and leave the grounds. Instead, after they left the press area they doubled back through the East Wing entrance where they seemed to be expected. That entrance was used for guests and visitors to the Oval Office. Sam Bixby made a mental note to find out if and where Alma worked now, although he had the distinct impression that she had married someone in Boston and retired to Florida several years ago. His efforts were to prove fruitless.

After a perfunctory budget meeting in Defense Secretary Mersky's office, the staff was dismissed with the exception of Phillip Margolin. The President, the Secretary and Margolin then took a private elevator, an addition to the Omega Center by the previous secretary, fourteen floors directly down to the main conference room, where Alicia Sanchez and her two assistants were putting the finishing touches on the Earthmother presentation.

Everyone else arrived within ten minutes of each other. The last to arrive, Amos Bright and Captain Walkly, were delayed in their Navy helicopter by heavy morning air traffic from National Airport before they were finally cleared to descend to the heliport at the Pentagon. Up to the last minute the President and Secretary Mersky argued, as only old friends in those positions could, about whether or not to bring the Secretary of State into the loop on the basis that Amos Bright was an emissary from another planet. He was, as far an anyone knew, the first alien to be officially greeted by a government on Earth.

Gideon Mersky stubbornly argued against involving the State Department. "They'll fuss and flutter about with all that time-wasting, ineffective diplomatic crap. Meanwhile we've got a spaceship to land and a mess of pregnant octogenarians to handle." He was adamant. The President eventually bent to his point of view but withheld any final resolution of protocol until the Geriatric Brigade was safely settled in at the Johnson Space Center Hospital in Houston. Secretly, he saw an official greeting of the Antareans as having immense importance for his historical legacy.

As Amos Bright and Captain Walkly descended in the main elevator, Ben Green informed the President. "Amos Bright is on his way down, Mr. President." Press Secretary Margo McNeil and the assigned Secret Service agent moved ahead of President Malcolm Teller to the Omega Center's doorway. Margo had a 35mm Nikon camera with her to record the historic event. The door opened. Captain Walkly preceded Amos Bright into the room. After acknowledging the President he immediately stepped aside. Amos Bright then entered the room. The Antarean commander, a powerful and revered member of his own race, stood face to face with the President of the United States of America. Malcolm Teller stepped forward and extended his hand in greeting. Then, in an extraordinary moment, Amos Bright peeled back the protective humanlike skin covering his own hand, revealing the Antarean's fragile opaque flesh and four tapered fingers. He extended it in greeting to the President, who gently took it in his own. The combined warmth, wisdom, honesty and genuine respect that flowed from Amos Bright was a sensation that President Teller would never forget. The others in the room sensed the importance of the moment.

Amos was then introduced to Secretary Mersky, Dr. Khawaja, Caleb Harris, who had come over earlier that morning alone, Margo McNeil and the Margolin–Sanchez–LoCasio–Berlin team. They all then gathered to hear reports on the progress of Operation Earthmother.

Everything in Florida was secure. Secret Service agent Benton Fuller and FBI Special Agent Gary McGill had Detectives Cummings and Betters in tow and were making the final security arrangements with trusted naval officers under Captain Walkly's special command. The transport from the Watership to Houston, in the stages previously agreed upon, was in place. They were prepared for any contingency with backup air and water craft. In addition, the captain proudly reported, a highly trained Navy Seal team had been brought in two days ago. Under the guidance of Amos Bright they had inspected the cocoon chambers. They had then plotted and inspected the underwater route that would be used in transporting the cocoons from the Stones to the parked and secured Watership. The Seal team's new amphibious assault with smaller high-speed boats and helicopters onboard, along with Jack Fischer's and Phil Doyle's boats, and the eleven Antareans aboard the Watership supervised by Amos Bright, would transport the nine-hundred forty-one cocoons and load them onto the single Watership storage tank brought down for the trip back to Antares. The time frame estimate, given good weather and a minimum of ship traffic in the area, was that the operation would take no more than two weeks—seventeen days at the outside. Other members of the Seal team were assigned as security in Houston.

"We toyed with bringing in a submersible like the *Alvin* that could handle up to twenty more cocoons per day. It could speed things up a bit," Captain Walkly concluded, "but that would mean involving more personnel, vessels and equipment. At this point we feel we have an adequate, secure manageable, well-trained and enthusiastic group necessary to aid Mr. Bright in accomplishing his mission." The President thanked the captain, making a mental note to propose him for promotion to admiral.

Dr. Khawaja spoke next, outlining how far they had progressed with staffing and outfitting the wing of the Johnson Center's Space Medicine Hospital in Houston. He circulated copies of a briefing book that contained floor plans, photographs of the four duplex chambers for the non-Earth human parents, and résumés of all the key staff now housed and secreted inside the secure hospital wing.

A team of medical specialists, along with state-of-the-art incubators complete with life-support systems, were currently being airlifted to Florida. "Led by Dr. Yee, they will be there to meet the Watership with us, Mr. President, and escort our visitors back to Houston," Dr. Khawaja concluded, "should there be any more pre-mature births."

A few moments were spent by the Secret Service agent discussing security for the President's apartment on the first floor of the hospital. He requested that Benton Fuller be allowed to inspect the facility before the President visited it.

Mary and Ben Green then communicated their own confidence in the facility and staff and praised Dr. Khawaja and Dr. Yee for their marvelous work.

All eyes then turned to Phillip Margolin and Alicia Sanchez. The group had been informed that a viable plan, approved by Joe Finley and Amos Bright, had been devised at the Roscoe think tank. Everyone eagerly awaited the presentation that would show them how an alien spacecraft the size of the Watership could be brought down from the moon to the targeted South Florida waters and submerge there undetected by a world bristling with satellite and earthbound detection devices. The moment Defense Secretary Gideon Mersky saw they intended to employ and deploy SSP, the top-secret Solar Screen Program, he was on his feet protesting in the strongest terms.

"Mr. President, I am appalled." He turned to Margolin. "How dare you bring top secret material regarding this program to this meeting? We cannot do this. Mr. President, I insist that Mr. Margolin's presentation cease immediately." Alicia Sanchez exchanged inquisitive looks with Phillip Margolin, both recalling their directive from the Defense Secretary some weeks ago. Had they misunderstood? Before the President could respond, Margolin confronted his boss.

"Excuse me, sir," he began politely, his voice controlled yet as forceful as Mersky's, "but our Earthmother directive, your directive, never excluded any programs, systems or facilities either operational or under development. SSP comes under that umbrella. I don't see where we've done anything improper."

"Idiocy," Mersky continued, addressing President Teller. "These 'yuppies' would have us compromise THE most secret project our military possesses. I'd resign sooner than reveal its existence to our enemies."

The Solar Screen Program, SSP, had been one of those far-fetched ideas that had been the brainchild of some long forgotten scientist back in the early days of the ill-fated Space Lab program. The basic theoretical idea was to develop a plasticized metal or ultra-thin metal alloy that might be deployed in space to act as a shield against solar particle bombardment or meteors and other space debris that might someday endanger a space station. It was one of those innocuous items that just slipped along unnoticed into budget after budget. Then, six years ago, two NASA chemists, one involved in ozone layer studies and the other in development of specialized polymers, came upon the previously gathered data and theoretical work on SSP. With new techniques developed for a future Mars exploration program, they made a breakthrough and created a new technology which they called vacuum deployment. Concurrently they developed a high-tensile, seamless polymer shield that could be manufactured by combining chemical and metal molecules on site in the freezing temperature and total vacuum of space. There was theoretically no limit to the size of the shield. All that was required was the proper amounts of raw materials and a curious multi-nozzle spray machine that was fashioned after the web-weaving spinnerets of the Wolf Spider.

Margolin and Sanchez proposed to install the technology on the shuttle *Remembrance* to deploy two polymer shields of several square miles, high above the earth, in a configuration angled to mask the movement of the Watership from the moon to South Florida.

"It's the only way we have to shield the Watership and one storage tank's approach and landing," Dr. Sanchez maintained.

"It's out of the question," Mersky said. "If the Soviet's or Chinese… if even our allies see we have this capability, it will scare the pants off them."

"And," President Teller responded, "if those same people saw a spacecraft and tank enter our atmosphere and land in United States territory, that wouldn't scare them?"

"We have to find another way." Secretary Mersky was adamant.

"Sir, with all due respect, there is no other way!" Margolin stated firmly.

"And if I might be permitted to add," Amos Bright said softly, "there isn't much time either."

As everyone in the room watched, the President silently reached his decision. He accepted the plan and ordered it to proceed.

The matter was then closed to discussion. The President's decision was that *Remembrance*, one of three shuttles standing by, would be readied immediately. The announcement of the SSP test would be made at a presidential press conference to be called as soon as the Watership was safely tucked behind the moon ready to descend to Earth. All he would say is that a new polymer solar screening device was going to be deployed by the shuttle science crew. It would be in two stages. The first screen would be deployed at an altitude of five hundred thirty-one miles and cover an area of sixteen square miles of space. The second screen, thinner and thirty times larger, would be deployed at an altitude of two hundred fifty-nine miles. The screen's purpose would be announced as an ongoing program to protect the Earth's delicate ozone layer, which many believed was decaying from our extensive use of fluorocarbons, and thus protect the Earth from the bombardment of harmful ultraviolet waves and particles produced by solar activity.

Any astute military planner, or for that matter any knowledgeable reporter, would immediately see the potential of those screens as they deployed out over hundreds of square miles of space. Although their stated purpose might make all the sense in the world, it would be obvious they could also be used as a radar and satellite detection shield as well as a deflector of ground and aircraft based radar. They could make satellite launched missiles obsolete. Perhaps all other missiles as well.

More out of curiosity than concern, Alma Finley tried to reach into Mersky's mind to track his thought processes as he heard the decision. She discovered herself blocked. Somehow Mersky was learning the commander's abilities. He would bear watching. Afraid that he might be able to intercept her own telepathy, she kept the discovery to herself, deciding to communicate to the other commanders later.

The President complimented Margolin and Sanchez on their work. Before he adjourned the meeting, as long as Amos Bright concurred, he gave the final "go" for Operation Earthmother to proceed to landing. Amos Bright was delighted. After a phone call Dr. Sanchez confirmed that the shuttle *Remembrance* would be ready to launch and deploy the SSP in five days.

The Watership landing time and date was set for 3:15 A.M. on June 12. Being on the water at night might add some difficulty to the landing, but it would also serve to mask arrival. It was time to bring the expectant mothers and fathers and newborn babies home.

CHAPTER TWENTY-ONE
THE PASSENGER'S DILEMMA

They crossed through the Martian orbit on schedule. The Parman guides disengaged and the ion accelerator took over. The Antarean flight crew plotted their final approach to Earth, keeping the unusual silhouette of the Watership blocked by the Earth's moon as they decelerated. The Antarean cocoon recovery team prepared their equipment. The four non Earth-human parents' living quarters were double-checked and the pregnant Brigade mothers examined for the last time before landing.

Panatoy, wearing a breathing device containing his planet's atmosphere, joined his wife Ruth in her cabin. They greeted and touched, embracing one another tenderly. Ruth's pregnancy, now in its seventh month, was a source of great joy to the tall, blue Subaxian. He stroked her firm, distended belly. A broad, proud smile froze on his blue face. He kissed his mate, as she had taught him, and she in turn stroked the pale bare spot on the base of his spine in an erotic circular motion as he had taught her. His body was warming rapidly, indicating it was time to return to the room next to Ruth's that had contained Subax atmospheric conditions. They parted physically but were able to see one another and communicate. They alternated visits. Next time, if the doctors allowed it, Ruth Charnofsky would go into his room, where she could, with protective clothing and breathing apparatus, spend time.

The three other mixed couples were getting ready for arrival on Earth.

The female of the first couple was an Earth-human named Karen Morano. She was from Mill Valley, California, who had been a widow and the cousin of a couple who lived at the Antares complex in Coral Gables. She happened to be visiting Florida when the Geriatric Brigade was formed. She and her cousins chose to join, leaving their homes and worldly possessions behind. She had no family other than her Florida relatives. Her mate was called Tommachkikla. Everyone called him Tom. He was a short, squat, powerfully built man, quite handsome with a rugged bearded face. His planet, Destero, was in the Axian system near the star called Castor. Its atmosphere is oxygen rich. Its gravity three times that of Earth. The average temperature on the giant planet, in the northern hemisphere where he lived, was 100 degrees Fahrenheit. Tom was a farmer whose spread was situated in a place topographically similar to the Australian outback; open, vast, deserted and lonely. He'd met Karen at the annual gathering on Destero when the Antareans arrived to trade off-planet goods to for protein-rich Destero crops.

The next couple had to meet in a special chamber that the Antareans had prepared. The female was from Wilmington, North Carolina. Her name was Ellie-Mae Boyd, an African-American. Her involvement with the Geriatric Brigade came quite by accident. She had been a nurse for most of her life. She never married, and had six children with her common-law husband, who she never legally married because of the miscegenation laws in North Carolina. He was a career solider, killed by Chinese troops when they crossed the Yalu River during the Korean War. She raised the children by herself. As they came of age, her children moved north with the exception of a daughter who had also become a nurse and worked in Florida. That daughter brought her aging mother to live with her, and to keep busy Ellie-Mae had taken a part-time job in a nursing home near Coral Gables. It was from that home that several of the Geriatric Brigade members were recruited, among them Betty, Bess Perlman's sister. Ellie-Mae had been the only person at the home who had been kind to Betty, a severe stroke victim. After Betty had been processed by the Antareans she went to Ellie-Mae and invited her to join in the adventure. Although reluctant to leave her daughter, Ellie-Mae chose to join Betty and the others, leaving behind the bigotry of the

American Southland.

Ellie's mate was a doctor named Manterid, a chemist; a humanoid native of Betch, the sister planet to Hillet in the Alphard system near the star Hydra. In fact, Andrea and Frank Hankinson's friends, the Messinas and the Erhardts, both of whom had given birth prematurely aboard the Watership, had conceived their babies on Hillet. The inhabitants of Hillet and Betch shared a common heritage and genetic background. Betch, a seasonal water planet, supports a controlled humanoid population. At first glance, Ellie's mate, Doctor Manterid, might be mistaken for an American Indian or Eskimo. But his pigmentation was capable of chameleon-like properties—a genetic adaptation. His eyes were set wider apart than Earth-human, nearly reaching to the side of his oval, weathered face. His hair was jet black, coarse and braided. His mouth was also wide, with teeth set in two rows that interlocked. That too was an adaptation developed to make efficient use of the high cellulose vegetation of the people of Betch, who were called the Hillet. They were a tall race, most males over six feet. On the nearby planet called Hillet, which was colonized millennia ago, the humanoids who evolved there called themselves Hilletoros. They were fiercely nationalistic, having won independence from Betch. Unlike Betch, Hillet's climate was warmer and dryer. The atmosphere was basically nitrogen with only five percent oxygen. Although their features were similar to the Hillet, Hilletoros ability to change pigmentation had been replaced by a dark, reddish leathery skin. They were also much shorter than their Hillet ancestors.

Dr. Manterid was a chemist. Earth atmosphere, which he barely tolerated, made him lightheaded. In order to room with Ellie-Mae, he put up with the discomfort for as long as possible. Their quarters had been designed so that after an hour in her atmosphere, nitrogen was pumped in and the temperature increased. Within fifteen minutes, which were uncomfortable for Ellie-Mae, he was recovered. This way he could be close to his mate, whom he insisted on calling *wife*. It was a word that he'd learned was important to Ellie-Mae. Dr. Manterid had questioned Commander Hankinson regarding Earth customs when he had decided to mate with Ellie-Mae. The concept of marriage was known on Betch. When the doctor discovered that Ellie-Mae had not ever been legally married, he insisted on a full-blown wedding, Earth style. One of the Brigade members, a retired Reform rabbi from New York, performed the nuptials, which were a mixture of whatever Baptist ceremony Ellie-Mae remembered, a little Judaism, a sprinkling of Parman philosophy and some Antarean words to bless the Master's wisdom in this unique joining.

The last of the mixed matings consisted of an Earth-human male and an off-planet female. He was Peter Martindale, a retired steel-worker and union organizer from Ashland, Kentucky. Peter was eighty-six years old when his friend Paul Amato, a resident of the Antares condo, brought him into the fold. Paul knew Martindale from their common union connection to the National Board of the AF of L/CIO. Peter was a handsome man who'd kept himself in good shape. But before he'd been processed for space travel with the Antareans he was dying of lung cancer. The processing restored him to perfect health.

After his two years on Parma Quad 2 he chose to travel with an Antarean Cargoship that was making a sweep of Quad 1. The first stop was Turmoline, the fifth planet in the Spica star system in the constellation Virgo. Their stay had been less than a month, but during that time Peter Martindale concluded that space travel was not his primary interest. Although he enjoyed the company of the small Antarean and Brigade crew, he found life aboard the Cargoship boring compared to life on Turmoline, a lush water planet inhabit-ed by a race of meat-eating humanoid hunters. They were called the Penditan and closely resembled Earth-humans but lived at a fairly primitive level as compared to Antares. Peter met Tern, a young fe-male Penditan who served as liaison at the Antarean cargo port facil-ity. He fell in love with the beautiful female. By custom he asked her tribal leaders permission for her to be his mate. They consented with the terms that he work one Turmoline year in the service of the tribe before Tern was his.

Martindale's skill as a steelworker came in handy. On Earth he had been a melter, the man responsible for operating the huge electric arc furnaces that made specialized alloy steel. It was his job to bring the furnace, initially loaded with scrap metal, to the temperature required. When the metal was molten and red hot, he supervised the addition of other elements such as zinc, nickel and titanium in order to produce the particular alloy steel the batch required. It was a highly skilled job with great responsibility. One mistake might ruin an entire melt. During his year of labor for Tern's tribe, he built a small blast furnace and taught the Penditan to make hunting weapons superior to those they normally used. Before doing this he had to ask permission of the Antarean envoy to Turmoline, since the improvement might be considered tampering with the normal development of a planet's indigenous population. The furnace was approved, because the Penditan already smelted metal and were sophisticated hunters on a planet that abounded with game and other fierce predators. It was also a fact that Turmoline skins and furs traded to the Antareans were coveted by many who populated or worked on less bountiful planets.

After his year of servitude, Peter Martindale and Tern were mated. They lived together on Turmoline for more than a year and then traveled to Antares on a Cargoship so that Peter might visit with Marie and Paul Amato. It was on that journey that Tern became pregnant. When they arrived on Antares the pregnant Brigade women were gathering. Tern had the choice of going back to her home planet to have her baby, staying on Antares, or going to Earth with the others. She chose Earth, stating that although hers was a mixed baby, her inner spirit voice, a feeling of deep religious significance to the Penditan, guided her to birth the baby to Earth. "Within me we have created a new race," she told Peter. "He must begin his life with the other babies of your kind." And so much to Peter Martindale's delight, they joined the passengers on the Watership.

As the Parman guides retired from their task, and the Antarean flight crew guided the Watership to the moon's hidden side, the returning Brigade members met to discuss how to deal with the families some of them had left behind on Earth. They had received a report from Mary Green regarding her visit to her daughter in Scarsdale. The sense that her family seemed to accept her extraordinary new life was a positive sign. But the fact that she hesitated to reveal her pregnancy to them weighed heavily on some minds. Of the forty-two returning couples, nineteen had family on Earth. Jack Fischer had visited each family, bringing the news of their parents' and grandparents' journey into space as well as personal letters left behind by the travelers. He had assured them of the goodness of the Antareans and that the decision made by their loved ones was a free and rational choice. But there was no mention of return, much less pregnancy. The families had eventually accepted their elders' decisions and all had promised to keep the secret.

The group aboard the Watership, along with the commanders on board, wrestled with the problem of family contact—if, when and how. Was it fair to rekindle relationships after departing in such a strange, abrupt manner? They were gone five years. What of grandchildren? How would sons and daughters take to newborn siblings? Emotions ran high, but cooler heads prevailed. Bernie Lewis said it best.

"This has all happened very fast. There was a time when five years, the time we have been away, seemed forever. But now we have been out among the stars, we have sampled other worlds, other beings, and we have come to gather a great deal of very special knowledge, powers and wisdom. But now we return, unannounced because something else has happened. Something that is common on Earth, birth, and something that is unheard of on Earth, birth from parents our age. And some from mates who would be immediately labeled as alien, while we know them to be as human as any Earth-human. There are many who would attach religious significance to this event. Many who would, because of their narrow point of view, look upon our return fearfully, hearing they are not the only life in the universe. We are here to bear our young. That is the way of the galaxy we have come to know. It is best that we go about our business first, meaning that we have our babies, bring them into life with health and love, and that we are firm in our plans for their future. When that is done, then it will be time for each of us to decide what is to be told, or not told, to those whom we love and left behind."

There was agreement. Family contact would wait. Bernie sent word to Ben, Mary, Joe, Alma and Amos Bright. They, in turn, had the word of the President that he would arrange private transport for the Brigade's families to Houston whenever it was requested. Everyone agreed. Family contact would wait.

An Earth-hour later, the conference room viewing portal opened. Ahead, looming majestically, was the moon. Just beyond a blue dot was dipping below the horizon. It was the Earth. It was home-planet.

CHAPTER TWENTY-TWO
A RECEPTION AWAITS

Manta III bobbed about like a cork on the rough sea. It was nearly two A.M. and the wind had shifted from east to northeast, a harbinger of bad weather. One hundred yards off the starboard, *Terra Time's* running lights were intermittently visible as it too was rocked in the ever increasing swells. Beyond the two sport-fishing boats, whose position was directly over the six-hundred-foot wreck, the rest of Captain Walkly's Operation Earthmother naval fleet waited in the ink-black night.

That morning, while Jack Fischer and Phil Doyle prepared for their part of the mission, President Teller spoke to the nation on television and radio at a press conference. He announced that a previously unannounced launch of the space shuttle *Remembrance* was taking place. He then proceeded to outline the test of the Solar Screen Program, the SSP, to be made that night along the eastern seaboard of the United States. He was questioned by the White House reporters as to why the test had not been announced and why it was being conducted now. The President stated that newly gathered data revealed considerable upcoming sunspot activity as well as a newly measured dangerous thinning of parts of the ozone layer. He also suggested that the moon was entering a waning phase and the sky would be darkest, enabling the NASA test instruments to study the highly reflective surface of the screens as they deployed. The program was of such a top-secret nature that no one in the press corps knew what technical questions to ask. By the time they had conferred with their editors and science experts, the President had left Washington, ostensibly to observe the screen deployment from a naval vessel at sea.

Remembrance, one of the third generation of shuttles built after the *Challenger* disaster, had a flawless lift-off from the Kennedy Space Center in Florida. The shuttle achieved its required orbit an hour later and one of the science teams aboard began their EVA outside the craft as they prepared the delicate and complex SSP deployment equipment. Inside the shuttle, the second science team began the intricate process of preparing the various chemicals that would eventually form the polymer screen in the vacuum of space.

The President's party that included Margo McNeil, Secretary Mersky, Alicia Sanchez and Phillip Margolin left Washington aboard Air Force One and flew to Shaw AFB near Columbia, South Carolina. From there they transferred to a Marine jet helicopter that flew them out to the Operation Earthmother flagship, the guided missile cruiser *USS Simi* where they were welcomed aboard by Captain Walkly and Benton Fuller.

Nearby, the smaller frigate, *USS Hapsas,* special agent Gary McGill watched over his charges, Detectives Matthew Cummings and Coolridge Betters. The two Coral Gables cops had been supposedly assigned as liaison for the massive drug bust that was about to commence. They were impressed with the scope of the operation and the efficiency of coordination between what appeared to be Secret Service, FBI and U.S. Navy forces.

Earlier that morning, after they had been on board for two days, the *Hapsas* had left its mooring off Key Largo and headed northeast toward their current position. The two detectives were fed only bits of information, but they were privy to the coded radio traffic in the area and knew that at least seven other vessels, a submarine and four or five aircraft were involved in what was now called Operation Earthmother. Cummings, a bachelor, had no one to explain his absence, but his partner, Betters, had been married for forty-three years to a woman who worried about her husband more and more as the day of his retirement neared. Rather than tell her it was a dangerous drug operation, Betters said he was going fishing with Cummings in the Keys for a few days on a friend's boat. Neither cop was much of a sailor, so as the weather worsened and the seas swelled, they stayed out on the second deck just below the bridge.

"How the hell are they going to chase anyone in this ocean?" Cummings asked. His empty stomach grumbled.

"They have some big boats out here. And choppers." Betters wished he had a bottle of Jack Daniels to settle his stomach.

"Why do I have this funny feeling we're being snookered?"

"That funny feeling is this damned ocean that won't stay still." Both men chuckled. Betters frowned and looked at Cummings. "What do you mean, snookered?"

"It just feels too pat. I don't trust those feds."

"You're gettin' paranoid in your old age, Matt."

"Hey buddy, not me. There's a lot of expensive hardware out here. Big bucks. So I ask you, why pull in two old farts like us?"

"Like the man said, we were onto his collar."

"Baloney. This ain't for those charter boat guys. I know Doyle and Mazuski. Small-timers, if that. And that Fischer guy doesn't have the smarts for something this big."

"What about the old people?"

"Right. That's what's bugging me. Where are they? See, we weren't on to them... at least not after they gave us the slip. All we were doing was watching a couple of boats."

"So what's your point?"

"That maybe there's something more going down here than our FBI keeper or that other fed is telling us."

"The Navy guy seems okay."

"You know who he is?"

"Captain Thomas Walkly?"

"Yeah. I asked if you know who he is?."

"Who? Spiderman? Batman? What?"

"Funny... but close. He's the goddamned Undersecretary of the Navy."

"You're shitting me." Betters forgot his queasy stomach.

"I checked it out with our underwater snoop photographer."

"Leiter?"

"Yeah. He was one of those Navy Seals before he went commercial. He knew Walkly as soon as I mentioned him. Seems the guy was heavy duty in Viet Nam when Leiter was in service there." Betters was beginning to feel uneasy.

"So what do you think a big shot like that is doing out here with us?"

"I don't know, but let's keep our eyes open." The frigate *Hapsas* turned into the rising swells. Above them on the bridge deck, a seaman flashed a lantern semaphore message to another vessel off to port.

That ship was the NOAA research vessel *Orca*—a seventy-foot, steel-hulled, bristling with sophisticated electronics and capable of supporting both submersible and free deep-diving scuba teams. The captain, Roger Hadges, was a forty-five-year-old veteran of five round-the-world cruises aboard *Orca*. His boss, Dr. Caroline Macklow, who had been working with the special Seal team attached to Operation Earthmother, was also aboard the *Orca*. The team was in civilian dress and was introduced as a new diving unit attached to NOAA, but Hadges wasn't fooled. He knew military when he saw it, and these divers were definitely military.

"We will proceed to these coordinates now, Captain Hadges," Dr. Macklow explained, pointing to the position of the six-hundred-foot wreck off the Boynton Beach inlet. "I want to arrive there no later than oh-three-hundred hours." Hadges looked at his watch. It was one-thirty in the morning. He peered outside at the black moonless night and felt the swells rising underneath his vessel.

"We've got four-to-eight-foot seas now, and predicted to get worse," he told the stately Ph.D.

"We have to be there on time."

"Then I'd say it's time to get moving now. I wish you'd told me this sooner."

"We all have orders to follow, Captain Hadges."

"Those Navy boys of yours sure know how to do that," he said, unable to hold back the sarcasm from his voice.

"I beg your pardon?"

"That new diving team. They're Navy."

"Who told you that?"

"No one. I've been around those boys before."

"Well, that's very interesting, Captain. If the seas are getting heavy, I think we'd best be heading up to Boynton Beach now." She gathered her chart, signaling the conversation was over.

"Whatever you say, Doctor." He turned to begin preparations to change course.

Dr. Macklow paused before leaving the bridge. "I'm sorry if this mission is a bit strange, Captain. It's not my style to be secretive. All I can say is that in a few hours it will all be quite clear to you. And after that I can promise you some of the most interesting work you or I have ever done." She smiled and left the bridge. He believed her.

The high seas and dark night were going to be both helpful and difficult. The original plan to take the people from the Watership to Elliot Key by helicopter had been abandoned because of the weather and the presence of a Soviet submarine detected in the area. Instead, the *Manta III* and *Terra Time* would be used to transport the visitors to the waiting helicopters now on the ground on Elliot Key. The fishing boats would be escorted by two Navy attack speedboats and, at a distance, by the destroyer *USS Metz*. A medical team from Houston, along with their hi-tech incubators and infant life-support systems, were aboard the speedboats.

Below the *Manta III*, ready to be jettisoned, the Antarean Probeship with Amos Bright, the Finley's and Green's on board communicated with the Watership flight bridge through the commanders.

Everything was in place. The Operation Earthmother flotilla began to converge toward the six-hundred-foot wreck off Boynton Beach where *Manta III* and *Terra Time*, their bows turned into the ever increasing swells, waited to gather in their precious cargo. From a distance aboard the navy vessels, the operation looked like a drug-running trap that was about to be sprung on the two charter boats.

The *Remembrance* reached the apogee of the first SSP release orbit at 11:17 p.m. Eastern Standard Time, 521 miles above Earth. The first solar screen was begun six minutes later. By midnight a polymer screen eleven molecules thick was spun and spread out over more than twenty-nine square miles of space, thirteen more miles than had been estimated. The screen, visible from Earth as a bright smear in the eastern sky, was awesome. The world began to pay close attention to this scientific phenomenon, especially since they had been told that in another two hours a second screen, thirty times that size, would be manufactured twice as close to the Earth.

On the dark side of the moon, two of the three storage tanks had been disconnected from the Watership and brought down to the moon's surface by Probeships. They were guided into a deep crater, fastened to the porous lunar rock, and then camouflaged to match the surrounding lunar surface. According to plan, the remaining tank, the one that would eventually carry the cocoons back to Antares, was brought alongside the Watership's main thruster unit and attached in a configuration that gave the smallest silhouette possible. Since speed was not a factor on their Earth approach, it was possible to present a very compact, almost spherical meteorite appearance, should the SSP fail to mask the Watership's entry into the Earth's atmosphere. On board, excitement grew among the Brigade members and commanders. But all was quiet with the Parman guides who were comfortably at rest, rejuvenating their outer crystal layer, which always suffered some wear and tear from cosmic debris and dust as they pulled and guided Antarean spacecraft throughout the galaxy. Everything was ready at 1:30 Eastern Standard Time. All that remained was for the *Remembrance* to release the second solar screen.

At precisely 2:13 Eastern Standard Time, the second solar screen, manufactured in space to a thickness of three molecules, spread out across the nearly moonless heavens covering more than one thousand square miles of the void above Earth. Every radar, telescope, military facility and research center in the world concentrated on the huge, oval-shaped cloud that glistened in the night sky from lights on the Earth below.

The Watership rose slowly above the rim of the moon. Ahead the Earth, a bright blue and white planet, appeared and beckoned. The Antarean flight crew aligned their approach with the coordinates

Amos Bright telepathed, aligning the Watership to make maximum use of the protective solar screen shield.

After the Brigade had travelled to distant planets in our galaxy, and discovered wonders never before dreamed of in human experience, the atmosphere aboard the Watership was charged with but one thought as they observed the blue planet set in the inky blackness of the cosmos. Home!

CHAPTER TWENTY-THREE
SPLASHDOWN

At 2:45 A.M. the thinner second solar screen's leading edge began to make contact with the edge of the Earth's atmosphere. The Watership was safely tucked in above it and beneath the first screen. In effect it was the meat inside a polymer sandwich. But in this case the meat was unobserved from the Earth below and the various satellites above. As more and more of the thin polymer entered the atmosphere, it gathered speed from gravity's pull and began to burn and disintegrate. The fire spread across thirty miles of the atmospheric envelope, a truly spectacular sight as observed from the Eastern seaboard and the Operation Earthmother flotilla below. As more of the screen entered the atmosphere the fire and debris grew more intense, and at a predetermined moment, when the fire was at its peak, the Watership slipped into the atmosphere, its outer skin turning red hot at great speed. It hurtled down toward the rough Florida waters, impacting with a huge, explosive splash-down thirty miles south and east of Elliot Key.

The burning screens were a large enough diversion to mask the entry of the Watership. From the point where it left the cover of the screens it appeared to be a large meteor that punched through the debris from the screens. NASA made the announcement about the meteor, stating that it had collided with the screens, pulling some of the material along with it, causing the test to be inconclusive. That phenomenon made the meteor appear much larger than it actually was as it plunged into the ocean off the Florida coast in deep water. They added that a NOAA research vessel was in the vicinity, as were two navy ships and an attempt would be made to locate the meteor and bring it to the surface.

Activities aboard the various ships involved in Operation Earthmother heightened as soon as the flaming Watership dropped from the skies above and crashed into the sea twenty miles away.

Cummings and Betters stood on the bridge of the *Hapsas,* awed by the sight of the blazing sky above and the fiery ball that lit up the rough waters around them before it crashed into the sea and disappeared. The small fleet was visible all around them. Then it was dark again.

"Jesus, Matt. Did you see all those ships?" Coolridge Betters asked.

"I counted eight, maybe ten. What the hell was that fireball?"

"A meteor."

"And the way the sky lit up. Did you see that?"

"Yeah. Some kind of test. They were talking about it on the TV this morning." Gary McGill stood near them on the deck, but the fireworks had been so distracting that the two cops hadn't noticed him come up behind them

"I saw Jack Fischer's boat. And the other one too," Betters said.

"The *Terra Time.* But the rest of the boats were pretty big, huh?"

"Too big to be chasing a couple of dope runners in slow charter boats."

Suddenly, the sea began to calm and glow with a yellow phosphorescence. McGill stepped between them and put his arms around their shoulders. "You're right about that, guys. I guess the moment for truth has arrived, or is about to arrive I should say." He indicated the calm, brightening sea around them as the submerged Watership approached.

Amos Bright had released the Probeship from the *Manta III* at the moment the Watership struck the ocean. He moved straight toward it to guide the huge spacecraft to the area above the six-hundred-foot wreck. Excitement coursed through the cabin of the Probeship as the Finley's and Green's anticipated their reunion with their fellow commanders.

The President's party aboard the *USS Simi,* Captain Walkly's flagship, were on deck to observe the Watership descent and arrival. The sight was spectacular. In the excitement of the moment, Malcolm Teller forgot himself and hugged Margo McNeil in front of everyone.

"Jesus, Mary and Joseph," he exclaimed, "will you look at that. Spectacular! And to think there are Americans on board that spaceship."

"Watership," Gideon Mersky corrected. He remained outwardly calm, but inside, especially when he noted the instantaneous deceleration of the Antarean craft just before it struck the water, his heart rate increased substantially as he contemplated the military significance of the technological secrets the Antareans and the Geriatric Brigade must possess.

"You want to tell me about it now, Doctor?" Roger Hadges, the NOAA captain asked after the fireball had submerged and Dr. Macklow had instructed him to head toward the meteor's entry point.

The tall marine biologist nodded. "To begin with, that wasn't a meteor."

"Part of that Solar Screen Program the President announced this morning?"

"No, not really. It's a spacecraft."

"Christ. Not another accident?" Hadges said softly, referring to the *Challenger* disaster.

"No. No!" she answered. "This spacecraft is not ours."

"Soviet?" he asked, then called out to the boson at the wheel, "Take her to 140…"

"Antarean," Dr. Macklow said matter-of-factly

"Antarean? Where's that?" The bosun spun the wheel to port.

"From Antares. It's a planet in another solar system," she responded calmly, watching the wily captain as he studied her unflinching weathered face.

"You're serious, aren't you?"

Dr. Macklow moved closer. She was five inches taller than the *Orca's* master. She put her hand on his shoulder. "Roger, my good man, we are both about to have the adventure of our lives."

He didn't have time to respond. The seaman on forward watch sounded the ship's Klaxon as a collision warning. The ocean was growing brighter dead ahead. Something was coming to the surface. Something very large. The Watership, having filled its ballast tanks with seawater and adjusted to Earth water temperature, atmosphere and gravity, was now ready to discharge its precious human cargo that had grown by three since departing from Antares two months ago.

Now it was time for Operation Earthmother's logistical plan to be executed.

CHAPTER TWENTY-FOUR
LOGISTICS

Ben Green left the Probeship and passed through the Watership membrane at a depth of three hundred feet under the sea. Ruth and Betty were waiting for him. They embraced. A moment later Mary entered the chamber and exchanged greetings with her fellow commanders. The Finleys would remain with the Probeship, on site, until the cocoons were safely retrieved and transferred. Then Amos Bright would return with the Watership and storage tankers to Antares while the Finleys took the Probeship to the port of Galveston, Texas. The Watership continued to rise toward the surface, guided by the Probeship toward the Navy and NOAA vessels.

Jack Fischer and Phil Doyle were in radio contact with each other as the water brightened below them. They saw the *USS Simi* heading toward them off the starboard while the *USS Metz*, the escort destroyer, moved closer in off their port.

"I hope those guys keep their distance," Phil said nervously as the big ships bore down on the much smaller charter boats.

"Walkly said the President's on the missile cruiser. He's gonna say hello to the folks before we shove off."

"Well, I hope he says it from a distance." The two attack speedboats now appeared. One of them headed for the *Simi* while the other came up behind the *Manta III*. "I don't think that's in the cards, old buddy," Jack told Doyle as he watched the activity on Walkly's flagship.

President Teller, Gideon Mersky, Margo McNeil, Alicia Sanchez, Phillip Margolin and Captain Walkly were about to disembark on a forty-five-foot ocean yacht that had been brought aboard the *Simi* and was now being lowered over the side to join. The speedboat reached the sleek guided-missile cruiser and stood off thirty yards. Benton Fuller and two other Secret Servicemen were already aboard the Navy speedboat. The ocean yacht, bearing the presidential seal and flying his flag, pulled away from the *Simi* and headed toward the *Manta III*. The sea was dead calm now. The pure yellow glow underwater had turned a bright orange-yellow. Obviously something was controlling the ocean surface.

The Brigade men and women prepared to leave the Watership. Time was spent with farewells to the Antarean flight crew and the Parman guides. Beam and her medical team would be going to Houston. The chamber inside the membrane was a domed room bathed in a deep blue night light to prepare the humans for their first exposure to Earth in more than five years. The excited passengers gathered as the Watership continued its slow ascent to the surface. The three infants were brought forward. Ben and Mary asked to hold them and passed the feeling if the young lives along to the Finleys.

The babies would be taken aboard the speedboat lying to port of the *Manta III* where a pediatric team waited with incubators. Beam and her two assistants would join them. The infants would be completely examined by the time they reached Elliot Key.

Phil Doyle saw the President first. "Hey, Jack," he hailed over to his friend, whose boat was now within thirty yards. "Check it out. The man himself."

"I guess we're A-list now," Jack joked lightly, but he was nervous and proud to be a part of all this. The President waved a greeting to Jack and Phil. They saluted back.

Matthew Cummings had trouble adjusting his binoculars. Betters was already absorbed as he watched the President greet their old adversary, Jack Fischer. Finally the senior detective, with some help from Gary McGill, focused in on the *Manta III* and the boats nearby.

"I'll be damned," was about all he could say. Then he saw the lights from the Watership rising toward the surface. These were the same lights he had seen when the Brigade left Earth five years ago. He put down the binoculars and glared at McGill. "So you guys knew all along that what I said to the DA was true," he said angrily. In the midst of the historic event unfolding before them, Cummings's remark was didn't register with McGill.

"Say what?" The FBI agent put aside his own binoculars.

"I told the DA five years ago that they had some kind of a rocketship. It was just like that one comin' up out there... just like I told them. And they said I was nuts. They said that if I started talking about spaceships and like that... that they'd have me off the force and in the funny farm."

"I'm sorry about that, Detective Cummings. Back then, no one really did know."

"That Fischer guy and his buddies knew, and I told that DA they did and..."

"Matt!" Coolridge Betters cut his partner off. "Take it easy,. So we were right and they were wrong and no one gives a good goddamn about it now. Our being here... it's their way of saying sorry. Kinda like eatin' crow. Can't you see that?"

"So?"

"So that's the payback, man. How many people you know are invited along with the President to meet some folks from outer space?"

Cummings chuckled and lifted the binoculars to his eyes again. "Not too many, pal," he said as he scanned the horizon, checking out the *Metz,* the *Orca,* and the *Simi.* Then he peered back at the President's yacht, *Manta III, Terra Time* and the two speedboats. "Maybe two or three hundred from the looks of the welcoming committee out here tonight."

Malcolm Teller could only think of Herman Melville's description in *Moby Dick* when the great white whale, having sounded, rose up from the depths, first just a tiny spot below growing larger and larger until he breached with all the power and majesty that that great leviathan possessed. He, too, peered into the ocean depths and watched the orange-yellow glow of the Watership grow ever larger beneath the ocean yacht. It was massive, covering the water beneath his boat, the two speedboats and the two fishing boats nearby. As it neared the surface the brighter lights emanating from it began to dim and a deep blue oval opening in the circular nose of the Watership became clear.

The Watership's flat dull white hull, with storage tanker attached, stopped thirty feet beneath the surface. *Manta III* and *Terra Time* were directly above the ship's membrane. The Probeship popped to the surface and came to rest between the two fishing boats. From beneath the Probeship, a laser-like ray of white light shot down to the membrane and split into hundreds of separate beams that encircled it. The beams then reflected back to the surface, forming a column of blue and white light. The water within the column drained and the membrane was exposed to the night air. Then as the membrane parted, the first passengers, led by Ben and Mary Green, ascended to the surface on a walkway that rose up out of the Watership's hull. At the same time Beam and her two assistants brought the three human infants to the surface on another walkway.

The President's yacht edged close to Ben's walkway, as did the *Manta III*. Ben waved a big hello to Jack and then boarded the President's yacht, which was now side by side with the *Manta III*. Mary followed. They both greeted the President and his party. Then one by one, led by Ruth Charnofsky, the commanders came aboard, were greeted by the President and then filed onto the *Manta III*. At the same time Beam and her party boarded the medical speedboat.

Everyone aboard the vessels had been briefed on the mission that morning. No one, not even the most hardened Seals or the experienced Secretary of Defense, even Caleb Harris who had been aboard the *Hapsas*, was prepared for the sight that now appeared rising out of the membrane of the Watership as all the Brigade couples on board, people in their seventies and eighties, up the walkways to the surface, holding hands. They waved a greeting to the people on the boats that surrounded them. Many of the women showed rotund bellies in which they carried and nurtured the first generation of Earth-humans conceived on other planets. Everyone cheered them and waved back. Even the sailors on the larger ships that stood off were heard cheering.

The President stepped forward onto the fantail of his yacht. The commanders stood behind him.

"My dear fellow Americans. I know that you still have a journey ahead of you tonight. A journey that will take you to the secure safety and expertise you require. I will personally visit each of you very soon. So all I want to say now, on behalf of your country, of your fellow Americans, is a sincere and heartfelt... welcome home." He waved to the group and they applauded back. The President's yacht backed away and headed to the *USS Simi*.

In a matter of a few minutes the Brigade couples and commanders boarded the *Manta III* and *Terra Times*. Slowly the two fishing boats backed away from the Watership, as did the speedboat carrying the babies. The President's yacht was already being lifted on board *USS Simi*. The beams of light from the Probeship retracted, and water once again covered the membrane. Then Amos Bright lowered the Probecraft down to the opening of the Watership where, in the near darkness of the warm Gulf Stream current, the three off-planet fathers—Panatoy the Subax, Tom the Desteran, Dr. Manterid from Betch, and Tern, the pregnant female Penditan from Turmoline— each wearing special protective covering and encapsulated in customized containers, were loaded aboard the Probeship. Their journey to Elliot Key and beyond would be secret, for as far as those who had helped with the landing were concerned, the only passengers aboard the spaceship were Earth-humans returning for a special visit, and the Antaean crew that no one saw.

As the Probeship moved away the lights aboard the Watership dimmed, and it, with its storage tank, sank quietly, settling on the ocean bottom, southwest of the six-hundred-foot wreck. The *Simi* and *Hapsas* remained on station. The *Orca* headed south to the Stones. It would be joined there later by the Probeship and the difficult task of moving the cocoons to the Watership would begin. The Presidential party returned by helicopter to Shaw AFB and from there to Washington. All the other craft were well on their way to Elliot Key, where eight Marine helicopters would ferry the newly arrived visitors to Homestead AFB, and a waiting C-5A would take them to their new home in Houston.

Everything went like clockwork, a tribute to Captain Walkly and the people in his command. The C-5A was met in the early dawn by Dr. Khawaja and his team, who now took over the responsibility of bringing new life into this old and troubled planet.

CHAPTER TWENTY-FIVE
SETTLING IN HOUSTON

After an uneventful flight from Homestead AFB to Houston, and as the Brigade members and commanders settled into their quarters, Dr. Khawaja called an emergency meeting after learning that the gas mixtures were showing signs of growing instability in the living chambers constructed for the four non Earth-humans. It was initially thought to be a computer malfunction, then a programming problem. Now it was unclear. The possibility of design and construction failures was now on the table as well. There was time to correct the situation, but not that much. Beam told those present that the off-planet beings, three males and one female, would be stable in their sealed environmental containers for another fifty-one hours. "But I do not have specific knowledge," she told Undersecretary of Health. "My training is biology and galactic navigation. What I can confirm is that so far the basic requirements are functional." In the end Dr. Khawaja would have responsibility for choosing the final course of action.

The chief chemical engineer, a man Khawaja had recruited from the Army's chemical, biological and radiological testing program at the Aberdeen Proving Grounds, was cautious. "The mixtures of gasses we had to manufacture for these folks were quite exotic. There just wasn't time to test every condition of temperature and pressure, but we feel we are within the parameters that the Antarean scientists supplied."

"Perhaps," Beam said, "but our containers are at variance with those in the chambers you have constructed."

"They're small differences," Angela Lippman, the computer specialist responsible for the program that controlled the environments said. "I think they'll be just fine in there."

"We are talking about lives here, Ms. Lippman," Dr. Khawaja interjected. "Think is not good enough." The programmer was embarrassed by his abrupt remark.

There was an awkward moment of silence in the room. Beam received a thought from one of her Antarean crew. "There is one being here who may be able to give us definite parameters for all the environments." That got everyone's attention. "Dr. Manterid, the mate of Ellie-Mae Boyd, is a chemist from Betch."

"Sure. But he's in a container," Angela Lippman said sarcastically, still smarting from Dr. Khawaja's chiding.

"He has been able to survive for some minutes in Earth atmosphere," Beam said. "He did so with his mate."

"You're certain?" Dr. Khawaja asked Beam.

"Yes, sir. I am certain. You can confirm that with Mrs. Boyd."

An hour later Dr. Manterid was removed from his container. A scuba tank with pure nitrogen and an ultra violet lamp was supplied which that enabled him to work for the rest of the day with the engineers, doctors and chemists as they fine-tuned the off-planet living quarters. They completed his first so that once it was controlled and functioning he was able to assist in stabilizing the other three. The only unresolved problem was the intensity of ultraviolet radiation that Panatoy the Subaxian, Commander Ruth Charnofsky's mate, required. Dr. Manterid examined the room that Panatoy would inhabit. He suggested they graduate the ultraviolet exposure across the room, producing different zones of radiation. When Panatoy was there he could tell them which was the most comfortable. They could then adjust the ultra violet accordingly. It worked. With ten hours to spare, the living quarters were functioning, and the off-planet visitors were comfortably in residence with their mates in adjacent Earth environment rooms.

After the Brigade parents were settled into their quarters, the first order of business was to perform a complete physical examinations on each woman to determine general state of health, the health and development of the fetuses, and the chronological birth schedule they might expect to have. In a part of the medical facilities on the top, or green floor, of the Space Medicine Center, units were converted into nine completely outfitted examination rooms. Each was staffed and equipped to perform the general examination as well as state-of-the-art ultrasound that enabled the doctors to observe the fetus in minute detail. Four highly specialized fetal surgeons in the country were also present, should any abnormality present itself. Their skills and their high-tech equipment enabled them to do lifesaving surgery on a fetus within the amniotic sac.

Mary Green, barely four months pregnant, resisted taking up residence with the other Brigade mothers on the third floor. She had conceived on Antares just before the Probeship left for Earth. She believed her time would be better spent working with the other commanders. Ben was insistent, but Mary adamantly resisted. Then she was visited by Bess Perlman. The two women had not had a chance to be alone until now. Mary's room was bright and sunny. The President had sent a bouquet of a dozen roses to each woman, and their sweet scent permeated the air.

Because time had been short, little attention had been paid to decoration. All of the rooms were Spartan, but neat. The couples had the choice of a large single bed or twins. They all chose the single bed. There was basic furniture and fixtures, a bath with tub and shower and a dining and living area. The Brigade traveled with little luggage, mostly personal items and uniform clothing. Their work on different planets required such a large variety of clothing that it was impossible to travel with all of it. In almost every place they visited, garments were supplied by their guests. The only exceptions were trips to unexplored planets. In those cases, the Antareans supplied the Brigade.

One of the amenities offered by Khawaja's staff was a large variety of clothing for the returning Earth-humans. For many of the women it was the first time they had been wearing something other than uniforms or off-planet dress. It was fun to see the latest fashions, but processing and life out among the stars had changed the Brigade. Those things were no longer important. All they were interested in now was comfortable maternity wear. Mary Green was still in uniform.

"You'll have to start wearing maternity clothing soon," Bess Perlman commented as she watched Mary Green cross the room on her way to get more coffee. She stopped and sniffed her roses. Many things that they had been without for the past five years now tasted and smelled wonderfully strange.

"I guess. This guy is going to be a buster."

"A boy? For sure?"

"I hope so," Mary said as she poured more coffee from the carafe supplied by the kitchen on the first floor. There was a printed menu. The visitors were served either in their rooms at any hour or in a central dining room during fixed hours. Room service was twenty-four hours a day.

"Well, they can tell you that with the ultrasound," Bess said as positively as she dared, knowing Mary was anxious about her pregnancy.

"I don't want to know. Ben doesn't either. We want to believe it will be a boy. You know… did I ever tell you that we lost a son in Viet Nam?"

"Yes. Scott, wasn't it?"

Mary nodded and sat down across from her old friend. They had not seen one another in more than three years. Telepathing was not the same as being face to face. "We should get a Mah Jong game going here," Mary continued, recalling how the four of them, Bess, Rose, Alma and she sat for hours playing the ancient Chinese game that had been adopted by immigrant Jewish women living on the lower East Side of New York in neighborhoods adjacent to Chinatown. When shopping, the women observed Chinese women playing the game in the street and learned it. Bess smiled, remembering their daily Mah Jong game at the condo in Florida.

"What if it's not a boy?" Bess asked. "Will you be disappointed?"

"No. Maybe. I don't know, Bess. It's not really important." Mary had wondered about talking to Bess about her miscarriage. Now she felt stupid worrying about the sex of her baby when Bess had lost hers.

"It's important that you take care of yourself, Mary," Bess said softly. "I wish I'd been able to get here before… you know… losing our baby."

"I'm so sorry, Bess."

"They said it couldn't be helped. Nature's way. But please don't be foolish. Don't take chances. We... you came all the way to our home-planet to have your baby. Betty, Rose, Alma and I will care for the others. The men have things well in hand. You have to promise you'll listen to the doctors." Bess was a dear old friend, pleading and making sense. It was a voice Mary had not heard for so long, but remembered well. She smiled at her old friend.

"Okay. I promise. And thank you." Mary stood. Bess stood. They embraced.

"That feels good," Bess said. They parted and sat down.

"Do you think that we, I mean commanders... that the special processing we had... that we might not be able to..." It was hard for her to ask. but Bess understood. Besides herself, Mary Green and Ruth Charnofsky were the only pregnant commanders. And Ruth had mated with an off-planet male, so her case might not be the same as two Earth-humans mating.

"I think it makes no difference. Art and I lost our baby because it was not meant to be. As Beam said, it was not part of the Master's plan. I accept that now. You be smart. Relax and let these doctors take care of you."

Mary smiled and nodded. "Okay. I'll go upstairs tomorrow."

"And be sure that Beam is involved too. She seems to have definite ideas about why all of this has happened to us, to the Brigade. Her people, the Antarean council, assigned her a special mission... aside from the medical aspect."

"What is it?"

"She said some on the council believe our children are special. They call them a new race in the Master's plan. If it's true, then it's one of the most powerful signs the Antareans have that they are chosen to execute the Master's grand plan."

For a moment both women stared at one another. There had been little, if any, discussion about the Brigade member's religious thoughts regarding their leaving Earth and their new life. Perhaps some of them had brought it up while making their decision to go, but as a group, nothing had been discussed openly. To hear that Antarean council considered this about the Brigade's offspring was curious.

"Do the others know about this?" Mary asked.

"No. Beam said that if she is asked she will speak about it."

CHAPTER TWENTY-SIX
EXPLANATION

The return trip aboard Air Force One had been jubilant. Alicia Sanchez and Phillip Margolin were congratulated several times by the President and Secretary Mersky. By the time they landed at Dulles International both young people were floating on a cloud of success.

"I want to meet with you two in a few days in my office," Gideon Mersky had commanded in a friendly, fatherly voice. "We've still got to get that Watership and storage tank launched and out of here in a few weeks."

"Yes, sir," the young scientists had said in unison. They stood next to the DOD limousine as Mersky closed the door and ordered the car to take him to the Pentagon. It was six A.M. The second DOD limo waited for Margolin. Dr. Sanchez and he walked slowly to the waiting stretch. They were euphoric.

"I can't sleep," she said. "It was the greatest night of my life."

"It's not over," he replied, looking at his watch. "The boss said he wants to see us in a few days. Why not keep the flavor going?"

"What do you have in mind?"

"How about breakfast at my apartment, and we take it from there?"

"To where?" she asked as they got into the limo.

"That," he said, "as Shakespeare wrote, is not in ourselves, dear Alicia, but in the stars." The car began to slowly pull away as the driver waited for instructions.

"You've got that backwards," Alicia corrected him.

"I hope so," he answered. "The Watergate apartments," he instruct-

148

ed the driver. Then he kissed her. She put her arms around him and kissed him back... hard, long and wet.

The DOD, NASA and the White House had their hands full with inquiries from the press, complaints from foreign governments including NATO, and outrage from the Soviet Union about the SSP experiment. The party line was simply that the test had been for peaceful purposes, namely *"An added protection for our rapidly deteriorating ozone layer..."* NASA announced that the program looked promising, but there was much data yet to be analyzed. They stressed that unexpected meteor colliding with the larger solar screen and pulling it into the atmosphere destroyed some critical data. Margo McNeil briefed the White House press corps the morning after what the media was calling the "Fire-in-the-Sky Show." She followed NASA's lead and only added that, *"The President was disappointed and has asked for a review of the entire SSP project."* He felt, she went on, that perhaps we launched too soon even though it was an unexpected event.

The Secretary of Defense had a different problem to handle. His counterpart in the Soviet Union, Marshal Pavel Kuzkonin, was on the hot line to the Pentagon moments after the test concluded. Their hot line was not a telephone, but a sophisticated series of word processors, translators, teletype machines and printers. The printed word is a far better tool when discussing details at a high level.

"Good morning, Mr. Secretary," the Marshal's message began. "We send greetings. The purpose of our contact to you this morning is to voice, in the strongest terms possible, our dismay and displeasure at your unauthorized use of international outer space last night between 0100 and 0330 hours Eastern Standard Time. This is a clear violation of the International Space Treaty accords signed by the United States of America and the Union of Soviet Socialist Republics two years ago in Phoenix, Arizona. Specifically, the agreement prohibits the use of space for weapons, or weapons defense research. The grave consequences of this flagrant violation are being discussed today at the highest levels of our government."

The message was clocked and answered: "Received. Please stay on the line." Gideon Mersky was prepared for the Soviets to be annoyed, but this was very strong language. As prearranged with President Teller, he responded.

"Good morning, Marshal Kuzkonin. To go straight to the point, we do not believe our SSP test yesterday was a violation of the Phoenix accords. In fact, we can prove they were in keeping with the stated purpose of the treaty—namely the peaceful exploration of space for the benefit of the entire planet. The Soviet Union is a major user of fluorocarbons, which research shows have a damaging effect on our precious ozone layer. The SSP is designed to protect the Earth. It is in no way a weapon or a defensive tool. The test was done on short notice because perfect weather conditions in the test area suddenly emerged, and because our scientists are predicting severe sunspot activity in the next six-month period. I trust this information will satisfy your government. In addition, may I now formally invite you and your staff to be my personal guests if and when we attempt another such test. As I am sure your scientists have reported, our test last night was a failure, due in part to the unexpected arrival of a meteor in the test zone. My best wishes to your family."

Mersky's communication was answered—"Received. Good-bye."

CHAPTER TWENTY-SEVEN
STRANGE COMMUNICATION

It took two days for all the expectant mothers to be completely test-ed. All of the fetuses were viable and appeared normal. The three human mothers who had mated with off-planet males and the one pregnant off-planet female, Tern, also appeared to be carrying normal humanoid babies. The only abnormal event occurred when Dr. Yee requested a second amniocentesis from Ruth Charnofsky. The obste-trician performing the procedure was Dr. Celia Fogelnest, a woman from Columbia Presbyterian Hospital's world-renowned Obstetric and Pediatric Clinic. When the long needle was inserted into the amniotic sac and fluid extracted for the second time in so many days, the fetus, a combination of Subax and Earth-human that was being observed ultrasonically, suddenly turned and grabbed at the intrusion in its warm, safe fluid world. Dr. Yee observed the baby's unexpect-ed movement at the same time Dr. Fogelnest turned her attention to drawing out enough amniotic fluid. Dr. Yee, his instincts still ra-zor-keen despite his aging body, quickly reached over the examina-tion table, firmly grabbed Dr. Fogelnest's hand, extracting the long needle just as the fetus grabbed at it.

"What the hell?" Dr. Fogelnest shouted. Ruth Charnofsky, who had felt the needle being withdrawn quickly, immediately went inside Dr. Yee's mind and understood what he had done.

"He was grabbing at the needle," he snapped back. "I had no time. It just had to be done." Dr. Fogelnest understood and apologized.

"A male, Dr. Yee? He's very fast, isn't he?" Ruth asked.

"And smart. He doesn't want us poking into his comfortable home,"

Yee answered as he motioned for Dr. Fogelnest to clean off Ruth's stomach with alcohol and apply a sterile bandage. He glanced at the slightly blue fluid in the syringe.

"When will you be able to tell me about the genetics?" Ruth asked. Dr. Yee hesitated, calculating how much time the geneticists would require and then how long it would take for Beam to assess her own input as well. The Antarean knew much about Subax. Her opinions would be invaluable, and she already knew much about human geneticists. Dr. Fogelnest finished and Ruth raised herself up from the table.

"Give us a day or so. I'd say you have at least six weeks before you come to term."

"On Subax six weeks is only about three weeks Earth time," Ruth told him as she stepped gingerly onto the floor. The tiny wounds made in her stomach wall and uterus were already healing. It was one of the benefits of being a processed commander. Her remark disturbed Dr. Yee, but he showed no emotion.

"Three weeks, six weeks. We have time. But he was concerned and Ruth knew it. There had been all manner of materials and cells never before seen by the geneticists in the first amniotic fluid sample. What was especially disturbing was the absence of antibodies and white blood cells normally present. "Just give us a little time. Beam is helping too. Everything will be just fine. Now you go back to that big blue husband of yours and have a rest." A nurse helped Ruth into a wheelchair and took her back to their special Subax-Earth-human apartment.

After two days of tests, the medical staff met and was confident they could perform their mission. Other than the unknowns that might present themselves in the mixed matings, everything else looked good. The three newborns were healthy and appeared normal. Their blood was exactly like their parents', like all the Brigade members'—no indication of disease, perfectly formed red cells, maximum organ function and efficiency, a huge variety of antibodies and the ability to repair cell and tissue damage rapidly. The physical state of all their guests was excellent.

What they didn't know, and something that the commanders agreed to keep secret, was that the mental status of the newborns was far from normal. The Messina girl and the Erhardt twin boys born aboard the Watership were communicating, telepathing with each other in a language none of the commanders nor Beam and her assistants understood. And beyond communicating with each other, the commanders strongly suspected the infants were also in touch with the unborn fetuses as well.

CHAPTER TWENTY-EIGHT
TRANSFER BEGINS

O*rca* and the Seal team were stationed over the Stones. The *Manta III* with Jack, Phil Doyle and Madman Mazuski aboard was anchored fifty yards off the *Orca's* stern. The Probeship with Amos and the Finleys on board was on the bottom, just south of the first cocoon chamber. The ocean floor was ninety-seven feet at this point. It slowly fell off from here as you traveled north toward the submerged Watership and storage tank that lay on the bottom nearly four nautical miles from the Stones at a depth of six hundred feet near the Boynton Beach wreck.

The plan was for the Seals, along with Amos and the Finleys, to operate as two teams. Dr. Macklow, on board the *Orca*, would supervise their activity and monitor the seawater taken into the Watership and storage tank to be sure that it remained chemically consistent with the water around the Stones.

The *Manta III* appeared to be a fishing vessel trolling for sailfish. Jack had the outriggers spread and four baited lines ready to go. The Seals, using scuba gear and supported by the *Orca*, would bring cocoons up to the *Manta III*, which would then transport them to the coordinates above the Watership. Four of the eleven Antareans remaining on the Watership would take the cocoons from the *Manta III* and bring them down to the waiting storage tank that now contained seawater.

The other team, Amos and the Finleys, would also remove cocoons and take them to the Probeship. They would then transport the cocoons underwater to the Watership and turn them over to the remainder of the Antarean crew working at the storage tank. Since the Antareans and the Finleys did not require any breathing apparatus, they could operate at these depths and pressures.

Between the two teams, it was estimated that fifty to sixty cocoons could be moved each day. At that rate Amos estimated the Watership would be loaded and ready to depart in nineteen days.

Although they were well within the United States territorial waters, operating at night was deemed to be risky. There was Soviet and NATO submarine activity nearby. Ostensibly the foreign sub's mission was to track the meteor, which NOAA announced it was trying to locate and bring to the surface. That explained the presence of the *Orca*. During the day, observation satellites had readings of a large metallic object off the Florida coast. This increased speculation that the meteor was large and intact. Further out in the Gulf Stream the *USS Simi,* the *USS Hapsas* and the *USS Metz* remained on station, keeping the area clear of nosy ships. Their presence was explained as drug traffic patrol and interdiction.

On the first day of operation both teams were able to move and store only forty-one cocoons. It now looked like thirty days would be a more realistic departure date and Amos so informed his council back on Antares.

Detectives Cummings and Betters, along with Special Agent McGill, had the responsibility of keeping the operation secure when the *Manta III,* with the Probeship attached to its hull, was in port. It was also anticipated that the *Orca* would have to make at least two visits to Miami harbor for supplies. That security was also assigned to the two Coral Gables cops and their FBI cohort. After finally understanding what had happened five years ago, there was an unspoken, half-spoken, continuing conversation between Cummings and Betters, always ending short of answering the question that was never directly asked.

"Those old folks sure looked good, didn't they?" Betters would say.

"Imagine, having kids at that age, huh?" Matthew Cummings had never married. Betters had no children. "Those guys with Fischer haven't aged at all. I swear they even look younger."

"They seem happy too," Cummings murmured. Betters silently nodded and wondered.

CHAPTER TWENTY-NINE
SPECIAL ORDERS

Alicia and Phil shared his dark blue tile and glass stall shower for the third morning since they'd returned from Florida. He reached around her and rubbed her smooth firm stomach with a soapy pink washcloth as he held her close against his own body. She leaned back and let the warm water hit her face as it rested on his shoulder. The water ran down her neck and between her breasts as Margolin slid the washcloth up along her belly. Then dropping the washcloth, he caressed her with his soapy fingers. She felt him growing hard against her buttocks.

"Again?" she whispered.

"I'll never have enough of you."

"That's my boy!" She turned and faced him, and then, with her arms tight around his neck she pulled her self up and wrapped her legs round his soapy hips. He was a short man, but strong and took her weight easily. *Twenty minutes, he figured. Then they would have to dress and head over to work. Of course, he then thought, there's always tonight.*

Their meeting with the Defense Secretary was brief and to the point. Their entry plan worked. Kudos. The heat from the Soviets and the media had cooled. He now tasked them to develop a plan for the Watership's departure. Casually, they suggested they would head up to Roscoe to work. Mersky rejected that idea.

"I want you two down in Houston with the visitors."

"It's sort of busy down there, isn't it?" Margolin suggested, not easily giving up the thought of being alone with Alicia in the cabin and getting some serious fly fishing in at the same time.

"Dr. Khawaja will set you up in a quiet spaced on the first floor. I have my reasons."

"Reasons, sir?" Sanchez asked.

"You two got along with that Finley guy, right?" They both nodded. "Okay. He's what they call a commander. He's operating with the Seal in Florida moving those cocoons. I want you two to get friendly with some of the other, uh, leaders... commanders."

Margolin was curious. "May I ask what you mean by friendly, sir?"

"Get to know them. Work with them. Ask questions. See if you can find out what their plans are after all the babies are born."

"I thought they planned to leave after the babies were born." Alicia said, surprised Mersky didn't know that.

"Well yes, they said that... but I have a feeling they might be convinced to stay, at least for a while. Just do your work and see how they feel about... you know... America, and maybe staying here. It can't hurt. But don't get too pushy. Okay?" They both nodded. "Good. One more thing. If you learn anything... about their plans, that is, don't call me or fax or anything. I'll have you flown up here once a week or so and we can talk then. Otherwise, keep that part of your mission within these four walls."

Sanchez and Margolin left the Pentagon wondering what their boss was up to. *Well, they thought, that's his problem, not ours. Orders are orders.* They realized they'd be working alone together for the next month. They couldn't wait to get back to Margolin's apartment and celebrate their good fortune.

Later that night, while the two lovers were asleep in each other's arms, Gideon Mersky placed a call on his scrambler phone to Colonel James "Jimbo" Smith, commander of the 1159th Light Infantry Brigade, stationed at Fort Campbell, Kentucky.

"How the hell are you, Jimbo?" the Secretary began, his voice jovial. He knew the colonel's habits and would bet he had roused him from a warm, but not empty bed.

"Mr. Secretary! Excellent, sir. How are you?"

"Just fine, Jimbo, just fine. You keeping busy these days?" Mersky's double entendre was not lost on Smith.

"Always alert and ready to go. Got something for us?" The colonel's voice was sharp and attentive. He lived for special, and preferably dangerous, missions.

"You still keep that special company... what'd you call it?"

"The Creamers, sir. The cream of my crop. Yes, sir. I've one hundred of the best trained, best equipped, travel light, ready for action troops the world has ever seen, or felt. Cocked, locked and ready to go."

"Well that's good to hear, Jimbo. You do me a favor and keep that cream right on top for the next month or so."

"Consider it done, sir."

"Thank you, Colonel. Sorry to disturb you. Good night."

"No problem, Mr. Secretary. My pleasure. Thank you, sir. And good night." The colonel had been seated on his king-sized waterbed. He hung up the telephone and looked over at the short blonde hair of the sleeping WAC Captain he'd invited to his quarters earlier that night. She was about to get awakened by an aroused American fighting man.

Back at the Pentagon, Gideon Mersky also felt excitement course through his body, but it wasn't sexual. It was the heady taste of power.

CHAPTER THIRTY
WE CAN HEAR YOU

Alicia and Phil were settled in on the first floor of the hospital; their equipment and computers hooked up and humming. The problem of getting the Watership off the planet with a minimum of detection was in the works. The size of the space vessel posed the greatest problem. Electronically its mass could be detected from anywhere on the planet. The data given to them by Amos Bright and the Watership flight crew suggested that it would take perhaps twenty to thirty seconds, once it surfaced, for the Watership to reach a speed where it would appear only as an anomaly on radar screens and satellite tracking systems. To launch it from American or even NATO territorial waters would alert the Soviets and Chinese.

The two scientists' quarters adjoined. They tended to gravitated to Alicia's room each night. It became their love nest. That was how they came to be friendly with the commanders. It happened the fifth day they were in Houston, just a week before Marie Amato was due to be the first to give birth on Earth. Ben Green was working with the Alicia and Phil, trying to compute the overall mass of the Watership, once fully loaded with the storage tanker attached, in relation to the amount of seawater it displaced. They were approaching the conclusion that the Watership, once loaded, would have to be moved from its present location to a more remote launching area. The possibility of the mid-ocean rift that was volcanically active near Iceland was under study.

Ben, who had made love with Mary earlier that morning, began to pick up on very strong feelings of love as he worked with Alicia and

Phil. He misread the sensation as Mary calling to him. He telepathed to his wife, who told him she did love him, but hadn't called to him. Ben then realized the emotions he'd felt were coming from Alicia and Phil. As a gesture of understanding he silently reached out to them and wished them well. Both the young scientists turned toward Ben at the same moment. Somehow they had heard him; somehow they understood what he had done. He tried to be nonchalant as they stared at him.

"Yes?" he asked, "did you say something?"

"Did you?" They said in unison, looking at Ben and then at each other. "I... we heard you say something... about us," Phil Margolin continued.

"About our being in love," Alicia said softly. It was very strange because they both had agreed to keep their affair a secret, but now she was blurting it out to a relative stranger. But was he a stranger? That was the interesting part of it. Both Alicia and Phil were suddenly comfortable with Ben Green as though he was an old friend. Ben understood their thoughts and feelings. He made his second mistake by thinking that and not blocking his thoughts. They read him again.

"You're talking without talking," Phil said incredulously.

"You can hear me?" Ben asked aloud.

"We can," Alicia answered. "How?"

"Telepathy," Ben responded. "Humans are capable of it. All in Brigade have had the ability since processing. We... the commanders have it and other uh, shall I say, abilities."

"But we heard you, and you heard us." Phil said.

"Can you teach?" Alicia asked.

"Yes. Jack Fischer was eventually able to learn to receive and send, but never consistently."

"Was that when the Antareans were first here?" Alicia asked.

"Yes. Shall we try some more?" Both Phil and Alicia immediately agreed without speaking. For the rest of that morning they communicated without words. It was difficult for Alicia to do directly with Phil, but with Ben joining in, acting like a medium, they could read each other's thoughts clearly.

Later that day, Ben reported the event to the rest of the commanders. It was then that Alma Finley, who at the time was under the sea in the first cocoon chamber, told them about Gideon Mersky's ability to block and read them as well.

CHAPTER THIRTY-ONE
POLLUTION

Dr. Macklow left the *Orca* and joined the Seal team at the Stones where the work was going well, but slowly. They were nearly finished emptying the first of the cocoon chambers. Two of the Antarean flight crew had also joined them. The Seals became fast friends with the Antareans. They dubbed them Ants, a nickname that spread to Houston as well.

Amos was concerned about the time it was taking to move the cocoons. There were three chambers to go. This first had been the smallest, containing only 217 cocoons. He'd noticed that toward the end of their work in that chamber the cocoons left were not as viable as those taken earlier from the same chamber. He discussed this with Dr. Macklow, suspecting it had something to do with their exposure to the fresh ocean water. He was correct. There was an increase in the amount of caustic chemicals and sewage in the water. Amos had her come back to the *Orca* when she did more tests confirming the change.

"In few days I have been gone, it has increased six percent," she told the Antarean leader.

"That is alarming. Five years ago we found the ocean contaminated. I fear the situation has gotten worse."

"I tested it when the storage tanker was filled and before any cocoons were moved. It has to be something being introduced within the past week."

"Are you certain?"

"Fairly certain," the tall marine biologist responded, her steel-grey eyes revealing a mind actively at work. "I'd like to find the source of this pollution. It has to be local. Perhaps illegal sewage, or industrial waste. Maybe a passing waste." She leaned over her charts and computer printouts.

"There is a water planet near the star you call Pollux in the constellation Gemini. It's known as Chexis Quad 3. On this planet there is a life form that must reproduce in the water—salty mineral water like your ocean. There is only a special time when they can breed, when the water is not poisoned. That is when the clean water flushes up from springs very deep in their seas. It rises up along fixed routes. These creatures, called Mellis, can follow the spring water just by tasting a few molecules. They can find it, they know when it is coming. They know where it is coming from."

"We have a species like that on Earth," Dr. Macklow said. "They are called salmon."

"I was fascinated with this ability," Amos continued, "so I experimented, with their approval of course, and was able to discover the means by which they could find the clean water. I converted that to instrumentation. Perhaps, I was thinking, if we could take some of this pollution and feed it to my instrument we might find the source."

"I have a sample right here," she said, picking up a jar of seawater.

"Then, Dr. Macklow, may I have the honor of inviting you aboard the Probeship?"

CHAPTER THIRTY-TWO
I HEAR VOICES

There was no doubt, with the exception of the mixed-mating babies, all of the Brigade fetuses seemed to be six to eight weeks advanced from the normal development of Earth-humans. During the ultrasound tests this sped up phenomenon gave the doctors pause. It was clarified when all the testing was complete and senior staff went over the results. Fetus size was deceiving—they were small, but their development was advanced. Beam was asked to join the meeting. Dr. Yee asked if she had ever witnessed this kind of change in the birth patten of any species.

"I cannot confirm that we have," she answered forthrightly. "But this is the first we have processed for space travel as though the subjects were Antarean. It was not our doing originally, as you know. The four male commanders, Green, Perlman, Finley and Lewis discovered our equipment and, thinking it was a health club, used it. They, in effect, processed themselves. As you know, all of the Brigade that were processed have changed. Many of their life functions have been enhanced. Their aging stopped and then some functions, including reproductive, reversed. This was a surprise for all of us on Antares."

"Well," Dr. Khawaja concluded, "we must assume that now a full-term baby for these mothers is possibly just seven months. Or that they all may be premature for a reason we don't yet understand. In any case, we must be alert to these possibilities and be prepared to adjust the schedule accordingly. Remember, the three births on the Watership were premature. That may have been due to space travel."

"There was also one stillborn," Beam reminded the doctors.

"I was told that labor of the mothers on the Watership was brief and the births came quickly and easily," Dr. Yee said. "One of the mothers, the woman who had twins, told me it was as though the babies were controlling their own birth. And something else," he continued. "The ultrasound tests. I watched all of them. Most of us did. Did any of you feel anything special when you were conducting them?"

For a moment there was silence in the room. Then Dr. Fogelnest, the specialist from Columbia Presbyterian, spoke. "I'm going to say something foolish."

"I don't think so," Dr. Yee said.

"Very well then," Dr. Fogelnest continued hesitantly, "during the ultrasound I did on the six women assigned to my team… well… I, uh, I had the distinct impression that I was being watched."

"By your colleagues, Doctor?" Dr. Khawaja asked.

"No. Not that way. It was as though… Oh well," she sighed, "I hate to say this, you'll think I'm crazy, but it was as though the fetus, the baby, was watching me as I was studying it on the TV screen."

"Yes. Of course." Dr. Yee announced. "I felt… I saw that too."

"They were speaking to me," Dr. Fogelnest admitted, encouraged by Dr. Yee's words.

"And me too," the obstetrician from the Mayo Clinic admitted. "I thought I was imagining things. We've been working long hours here and…"

"It is true," Beam said. "I have seen it. I have heard of it before. There are species that communicate with their young before birth."

Dr. Michelangelo Yee leaned back in his leather chair and smiled. "Well," he said, "if we can find a way to get those little beggars to help us, to talk to us somehow, our job here might get a whole lot easier."

"And safer," Dr. Khawaja added.

Alicia could not sleep. She watched Phil Margolin peacefully sleeping next to her, and though tempted to wake him, she resisted. Something was gnawing at her. Something weird. Then she heard a voice. "Protect us. You must protect us." It was a child's voice, far away, tiny. Then it was gone. She got out of bed and to relax, took a hot bath. When she returned to the room Phil was awake, sitting up in bed with the light turned on. He was writing on the yellow legal pad that he always kept nearby in case an idea or solution or a problem came to him in the middle of the night.

"An inspiration?" she asked, toweling off and sitting next to him. He kissed her shoulder.

"I was sleeping… dreaming I guess. Then I was up. I heard you in the bathroom and thought maybe that's what woke me. But then I began to hear strange voices." A shiver coursed down Alicia's spine. "They sounded like little kids… no, maybe like…"

"Angels?" she asked.

"A choir. Young, clear voices. No words. Just thoughts vocalized. Maybe some backlash from that telepathy we were doing with Ben Green. Whaddya think?"

"I heard them too, love," she said, leaning over to see what he had written. "Protect us. Protect us," she read aloud.

"Protect who?" he asked.

"The babies."

"From whom?"

"Gideon Mersky, I think." They dressed quickly, calling out to Ben Green silently as they did. He met them at the door to Phil Margolin's room.

CHAPTER THIRTY-THREE
THE FIRST EARTH BORN

Marie Amato's husband Paul was awakened by his wife at three in the morning. She was in labor. He pressed the medical call button installed in every room. In moments an emergency team was at their door. The team chief, an obstetrician from Walter Reed, sized up the situation immediately. He ordered Marie be taken directly to prep and at the same time ordered delivery complex Alpha staffed and readied. The team rapidly deployed. The ruckus awakened everyone on the top floor. There was concern and at the same time anticipation that the first Earth-born Brigade baby was on the way.

It was a girl, perfectly formed and appearing to be full-term. She was, as Dr. Khawaja suggested and the ultrasound confirmed, two months early and quite normal, no matter that earlier tests and confirmation of the time of conception suggested. The baby was kept in the pediatric intensive care unit for the maximum four hours allotted, then released to the transitional nursery, where Marie Amato nursed her. They named her Beam. Her namesake, the Antarean medical officer, was honored and delighted.

In the morning, a staff meeting was called by Dr. Khawaja as soon as things settled. The senior staff would have to reevaluate their schedule. Reexamination of all the expectant mothers, with careful attention to changes indicating time of birth, was initiated by Dr. Yee. He thought back to the incident with Ruth Charnofsky when the fetus seemed to grab at the intruding amniocentesis needle.

"We should consider that these babies might be somehow more advanced and different than other human children. If they are coming earlier and normal, and that certainly seems to be the pattern, we must be ready. I want all the women, including the mixed couples, all of them, to be scheduled for ultrasound. I think we'd better have a closer look at those fetuses."

The commanders also met that morning, gathering in one of the large examination rooms on the top floor. During the night, just before Marie Amato went into labor, Mary Green had been awakened by someone calling to her telepathically. It had happened before to all of them, but their minds were able to block a disturbance when they slept. There were ways to awaken one another if the situation was critical. But this intrusion into Mary's subconscious was different.

"It came from within," she told the others. "I heard something too," Ruth Charnofsky admitted, "but I couldn't understand the message."

"It woke you?" Frank Hankinson asked.

"Yes. I think so. I may have been awake before... a moment before. I'm not sure."

"What did it sound like?" Ben Green asked his wife.

"A voice... no, voices. But speaking in a strange tongue. Yet I thought I could understand. It was like the time when we had just arrived on Parma Quad 2. We knew the Parman language, but other than the guides, we had never actually met any of them."

"You mean the dialects," Bess Perlman suggested.

"Not exactly," Mary Green answered. "I mean the way they spoke to one another sometimes. The lost language, they called it... something like that..."

"The ancient language," Betty Franklin remembered. "That's what they called it."

Betty, Bess's sister, had been one of those who stayed behind on Parma Quad 2 after the two years of training. She had studied hard and came to know the Parman culture as well as any of the Antarean ambassadors who lived there. "It was the way of communicating before their race evolved to a total crystalline form." An uneasy feeling passed through the room.

"I believe we are all thinking the same thing," Bernie Lewis said. "What woke Mary and Ruth was from within our own. Within the mothers."

"The babies," Rose said aloud. "The babies are calling to us."

"No," Ruth said firmly, "Not to us; to each other. Somehow they know about each other. I believe that they are speaking from the womb in a language we once knew and have long forgotten."

"We must reach out to them," Mary stated matter-of-factly.

CHAPTER THIRTY-FOUR
ENVIRONMENTAL CRIMINALS

There were two distinct sources of the pollution around the Stones. The worst of it came from a phosphorous processing plant in Lake Worth. The people there produced fertilizer and had a breakdown of their waste-material filtering system. While it was being repaired, the plant, recently acquired by a Japanese consortium, continued to operate under the orders of the new Japanese plant manager who brought with him a fierce desire to improve the bottom line. He simply stored the caustic waste material during the day and then ordered it dumped into the ocean at night. After all, he reasoned, this ocean was a long way from Japan. The most important thing was that his management efforts succeed.

It was an easy matter for the Probeship to locate that culprit because Amos and Dr. Macklow had to track the source at night since the Probeship had to be used to transport cocoons during the day. When they found the plant's location they sent Cummings and Betters up to Lake Worth the next day to have a good look around. The manager proudly showed the two detectives that he was storing the waste material. At the same time NOAA Captain Hadges aboard the *Orca* notified the Florida office of the Environmental Protection Agency of the violation. That night, as the plant spewed its killing waste, they were caught red-handed and eventually fined seven million dollars. The manager was recalled to Japan and disgraced as his government chastised him publicly and apologized to the American people.

The sewage was more difficult to trace. It took three more nights, but eventually a barge leaving a trail of sewage just off Jupiter Beach was discovered. They did not know where the barge originated and they were sure it was, at best, an intermittent thing. All Amos could do was to notify Captain Walkly aboard the *USS Simi*. The captain dispatched the *USS Metz* to intercept the barge and put the fear of the U.S. Navy into whoever operated it.

The sight of a Navy destroyer bearing down on them in the middle of the night was frightening enough, but when the *Metz* loudly hailed the errant barge with a warning that they were polluting a government area and could be fired upon, the crew aboard the barge came out of the deck cabin with their hands high in the air. The *Metz* came to a stop and turned on her bright searchlights. The forward machine guns were manned, aimed at the three quaking men. Satisfied, the *Metz's* captain turned abruptly and put a wash across the deck that soaked the barge operators. They were not seen again in the area.

CHAPTER THIRTY-FIVE
THE SECRETARY'S PLAN

In Washington, Gideon Mersky, who had begged off accompanying the President to Houston, called Phillip Margolin to DC from Texas for a quick meeting the night before the President left. He wanted Margolin back in Houston the next day when President Teller arrived, ostensibly for a visit to NASA. The real purpose for the President's being there was to meet personally with the space visitors at the secreted hospital. Both Margolin and Sanchez were scheduled that same day to brief the chief executive on their progress in developing a plan for the Watership's departure.

It was Friday afternoon and Washington was emptying out for the weekend. The Defense Secretary kept Margolin waiting for nearly an hour. When Mersky finally emerged from his office he was with a tall, severe-looking man who Margolin immediately pegged as military, although not in uniform.

"Phillip Margolin, I'd like you to meet an old friend, Jimmy Smith." Margolin, who was quite strong himself, tensed at the viselike grip of Smith's handshake.

"Very nice to meet you, Mr. Margolin."

"My pleasure, sir." Smith released Phillip's hand and smiled. He then reached a softer handshake to the Defense Secretary.

"Good to see you, Mr. Secretary. You take care now. And don't worry about that little problem. We'll be able to handle it."

"I'm sure you will, Jimmy. Thanks. I'll be in touch." Smith left. Mersky signaled Margolin into his office where Margolin, who had developed the beginnings of a plan to launch the Watership as secretly as possible, presented his ideas. The Secretary listened intently, but made no comment until the presentation was finished.

"The plan sounds fine, Phillip. I think it needs some refining, but you've broken its back for sure."

"Sounds like a good beginning you've got there Phillip."

"Dr. Sanchez and I both worked on it."

"Of course. I'm sure the President will like it. I'll be talking to him in the morning before he leaves for Houston." Mersky shuffled some papers on his desk. He had no idea that Phillip Margolin was, in a very crude manner, trying to reach into his mind to read his thoughts. Ever since he'd discovered the Brigade commanders were able to telepath and auto-suggest, Mersky had practiced and sharpened his own abilities to block their intrusion. He never believed or accepted Alma Finley's contention that they were not permitted to interfere with people's actions by mind control. But not suspecting that Margolin had been developing his own telepathic abilities with the commanders' assistance, the Secretary was not blocking.

"That's encouraging, sir," Margolin answered, knowing now that their meeting had an additional agenda. Mersky continued playing with the papers for a moment, then looked up.

"How're you doing with those commanders?"

"Very well, sir. I've become friendly with Mr. Green and Mr. Lewis. Dr. Sanchez has also met them and gone out of her way to become friendly with their wives. Of course, with the birth schedule moved up, things have been pretty busy for them."

"So I understand. How many born so far?"

"Ten, I believe. And Dr. Khawaja confirms they're not premature at all."

"Interesting. These babies take only seven months to fully develop."

"They seem to be somehow evolved."

"More than you know." Margolin was inside Mersky's head, but his exact thoughts were difficult to read. The Defense Secretary was excited. "That man you met before…"

"Mr. Smith?" Margolin said, unable to hide the slight tone of sarcasm in his voice.

"That's really his name. He's a bird colonel stationed at Fort Campbell."

"The one-oh-one?"

"No. A newly formed light infantry brigade."

Margolin knew something about those new brigades. They were part of the RDF—Rapid Deployment Force, a product of the need for the military to respond quickly to trouble spots on a global basis. The unit could move on a moment's notice. From a single squad to the entire brigade, they were always combat ready. They airlifted by jet transport with all their equipment. From that point on they operated with a minimum of support and a maximum of deadly force.

"I'm concerned about the safety and security of those people down in Houston," Mersky continued. Margolin knew Mersky was lying.

"They seem quite secure in the hospital," Margolin offered with a faked naiveté in his voice.

"Well, they're not. I'll be giving Colonel Smith the task of relocating our visitors to a more remote and secure facility."

"What about the babies?"

"Of course we'll take the babies."

"No, sir. I mean what about the medical attention they need, and the ones not yet born?"

"We're not planning any moves until all the births are done. The last thing I want to do is run a hospital. No. It'll be done in a few months."

"Will the President tell the visitors about that tomorrow?" Mersky leaned forward in his chair.

"This is extremely confidential, Philip. The President has approved it, of course, but he wants time to develop the plan completely, covering all contingencies, so when he does present it to the, uh… to our visitors they will have all the information and understand our reasoning. These old folks are Americans. They aren't sedentary retired people anymore. The knowledge and abilities they now possess… well it's all very important to the nation. I'm sure you understand that, Phillip. Its to remain top secret—need to know only"

Margolin still couldn't read all of Mersky's thought processes, but he knew the Secretary was lying. He was sure Mersky believed that part about the Brigade folks being important to the nation, but he was sure Mersky had no intention of allowing the visitors the freedom to choose where and how they wished to live. At least there was time before Mersky made his move.

The Defense Secretary leaned back in his chair. "Now tell me more about these two commanders you've befriended, Green and Lewis."

Margolin talked innocently about them, explaining that they were the leaders and had developed certain abilities beyond the other Brigade members. He talked a little about their adventures on Parma Quad 2 and gave the Defense Secretary a brief explanation on how the Parman guides were used for deep-space travel. He knew that kind of talk would tweak Mersky's curiosity to know more. That way, Margolin assured himself, he would be asked to continue his spying assignment. But he told Mersky nothing of the commanders' plans. That was the last thing Gideon Mersky should know now that he intended to hold the Brigade visitors on Earth by force.

CHAPTER THIRTY-SIX
A MESSAGE TO THE GALAXY

The President arrived in Houston ostensibly to review the progress of the NASA Office of Exploration, a position created to put men and women in space. Some time after the *Challenger* accident some in the government complained that we were no longer pursuing the dream of exploring space, but rather running a transportation and hardware hauling business. President Teller took that realization one step further in his first inaugural address when he stated, "The time has come for all of us on this planet to get up off our tails and dream again to walk among the stars." Prophetically, that was only a month after the Geriatric Brigade had left Earth and begun their journey to Parma Quad 2.

The meetings at the Johnson Space Center had minimal press coverage. The President then went on a private tour of the sprawling NASA facility with his last stop being the newly renovated Space Medicine Center Hospital.

His arrival coincided with another birth. A son was born to parents who originally lived in New York City and were old friends of Ben and Mary Green. President Teller was delighted to personally witness the birth from an observation room outside the Beta delivery suite. Chief obstetrician, Dr. Fogelnest, delivered the baby easily. Dr. Khawaja was with the President observing.

"The births are consistently the easiest we have ever witnessed. They all leave their womb in a similar manner. There is very little labor and the infants emerge at the correct angle and position. One of our doctors maintains they come with their arms extended as though they were asking to be held."

While the President visited with the Brigade parents and parents-to-be, Margolin and Sanchez met with the commanders who were in residence at the hospital. The Finleys were still on site with Amos Bright transferring the cocoons to the Watership's storage tank. Margolin reported on his meeting with Mersky. He had researched Colonel Smith's special RDU.

"It's an elite group—highly trained. Colonel Smith was combat hardened in Viet Nam and quite experienced. And I'm certain the President has no knowledge of their plans."

"If we assume President Teller knows the plan," Art Perlman suggested, "we can use his ignorance to our advantage. Let him be truly surprised when Mersky makes his move."

"If Mersky makes his move," Ruth Charnofsky said. "I think it best to make our plans to leave before it comes to a confrontation."

Ben Green agreed with a reservation. "I agree. But we'll need help to reach the Watership."

"And to a Mothership to transport all of us, the babies and the two storage tanks we left on the moon. Don't forget the Watership will have a fully loaded storage tank transporting the cocooned army back to Antares.

"To play it safe," Bernie Lewis interjected, "I think I'd better contact Amos and have that Mothership leave Antares as soon as possible." They all agreed and telepathed their concerns to the Antarean leader.

"We have to present our plan for the Watership's departure to the President in an hour," Alicia Sanchez said. She had filled the commanders in on how they proposed to have the Antarean craft depart Earth. "But," she continued, "I think that Phil and I should begin to develop a plan for your own departure as well."

"We assume you will need special arrangements for the children," Margolin suggested. For a moment the commanders linked their thoughts, blocking all others.

"We will need to discuss that with Beam and the off-planet parents," Bernie Lewis answered, "but for now we must assume everyone here in Houston, other than Alicia and Phil, are involved in Mersky's plan to hold us against our will. Our plans must be kept secret."

"Do we have a departure date we can aim at?" Margolin asked.

Betty Franklin, Bess's sister who had been assigned the task of liaison with the still expectant mothers, spoke up. "As best we can determine it will be two months and three weeks. Let's say mid-October to be safe. Mary will be the last according to Dr. Yee's new schedule."

"Of course we can't be certain about the mixed babies yet," Ruth chimed in. "On Subax a pregnancy might last as long as a year, depending on the time of conception and weather conditions."

The newborn boy was transferred to pediatric intensive care as standard procedure. The initial tests and examinations showed another perfectly formed, healthy and extremely alert baby. The President, accompanied by Margo McNeil and Benton Fuller, visited the transitional nursery near the intensive care unit. There were six infants in there. The procedure was to move them down to the second floor after five days. As soon as the President arrived at the nursery, the babies awoke and became very active. Down on the second floor, in the main nursery, the older infants stopped their activity and suddenly became quiet and still. It gave the chief pediatric nurse quite a scare. She immediately called for an emergency unit, but when they arrived they could find nothing wrong. All of the babies, nine of them, lay in their bassinets on their backs, eyes open, staring up at the ceiling. Their breathing was normal.

Back at the commander's meeting Alicia Sanchez suddenly stood up. She covered her ears with her hands, her face contorted in pain. Phillip Margolin's body stiffened, his feet shot out under the table.

"Jesus!" he gasped.

"What's wrong?" Ben Green asked. He reached into their minds but he was blocked.

"The children," Alicia said, "they want us to come to them… now." She relaxed, as did Margolin. Everyone stood up.

"No," Phillip said, "they only want us."

President Teller stood among the bassinets in the transitional nursery admiring the calm but alert babies. Yet he was uneasy. He watched Margo McNeil as she held one of the infants who had been handed to her by the chief nurse. That baby, in fact all the babies, were staring at him.

Sanchez and Margolin entered the nursery. All the babies turned their attention toward the couple. The baby being held began to squirm, and Margo had to give her back to the nurse who put her back in her bassinet.

"Hello, Mr. President," Margolin said.

"Ah… the two geniuses from DOD. How are you?"

"Very good, sir," Sanchez answered.

"Quite a bunch we have here. They seem so healthy."

"They are, Mr. President," Margolin answered. Then he heard the voice. So did Sanchez. They spoke rapidly, alternating with each new thought. Alicia spoke first.

"These are the children of the new race."

"These are the children of off-planet human-mankind."

"These are the children who will teach many."

"These are the children who must be protected."

"These are the children who will serve all races."

"These are the children who will lead you to peace."

"These are the children of the beginning."

Alma Finley heard the voices deep beneath the ocean as she swam outside the Watership's flight bridge. She was transporting the cocoon of an Antarean commander at the time, guiding it toward its berth within the Watership's storage container. She swam past the green translucent bubble that housed the Parman guides. They were sealed inside, replenishing themselves with chlorine. They transformed the gas into an absorbable crystalline form. At first she thought the voice was coming from the Parmans. Then she realized it was coming from the cocoon she carried. It was pulsating with a reddish light from within. Amos swam up next to her.

"Do you hear it?" he telepathed.

"What is it?"

"The children. They are calling to us. They are announcing their arrival in the galaxy. Today the fifteenth baby was born. Their power increases geometrically as more join them."

"This sleeping commander also hears them," she thought as she touched the glowing cocoon.

"Yes. I think it is possible that the entire galaxy hears them. Commander Lewis is correct. I will send for the Mothership immediately."

Phillip Margolin brought the President back to their work area on the first floor. The shock of what had happened in the nursery remained with everyone, but they had not discussed it yet. Sanchez prepared the preliminary presentation for the Watership's departure, but the President told her not to bother.

"Secretary Mersky filled me in on everything. It sounds fine to me. You coordinate with him." The work area was one large central room with four computer terminals, TV monitors, two laser printers, a FAX machine and a teletype link to the Pentagon Communication Center. Maps and charts, mainly of the mid-Atlantic Ridge, a chain of huge underwater mountains that stretched from Greenland down past both North and South America to the Antarctic, were prominent. Two smaller rooms off the main room were used as offices. LoCasio and Berlin, the two assistants who worked with Margolin and Sanchez, occupied those offices now. President Teller indicated for Benton Fuller to close the doors to the offices.

"What happened up there?" he then asked.

"I'm not sure, sir," Sanchez answered.

"Those things you said about the babies. Who told you?"

"Again, we're not sure, Mr. President," Margolin said.

"When I first met Alma Finley, she was able to... well, sort of hear what I was thinking. Afterward I talked to Caleb Harris and he told me that these commanders can put thoughts into your head too."

"I wasn't aware of that, sir," Alicia lied.

"Well," he continued, "whose voice did you hear telling you to say those things?"

"We don't know," Margolin said quietly. "Perhaps it was the commanders." The President was disturbed. He had a sense that things were getting past him; that he had somehow been duped by the commanders and that he was being used.

"It sounded to me like someone was warning me about something."

"Did it sound that way?" Alicia asked, "Or did you feel it inside?" President Teller didn't answer. But Alicia knew the question gave the President pause to wonder exactly what had happened. He didn't like it.

CHAPTER THIRTY-SEVEN
THE OLD GREEK

Bad weather and the pollution problem had slowed them down, but in four weeks they had completed moving half the cocoons to the Watership. Another storm system was moving into the area and they had to stop work for four days. The *Orca* put into the port of Miami for supplies and fuel. None of the crew or the Seal team left the vessel for security reasons. Jack Fischer brought the *Manta III*, with the Probeship attached to its hull, to his dock at Boca Raton as he had every night since the operation began. He stopped at the fuel barge to fill his gas tanks. Nick, the old Greek at the gas barge, watched Jack and Phil Doyle carefully. They had come and gone each day, but without the submarine because the Probeship had remained at sea next to the Stones. But as he pumped the gas, he noticed the *Manta III* had the submarine attached to it again.

"You for to use gasoline in that boat too?" he asked, pointing with his bent cigar to the waterline of the *Manta III*.

"Yes. I use gasoline in this boat," thinking he meant the *Manta III*.

"You want me to fill up?"

"Yes, Nick. Like always. Both tanks." Jack went back to his conversation with Phil Doyle.

"Where is gas cap?"

"You already have the caps off."

"Not these, Captain Jack. I for to mean the cap for your submarine under the boat. I need to know how to put gas." Jack and Phil understood immediately that the old man had seen the Probeship. Jack made light of it.

"Submarine? That's not a submarine. It's a, uh, special fishing thing... a sonar... like a fish finder."

"It's a big one, huh?"

"Big finder for big fish." Jack laughed. Phil laughed. The old man turned away to get the gas hose from the pump. *Okay,* he thought to himself...*you want for to get your gas somewhere else... that's your business.* But he was annoyed that Jack felt he had to lie to him. Below, inside the Probeship, Amos Bright heard the conversation. His mission was to get the cocoons safely home to Antares. Nothing could stand in the way of accomplishing that. He decided to have a talk with the old Greek at the same time he spoke to Cummings and Betters. The Brigade could always use some more members.

CHAPTER THIRTY-EIGHT
CAN THE BABIES TRAVEL?

Leaving Earth was never a question. The Brigade had come to their home planet for births, nothing more. But the question of what they might do with the babies could not be answered until they knew exactly what these babies were. It was clear now that physically the babies were human in every way. They all had inherited the disease-free blood, organ and muscle tissue their parents had as a result of the Antarean processing. The preliminary tests showed no genetic abnormalities. There was a question about what the effect of two new sets of chromosomes, present in the infants, meant. And the growth rate of those already born seemed to be much faster than normal Earth-human babies. What that meant could not yet be determined. The chief pediatrician needed at least six weeks to hazard a guess as to how advanced the development of these infants might prove to be. He would base his estimate on comparison with a group of human babies being born in the nearby Houston Children's Hospital during the same time period. Until that data was in, the decision as to how soon the infants might be able to travel in space, if at all, would have to be deferred.

The Mothership had left Antares. Its tactical route and approach to Earth was similar to that of the Watership. In fact, if the cocoon retrieval went according to schedule, the Mothership, using stars and planets to block it from instruments on Earth, and the Watership and storage tank would rendezvous on the moon's far side undetected. But the means of masking the Watership and its cargo containers departure was still being developed.

185

As requested by Amos Bright, the Mothership had aboard the means to process and cocoon the infants for space travel. How long they would have to remain in suspended animation was not known, and Beam was deeply concerned that this might prove a dangerous, if not impossible task.

"We have processed our own kind this way," she told the Brigade Commanders. "We know that for us, and several other humanoids, cocooning works. But for Earth-humans... for ones so young, who can say?" Her apprehension was disconcerting to the commanders.

At a meeting of the Brigade in the dining room, the commanders informed their comrades about the potentially hostile plans of the Defense Secretary and the departure problems they would have to solve. Alicia and Phillip were working on those. Of course Mersky knew nothing about that.

Beam then addressed the gathering. "We will have to wait and see what condition the infants reach in the next month, and how they compare with normal Earth-human babies."

"And we will need to see what surprises the mixed babies bring to us as well," Ruth added as she felt her own baby move as if in response to Beam's information.

CHAPTER THIRTY-NINE
THREE MORE FOR THE BRIGADE

Detective Betters' wife listened patiently as they sat alone in the Florida room sipping cool white wine spritzers, while her husband related the story. He began by going back five years to the chase up Red Lake Canal when his speedboat was lifted from the canal, hurled across the manicured lawn of a wealthy Coral Gables resident and dumped into the man's green and red tiled swimming pool. When he got to the part about seeing the President of the United States, Paige Betters thought her husband had finally lost it.

"Stop right there," she insisted, getting up from her chaise, hovering over him as he lay prone on his own lounge chair. "The story was good, damned good. One of the best you've told. But just what do you think I am? The President? Give me a break."

"I swear, honey."

"Don't you swear about those lies. You've been with Matt too long. Both of you have carried around this condo story from five years ago like heavy baggage. Now that retirement is near I guess Matt wants to clean up old business. But that doesn't mean you have to be involved."

"Honey. Please," he begged. "Everything I say I can prove. It's not the story that matters. It's what we want to do about this offer..."

"Someone offered you a job after you retire?"

"Sort of... like that. But it involves you too." She walked over to the wet bar they had built in the corner of the tropical room and fixed herself another drink. They had both worked hard for this house. It was in a good section of Kendall. They had paid sixty thousand dollars twenty-two years ago. Now it was worth over two hundred seventy thousand. It was their equity. Paige was extremely proud of the house and loved her husband dearly. Police work, even in the Coral Gables sheriff's office, was dangerous. They'd had no children. Once, after they were settled in the house, they discussed adoption, but were told they were too old when they finally applied.

"I want you to listen to me, honey." Betters' voice was serious. She came back to the chaise and sat down.

"Okay. I'll listen." And she did, although she couldn't possibly believe the "offer" he described. Yet she had never seen him so insistent and as far as she knew he'd never lied to her. They were up most of the night until she decided that if, and she used the word *if* advisedly, the story was true then she would go if he wanted it. He said he did. She was suddenly frightened, realizing either way her life would change radically. If he was lying then it was obvious he was ill—perhaps Alzheimer's. And if he was telling the truth, then they were about to begin a life she really couldn't comprehend.

Paige and Coolridge Betters were at the *Manta III* dock before dawn. Matt Cummings had brought a small suitcase. Amos told him to leave it behind.

"You'll have plenty of time to gather personal things before the Watership departs," he told the aging cop. Then he welcomed Paige and suggested they board the *Manta III*. They found the Joe and Alma Finley, Phil Doyle and the old Greek, Nick Sorukas, on board having breakfast in the spacious cabin. Introductions were made. As they cast off, Nick smiled a toothless smile.

"They say I will for to grow teeth again," he told Paige. Then he laughed. "And maybe babies too. Many babies." *Could this really be happening? This is crazy, she thought.* Alma Finley understood her panic. She telepathed comfort to the sixty-seven-year-old woman, a retired schoolteacher who was on her way to an unimaginable life. Then she spoke softly to her.

"It's a little disorienting, isn't it?"

"I don't know what's happening. I listened to my husband all night. I had to come. I mean I wanted to come. But is this really true?"

"Yes," Alma assured her. "It is. The decision to ask you and the others came from Mr. Bright. He is the only one who can invite us, Earth-humans, to join the Antareans on their voyages."

"Well," Paige Betters then said, taking a cup of coffee that Jack Fischer offered her, "I always believed that life didn't end on this Earth of ours; that there had to be something beyond. I guess I'm about to find out that's true."

"It is," Alma said. "But you'll see it's not exactly what our religions taught us."

CHAPTER FORTY
THE FIRST DIFFERENT BABY

Eighteen babies had been born. The first three who were born on the Watership were nearly two months old and showed remarkable progress. The pediatric nursing staff had grown because the mothers ceased nursing their infants. The babies were controlling their feeding and general care by communicating their needs telepathically. The parents knew why they had gone to bottle feeding. Two reasons caused the decision.

First, it seemed a possibility that the parents would have to separate from their children at some point in the near future. Unless it was deemed safe for the babies to endure space travel with the Parman guides, which seemed highly unlikely, they would have to be sealed in life-support cocoons and de-metabolized until arrangements could be made for them on an Earth type planet. All were certain that their young bodies could not be processed with the Antarean equipment used on the Brigade five years ago since that processing only worked on human bodies that were well along in the Earth-human aging process.

Second, because the Mothership was now on the way to Earth to pick them up, it was time for those who had families in the United States to visit them if they wished. Of the humans who'd returned to Earth, only thirty-one who had become parents had any family they knew how to reach. Of these, twenty-seven wanted to pay a visit. Dr. Khawaja mentioned this to the President, and he arranged for small jet aircrafts, normally assigned to cabinet appointees, be used to transport those who wished to see their relatives.

Before the twenty-seven Brigade parents departed, the commanders insisted that, for security purposes, nothing be said regarding babies or the hospital's location. A deadline was set for the return of everyone to Houston six weeks hence. They were to check in by telephone weekly. And before they left, those Brigade parents once again listened to Mary Green recount her visit to family. She counseled them to be positive and resist giving too much detail about the other worlds they'd seen.

"It will only cause them worry and runaway imaginations. Try to make it sound like a long vacation overseas. Use that analogy. And little white lies about harsh weather, poisonous atmospheres and hostile inhabitants are in order. Remember, especially with grandkids, their image of life on other planets is limited in great part to the horror and fantasy movies they see."

Ruth Charnofsky put it another way. "We know how much we have changed and how fortunate we are. They do not, and most likely will not, have that same opportunity. They do not understand death as we now do. They do not accept the gift of life that we have learned to cherish. Be kind and loving, as we all have become, but do not let them peer too deeply into your heart and mind. And, of course, likewise respect theirs as well and refrain from reading their thoughts."

Three days after the twentieth human baby was born, Tern, the female Penditan from Turmoline, felt the onset of birth and left her husband, Peter Martindale, sleeping in their bed. Their specially prepared living quarters were kept at a temperature of ninety degrees Fahrenheit with a humidity level close to eighty-five percent. The air was oxygen rich and filtered. All this approximated the jungle conditions where Tern's tribe lived and hunted.

Tern had prepared a corner of their living room for the occasion. She rolled back the carpet. She picked fresh leaves from the lush house plants provided in the habitat and gathered them in the corner, placing them on the floor to form a nest. She then removed her human clothing. Naked, she squatted over her nest and began to bear down, helping her baby into the world. It took thirty minutes. The boy dropped onto the leaves without a whimper. Tern gathered him up and blew into his tiny mouth. He began to breathe. Then she cleaned his body. His skin and hair was lighter than a Penditan baby. His milky eyes looked as though they might be blue someday, like his father's. Tern was pleased that the child was a male and that it resembled the other human babies she'd seen in the nursery. She bit the umbilical cord and ritually tied a knot through which she placed a curved bone amulet with Penditan markings along one side and the symbol of their deity, three circles in a line. The one in the middle was black. Standing, she placed the infant at her full breast and it began to suckle. Her milk flowed easily. She walked proudly back to the bed and got back into it, still holding the nursing baby. Later that morning when Peter Martindale awoke, he rolled over to say good morning to his wife and discovered he was a father.

It took some time for the doctors to convince Tern to let them examine the baby. Martindale's coaxing finally prevailed, but she insisted on staying with the infant in her sight at all times. The baby was healthy and vital. He was larger and heavier than the Earth-human babies. He did not cry as long as he felt his mother's presence. When the medical team moved him to the transitional nursery, he became agitated. There were four new Earth-human babies in there at the time. Tern heard her baby cry and rushed to take him from the nursery. As soon as she had him out of the room the crying stopped. The doctors tried to have her return the infant to the nursery but the same reaction occurred.

While this was happening, Alicia Sanchez was working on the final details of the Watership's departure. Two floors below the nursery, she suddenly felt uncomfortable and agitated. She heard the voices of babies in her mind. One of them was frightened, calling out for help. Then the cry was gone. Then it came back, this time stronger. She left her work and was guided up to the third floor where she saw Tern, Peter Martindale and their new baby. Alicia then knew why she had been called.

"He has to stay with you for a while," she told the parents. The doctors were annoyed, but knew that Dr. Sanchez was on the President's personal staff and had seniority in Operation Earthmother. "He is not yet in tune with the other children," she explained quietly. A moment later, Rose Lewis arrived. She had also been called by the new baby's cries. She understood his discomfort and suggested that Martindale take Tern and the newborn back to their quarters.

"He needs the warmth and humidity. He needs his mother's smell and touch. He wants her breast. Go now," she commanded gently, "I'll speak to the doctors." She then turned to Alicia. "Did you hear the child?"

"Yes. He was afraid."

"He will learn to communicate with them. The fact that he can hear them is good."

"I wish we could tell them why he is different, and that there will soon be others that will also be different."

"Maybe if we allow them some time to absorb those differences they will learn and teach," Rose suggested. The idea of newborn infants being able to construct their own complex social structure telepathically was too much for Dr. Sanchez to fathom. But there was enough conviction in Rose Lewis's voice for the scientist in Alicia to respect her theory. Rose was the one commander who seemed to have a special way with the babies and they responded to her presence.

Back in their quarters Tern and Peter Martindale comforted their new son. The infant was content to nurse and sleep in his mother's embrace. Once in a while he would awaken, as though called by a voice. He concentrated, his tiny brow frowned once or twice, and then he would go back to sleep. Rose Lewis knew that the other babies had understood the new baby was different. They were trying to communicate, but this time they called to him in their special language, one at a time and softly.

CHAPTER FORTY-ONE
IN THE COLONEL'S MIND

The morning of the Martindale birth, Brigade Commander Bernie Lewis had boarded an early flight from Houston to Nashville. From there he rented a car and drove northwest across the Kentucky border to the Fort Campbell Military Reservation. Bernie was a World War II veteran. He entered Buchenwald, the Nazi concentration camp, near Weimar, Germany on April 11, 1945. A month earlier, his kid brother Marty, a Marine, had been killed on Iwo Jima. He was a much decorated soldier and active in the Jewish War Veterans Association. It was easy for Bernie to get onto the post. He showed his veteran's ID and said he was looking for the son of an old buddy who he'd served with in Europe.

"Smith," he told the MP at the gate. "He's a bird colonel, I think."

"With the 101st?"

"No, I don't think so." Bernie put on a forgetful old man act. "Infantry. I think it's that new infantry with the letters... R something."

"RDF?"

"Yeah. That's it." The MP checked his officer roster on the computer screen in the guard post. He found it in a minute. "You'll want the 1159th Light Infantry. That's in a restricted zone so you'll have to go to base headquarters and call him from there." The young Airborne MP politely gave Bernie directions. As Bernie drove away he thanked the soldier. The young man snapped to attention and saluted. "My pleasure, sir. Welcome to Fort Campbell."

The commanders had discussed the propriety of Bernie's visit to the Army base. After Phillip Margolin revealed Gideon Mersky's plan to put the Brigade under the military "protection" of Colonel "Jimmy" Smith's elite company, Bernie and Ben wanted to know first-hand what they might be up against. The last thing they wanted to do was get into a power struggle with innocent soldiers, not to mention the possibility of hostility around their newborn babies.

"Having a look wouldn't hurt," Ben had argued.

"I'm a veteran. An old man. I'm just visiting to say hello. These soldiers love to put out for old guys like me... to show that they are as tough and ready as we were way back then." Bernie was persuasive.

Head Commander Ruth Charnofsky finally agreed, but warned him. "No interfering, Bernard. Stay out of that colonel's mind."

A man can have a head without a mind, Bernie thought to himself as he waited in the post headquarters dayroom remembering Ruth's warning. The OD, officer of the day, was a portly major whose uncle had served in Europe at the same time Bernie was there. Bernie told the major he wanted to surprise "Jimmy," so the message only requested that Colonel Smith come as soon as possible. He arrived twenty minutes later in combat dress, having been in the field preparing a night exercise with the firing range officer. The major brought Colonel Smith into the empty dayroom. As he came through the doors Bernie jumped into his mind with the impression that his was a familiar face.

"Mr. Lewis," Colonel Smith said, beaming as he approached Bernie. "What a surprise." He extended his hand. The major stood nearby smiling.

"Jimmy," Bernie began, "I'm sorry to bother. I was going to be nearby and I promised your dad I'd stop in. He says to give you a hug." Bernie opened his arms and embraced the colonel. As he did, he was back into the officer's mind, exploring his subconscious. Colonel Smith's father was retired in Arizona. His mother was dead. Bernie peeled some more layers and found the secret place where Gideon Mersky's mission against the Brigade was stored. He absorbed it in an instant and stored it away to be examined later. While he did that, which took a matter of seconds, he blocked the other commanders. Aunt Ruth would have cause to be very annoyed until he could tell her what Gideon Mersky was planning to do. Bernie spent the next hour passing the time pleasantly with Colonel Smith. They discussed his father at great length and the days they'd spent together in the "big war." After Bernie left Fort Campbell and was on his way back to Houston, the autosuggestion he'd left with Colonel Smith occurred. At the start of the night firing exercise for an inexplicable reason, just as Colonel Smith began briefing his staff, he urinated in his pants, wetting his camouflage fatigues and steel-plated, spit-polished, paratrooper jump boots.

CHAPTER FORTY-TWO
THE RELUCTANT INFANT

Three days later the third underwater cocoon chamber near The Stones was empty and the teams began work on the fourth and final chamber. Amos estimated that if the weather held they would be ready to leave Earth in two weeks at the most, maybe less if Cummings, Mr. and Mrs. Betters, and the old Greek Gabe, were able to help with the loading. Their processing was nearly complete.

Ellie-Mae Boyd, the African-American nurse and close friend of Commander Betty Franklin, went into labor five days after Tern gave birth. Her case was quite different. Her mate, Dr. Manterid, the chemist from Betch, could not help her. He had to remain in his controlled environment—a nitrogen-rich atmosphere, high humidity and moderate temperature. Ellie-Mae was familiar with the signs of labor. She'd given birth to six children in her Earth-life in North Carolina. But these pains were much more acute. At first, she and the attending doctors joked nervously, citing that a woman of her age should expect a little reminder that some time had passed since her last pregnancy. Beam did not see the humor. She was concerned. This baby was not coming as easily as any of the others.

After two hours of labor, they all agreed something was very wrong. Her cervix had dilated, her contractions were normal and strong, her muscle tone perfect. They decided to try a mild drug to stimulate more contraction. That only caused more pain. The medical team was anxious. Beam tried to telepath and relax Ellie-Mae. But something, or more to the point someone, was interfering. The two other Antareans present confirmed the birth procedures of the Hillet, Dr.

Manterid's race on Betch. It was very similar to Earth-human birthing. There was no answer there.

Another hour passed. The doctors began to discuss doing a cesarean section. Dr. Manterid was given a breathing source, rich in nitrogen, so he could be with his wife. He was deeply concerned. His anxiety and Beam's worry forced the medical decision. They prepped Ellie-Mae for surgery.

The cesarean section took only a half hour. The baby, a female, looking very much like a Hillet, only with darker pigmentation, was removed from her mother's womb. During the surgery it was noted that the placenta had an unusual growth on it. It resembled a small starfish and was attached to the umbilical cord where it joined the placenta.

After the cord was cut, the baby was rushed to the pediatric intensive care facility that adjoined the operating room. It was kicking and screaming. It was immediately apparent that the baby was in trouble. She began to gasp and turn crimson. Beam, satisfied that Ellie-Mae was recovering, went to the intensive care nursery where there was a crisis atmosphere surrounding the newborn. Then an idea rushed into her mind. Beam ran back into the recovery room where Dr. Manterid sat with his wife. She took his breathing apparatus from him and ordered, "Get Dr. Manterid back to his chamber!" Them she rushed back to the baby and exposed it to the nitrogen-rich mixture. The infant responded immediately by reaching for the breathing mask to pull it down to her face. "How did we miss that? Let's get this little girl down to her father's room." Later they learned that the babies in the nursery on the second floor had been agitated throughout Ellie-Mae's labor. They calmed down only after the baby girl was safely in her father's native atmospheric conditions.

The medical team was exhausted and embarrassed. This became more acute when Beam reasoned that the baby didn't want to be born. The prolonged labor was caused by the little girl refusing to leave the safety of her mother and enter an atmosphere that she knew was not breathable. The small starfish-shaped organ that had been attached to the umbilical cord proved to be an oxygen to nitrogen converter that Ellie-Mae's stem cells created.

It was, Beam remarked, a giant genetic leap forward. "It is long known that humanoid species interrelate and interbreed. But this mating was radical. Yet the Earth- human body adjusted and adapted. The infant survived and flourished in the womb, and then amazingly, she had the good sense to resist entering a lethal atmosphere."

"She was trying to tell us, and we were not able to understand," Beam said.

"But somehow you did," Dr. Fogelnest remarked wistfully, feeling inadequate at the moment.

"I was moved to do it," Beam suddenly recalled. "I believe it was those infants in the nursery below. I think they were warning the baby and then, when we took her out, began to warn me." Beam reflected silently for a long moment. "What are these children?" she finally asked herself.

CHAPTER FORTY-THREE
GETTING READY TO DEPART

Finally, with some luck with the weather and help from the Finley's, the last of the cocoons were loaded aboard the Watership. Dr. Macklow made a final dive aboard the Probeship to the chamber filled with seawater and checked the quality of the water with a sample taken from each chamber before they'd begun work. The salinity, temperature and viscosity were correct. The cargo chambers of the storage tank and Watership were sealed and put on automatic controls. Final plans for departure were computed and the flight crew did a thorough check of their massive, fully loaded spacecraft. Lift-off was scheduled for eight days hence, but they had some underwater traveling to do before then.

The Finleys would take the Probeship to a safe anchorage that Ben Green had located in the backwaters near Galveston Bay. At the last minute Amos Bright decided to go with them. They would all say their good-byes to the commanders and the Brigade people that were to remain behind. The Finleys, Perlmans, Hankinsons and Betty Franklin would return with Amos Bright via military aircraft to Homestead AFB.

They would then be driven to the *Manta III*. Jack Fischer and Phil Doyle would take them out to the Watership. By then Matthew Cummings, the Betters and Gabe would have cleaned up their earthly business and be on board. The rest of the Geriatric Brigade, scattered across the galaxy, needed their commanders.

The commanders gathered in a meeting room with Amos Bright, Beam and two Antareans. It was the first time they'd all been together in nearly eight months. The Mothership was on its way. The discussion centered mainly on the babies and their future. Mothership would bring the means to cocoon the infants and secure the mixed babies and off-planet parents as well. Bernie Lewis assured the commanders that there would be no trouble with Gideon Mersky once the President was informed of the Defense Secretary's maverick plan. Ruth Charnofsky, as Head Commander and the only human with Antarean citizenship, spoke last. She thanked Amos, Beam and the Antarean crew for their kindness and help in Operation Earthmother. Then she surprised everyone by putting forth a new idea that had been formulating in her keen mind for several days.

"There is no doubt that Ellie-Mae's infant girl will have to return to Betch," she began, her voice talking to no one in particular. It was more a stream of consciousness. "And of course we must anticipate that the two other mixed babies, when they arrive, might be faced with the same imperative. But the others, the Earth-human babies… well… I've been watching them and listening to them. They telepath to one another, you know. Yes, you know that. They seem to prefer speaking to Rose and those two nice young people downstairs. I think we must consider a very difficult possibility… it is that we might have to leave our babies here on Earth. I think this may be the place where they will grow the best and become whatever God has brought them to us to become." Then before anyone could comment, she gasped and doubled over in pain. It was not a labor pain. Something was radically wrong. Bess's thought passed to all the others. Ruth was the Chief of Commanders. Did this mean that because of the special processing and adaptations done to them, the commanders could not bear children?

CHAPTER FORTY-FOUR
LISTEN TO THE CHILDREN

Ruth and Panatoy's baby had been developing well inside the ninety-year-old Chief Commander. At her last examination, five days before the pain began, everything looked normal.

"Ultrasound is a great tool," the young doctor, Robert Chollup, from New York's Albert Einstein Hospital, said to Beam and the medical team assigned to Ruth Charnofsky's case, "but you have to know what you're looking for." His arrogance was exceeded only by his amazing, almost legendary skill as a fetal orthopedic surgeon. Fetal medicine had made slow but substantial progress in the past decade with the advent of high-resolution ultrasound examination procedures and genetic research.

"No one can be faulted for not noticing these changes, Doctor," Beam told him. "The baby's skeletal structure, especially the legs, developed at an abnormally accelerated rate during the past four days."

"Yes," Dr. Chollup agreed, nodding as he examined the ultrasound recording of the fetus taken the week before. "I give you that. But I would have anticipated some additional growth near term just by examining the father. His bone structure is very different from ours. As you can see, the fetus is now growing toward a pattern more in keeping with the ah... what is it? Subax?"

"Yes. Subax," Beam answered. "Can you do anything to alleviate the problem?"

"I can't stop the fetus from developing, unless..."

"Unless what?" Dr. Yee asked.

"Unless you want to terminate the pregnancy."

"That is an option of last resort," Beam suggested.

"Well," the young surgeon said, peering once more at the row of illuminated X-rays displayed on the wall next to him, "let's have a look again."

Beam knew the man had an answer to Ruth's problem, but she let the surgeon play out his game. "I think we can take a shot at something here. I look upon a fetus as a patient separate from the mother. I treat it as though it were out of the womb. But in this case I think the relief will be temporary. If the fetus continues to develop the way I think it will, we'll be back in the same boat next week, maybe worse."

"Then, Doctor, may I suggest you take care of the short term," Beam answered curtly, "and I'll see what I can do about the longer-range problem." Dr. Chollup smiled at the attractive female Antarean medical officer, acknowledging her with a patronizing tilt of his head. He was unaware her human appearance was only a protective skin covering. Had he any idea that she was reading his thoughts, understanding that the exterior bravado covered his insecurity about this case, he might have put aside the pretense. But that was his way and Beam knew it. *Let him be what he must,* she thought. *He is skilled regarding the Earth-human body. That is what Commander Ruth needs now.*

Subax is a tall race, living on a dark, cold planet rich in minerals and medicinal fungi. Their bone structure has evolved to accommodate the high gravity of the huge planet. Notably, their legs are long and muscular. In particular, their femur, the large upper leg thigh bone, and tibia, the main lower leg bone, are twice the weight of human bones and a third longer. The development of these bones in Ruth's baby had crowded the Subax-Earth-human fetus inside a human womb. The bones were pressing on the base of Ruth's spine, compressing nerves and threatening paralysis.

Dr. Chollup prepared Ruth with a local anesthetic. That relieved the pain and relaxed her. He then entered the amniotic sac with delicate instruments guided by a miniature video camera and light at the tip of a needle. The progress of the surgery was followed closely on the high-resolution ultrasound TV monitor. The baby reacted to the intrusion immediately, reaching for the needle and twisting violently in its warm safe fluid world. Dr. Chollup withdrew his instruments.

After carefully examining the blood flow and heart rate of the fetus, he decided sedation was necessary. "She's not going to let us in without a fight," he commented coldly as he inserted the needle again and with cool precision injected the fetus with a mild opiate derivative. The baby had a spasm, and then relaxed. Dr. Chollup then moved quickly to reinsert his instruments and operate. He placed tiny metal pins in the femur and tibia of each leg. Then, in a display of incredible manipulation, he stitched a thin, sterile wire between the pins. When he tightened the wire the baby's legs bent backward in a froglike manner. When they were bent at about forty-five degrees, he tied off the wire and withdrew. Beam was impressed.

"That was quite something, Doctor," she said with professional admiration.

"Thank you." His voice and manner were much calmer now. He knew he'd done a good job. His concern was now for the future. "The longer term is now in your hands, Doctor." That was the first time anyone had called her doctor on Earth. She felt accepted and proud.

"It's being taken care of, even as we speak." Her thoughts then went to the main nursery on the floor below where Alicia Sanchez and Phillip Margolin were trying to communicate with the more than twenty infants in residence there. But they were having no success. The babies did not understand what the images Alicia and Phillip were trying to project to them meant. Rose Lewis was also in the nursery. More and more, she was the one with whom the babies communicated. Perhaps because she was the only female commander who remained who was not pregnant? They loved when she held them. The older ones were now capable of smiles and laughter, especially when she telepathed love to them.

"They don't understand what we want," Rose told the two young scientists. Then she hit upon an idea. Telepathing up to Beam, she asked if Ruth was recovered enough to be brought down to the nursery. Beam asked Dr. Chollup, who said, "Yes."

A few minutes later Ruth Charnofsky was wheeled into the main nursery room, a large pale blue facility with bassinets and cribs in five neat rows concentrated in the center of the room. Along the walls were all manner of emergency equipment, ranging from incubators to complete life-support systems, specially engineered for infants. Off the main room were two laboratories for blood workup and immunization testing as well as genetic follow-up studies. The hospital was gathering quite a mass of data on these special infants.

"Put her in the middle of the room," Rose commanded, sensing the babies were beginning to understand they had a chore to do. She then turned her attention to her Chief Commander, "Ruth, honey. How do you feel?"

"Better. What are you trying to do?"

"I want to see if we can get these little ones in here to talk to your daughter in there," she whispered, stroking Ruth's distended belly.

"To tell her what? To stop growing?"

"No. To tell her to stop moving around so much because she's hurting her mother."

"If they can do that, tell them I'll give them all lollipops tomorrow."

"It's going to have to be a three-way conversation. Open yourself up to them. They're really quite delightful. But no words. They don't know many of our words yet. Give them images of Panatoy, the Subax, long legs, of your pain… whatever you can send them to tell the story."

"And then?" Ruth asked, whispering back to her fellow commander.

"And then they will send their thoughts to your baby… I hope."

Ruth began to reach out mentally to the babies around her. At first she felt nothing. Then, after a moment, she experienced a delightful, lightheaded sensation. Her mind was full of sparkling colors and laughter. There was joy in her heart. She was in the children's minds, innocence and love as they came to hers. She sent an image of the baby girl in her womb and the problem they were having. She sent images of what the doctor had done to keep the long legs away from her spine. Then, for a moment, the children left her conscious mind. When they returned only one came forward. It was the first-born girl, the daughter of the Messina's, whose name was Melody. Ruth felt her baby stir inside her. She then heard a stream of language that sounded like a song or chant; but in tongues—the babble that some possessed people, caught up in religious fervor, spew forth. Melody's conversation with Ruth's unborn daughter flowed through her. Then it ended abruptly. She had the sensation of her baby turning, adjusting her body. Then a voice...

"In one week take away the wires," Melody said. "She will lie still and not hurt you after that. She loves you."

Beam explained what was to happen to Dr. Chollup. At first he didn't accept her explanation that the babies communicated the procedure. But then Beam continued the story without speaking words and the good doctor understood that the universe held many secrets and wonders beyond his ken.

CHAPTER FORTY-FIVE
WATERSHIP AWAY

The *Manta III* arrived above the six-hundred foot wreck. It was time to say thanks and bid good-bye to Jack Fischer, Phil Doyle and Madman Mazuski.

"This time we are not as rushed to say farewell," Amos said to Jack after embracing the charter boat captain. "No old Earth-human jumping overboard." They all laughed, remembering that night five years ago when they made a hasty departure while being pursued.

"You got that right," Mazuski chuckled. "No Coast Guard choppers tryin' to shoot me down."

"Hey, guys" Jack said, extending his hand to the Finleys and Perlmans. "You guys take it easy now. Not too many space walks." He hugged Betty Franklin and the Hankinsons. "Good luck. Safe journeys." He turned back to Amos Bright. "And the next time you're coming, give us a little head's up. We'll get you some decent digs."

The visitors began to slip over the side and swim down to the Watership six hundred feet below. Amos embraced Jack again.

"I am forever in your debt. May the Master watch over you... all three of you."

"Thanks, Amos. Just remember we've got a date in about forty years or so..."

"That is my promise, dear friend. Farewell." He dove over the side and disappeared into the depths of the Atlantic.

A short while later, they were ready to begin the journey home. Light years across the Milky Way Galaxy, an entire planetary civilization on Antares waited to welcome home their brothers and sisters who had been asleep in their cocoons for over five thousand Earth years. The mission that had begun five Earth years ago was finally going to be completed.

The last operation to be done before departure was to bring the Parman guides inside from their chlorine chamber atop the flight deck. The storage tank, filled with the sleeping Antarean cocoons suspended in seawater, was safely attached beneath the Watership. Three of the flight crew helped the last of the glowing green Parman guides into the main deck. There were six of them, alert and satiated, ready to bring the Watership to Antares, or rather Antares to the Watership, depending on how one thought about travel with Parman guides.

In a brief ceremony before leaving their ocean bottom mooring near Boynton Beach, Amos introduced the Parman guides to the new passengers aboard. Having spent years on Parma Quad 2, the Finleys, Perlmans, Hankinsons, and Betty Franklin knew their race to be open and giving beings. But for Cummings, the Betters and Gabe, although they'd been processed and their senses enhanced, Parmans were only the second non-Earth-human life form they'd encountered. The Antareans had shed their human coverings and the three new space travelers adjusted to their ephemeral appearance. The translucency of their skin and lack of facial features was hardly alien as their presence was strong and assuring.

The Parmans are crystal-base beings with the green quartz-like covering and amorphous shape similar to crystalline structures on Earth. But they did have language, and projected waves of friendship and trust. Gabe greeted them first. He smiled, newly budding teeth popping through his now pink gums.

"Calimera," he said. "Good morning."

"*Calimera,*" the Parman nearest answered.

"Hey," Gabe chirped out, "these guys speak Greek."

"They can speak any language, if you teach them. They enjoy learning," Amos told the three newcomers. "We play a kind of game with them. We give them a new thought, a new idea for us, and they give us one back."

"I never thought I'd ever talk to a crystal," Coolridge Betters said aloud.

"Nor I a policeman," the Parman nearest to him answered.

"I think you all look beautiful," Paige Betters said.

"We cannot see the way you do. But we know of your beauty from within."

"And I never thought I'd be going traveling in space," Matthew Cummings said to the largest and oldest Parman guide.

"You are not yet," it answered, "and if we do not depart promptly, this old crystal will need another feeding."

Amos laughed as he removed his four molecule thick human covering. He then gave the order to the flight crew to begin the journey. Ahead of them, the nuclear submarine *USS Schulman* also moved east, running a mile or so in front of the Watership. It would keep an eye and ear out for intruders who might detect the huge Antarean craft deep beneath the surface. Above, the *USS Hapsas, USS Metz* and *USS Simi* also got underway, all heading due east toward the mid-Atlantic Ridge.

Two days later, after being shadowed by the Soviet submarine *Pomorze* and its companion guided-missile cruiser *Novosobirsk*, the Watership cover fleet reached its destination. Throughout the journey the American and Soviet vessels played a game of cat and mouse. But instead of the American ships and submarine, the Soviets were confounded by the huge metallic mass that filled their sonar screens. Playfully, the Antarean flight crew electronically changed the shape of their craft. At times it was another submarine. Then a mountain ridge... a school of blue whales and at times it completely disappeared. The captain of *Pomorze* reported to his fleet command that the Americans had developed a new, sophisticated sonar jamming device.

The Watership took leave of its escort, bidding Captain Walkly and the Navy Seal team that had been transferred from the *Orca* to the *USS Simi*, farewell. The Watership then dove rapidly to the deepest part of the Atlantic Ocean where no submarine could dive and where no sonar could see them. Three and a half miles down they reached the mountain peaks of the mid-ocean range. They continued diving until they reached the valley floor and the mid-ocean rift, an area of volcanic activity and geothermal upheaval. This was the place where two tectonic plates met. The Watership followed the rift valley north, steadily increasing speed, slowly engaging its ion drives. The pressure outside the spacecraft was hundreds of thousands of pounds per square inch, capable of crushing almost any manmade object. But the Watership was built to withstand pressure many times this load. It moved through the ocean depths as though it were air.

As they neared Greenland, where the volcanic activity increased, they turned northeast, skirting Iceland, up into the Greenland Sea, then under the thinning summer pack-ice, due north toward the magnetic north pole. At the predetermined time and place calculated by Phillip Margolin and Alicia Sanchez, the Watership engaged full power to its ion engines and sped toward the surface. It exploded through the pack-ice and soared into the bright arctic summer sky. The flight crew overdrove the ion engines so that an excess of negatively charged electrons flooded the atmosphere behind it. It sped away from the Earth at incredible speed. By the time human detection devices recorded it, it was gone. All that remained was a negatively charged image—a polar anomaly. The Soviets chalked it up to electric disturbance. The Chinese listed it as a solar disturbance that activated the Earth's northern magnetic field. The American observers on station in Greenland and along the Canadian DEW line filed a variety of reports. Among them, one young Air Force lieutenant with an active imagination suggested it was a UFO that had been submerged under the ice-pack.

A short time after that, the Watership picked up the two storage tankers left on the moon's dark side and set a course for Antares.

CHAPTER FORTY-SIX
A QUESTION POSED

By the beginning of September, three more babies had been born. Everything was normal. The nursery was flourishing. Ruth Charnofsky and her unborn Subax daughter were on good terms. Dr. Chollup had removed the wires and pins, and to his amazement the fetus had remained stationary. Studying the Earth-human-Subax female with extremely high-definition ultrasound, a machine he had specially flown in from New York, he watched in fascination as the baby flexed and toned its own muscles in her mother's womb. But the baby never stretched or pressed near Ruth's spine or other organs. As it grew larger it huddled tight into the fetal position, moving slowly, deliberately and only when necessary.

The parents who had gone to see their families began to return. For most it had been a magical, wonderful time, especially seeing children and grandchildren. None of the couples went to see old friends. What could they say to them? There was no more processing room, no way to take them along into their future. Many came back to Houston ahead of schedule. They had missed their babies, but in fact, also wanted to escape the reminders of what growing old in America, and the state of the world meant. Television news was filled with poverty, the homeless, brutality, war, religious and racial hatred—life here had not changed since they left. Earth-humans seemed intent on destruction and hatred compared to so many other worlds they had seen.

Marie and Paul Amato had gone to see their son in Boston. He was a Speech and English professor at Tufts. After the initial reunion with him, his wife and their two grandchildren they decided to take a week and drive into the New England countryside. It was a beautiful trip. "We've missed so much," Paul told Ben Green, "and left behind a part of our lifetime."

Marie saw things differently. "Our life is changed forever. This is our home-planet, but it can't be our home anymore. The steps we've taken, the places we've been... the long life ahead.... Well, I can't relate to Earth anymore. I feel as though I'm a visitor. It's the same way we felt on Hillet. Visitors."

"And what of our family?" Paul asked his wife, unhappy with her because she wanted to leave their son and grandchildren earlier than planned.

"Our family is now the Brigade. Our family is lying asleep in that bassinet on the second floor." She had tears in her eyes. "Our family now travels to every corner of the galaxy."

Another couple, who had gone to Denver where both their married children lived, told Beam similar things but in a different way. "We became intolerant of our children and grandchildren. Probably much the way they were intolerant of us as we grew old and set in our ways. But now we're the ones who have stretched... expanded. We can't go back to who we were before. When we left this planet, we left its ways forever."

"Not exactly," Beam answered. "You are back here for good reason."

"But not to stay," the couple answered. "What we mean is that we can never live here permanently again. Certainly not after what we have seen and done out in the galaxy."

No one was sure just where the idea was coming from, but after returning from their family visits several Brigade members began to have doubts about the wisdom of cocooning the babies. Even Beam was not convinced that was the best course of action. The closer the parents bonded with their children, the stronger the fear and doubt grew.

Peter Martindale's mate, Tern, asked the question as she held her son while he slept in their quarters. "Are there no places on Earth where it is warm and humid like on Turmoline?"

"Many," he answered.

"Then why take the child so far? This is home-planet for you. I am your mate. I can stay here with you and hunt."

Besides being a steelworker in his former life in Kentucky, Peter had enjoyed teaching others. He had dreams about taking his new son fishing and hunting in those Appalachian Hills he knew so well. He had thought about asking the commanders to allow him to stay behind. Some other parents had similar thoughts. And no one was very comfortable with the idea of putting the babies in suspended animation for such a long period of time.

Ruth, Beam, the Greens and Lewis sat with Alicia and Phil in their office on the first floor. LoCasio and Berlin, the two NASA assistants, had gone back to their regular jobs at the Johnson Space Center. Rose Lewis had called the meeting. She had news.

"Some of the babies are communicating in English," she began.

"Three can speak the language of the Penditan, Tern's tribe," Beam interjected.

"And the language of Betch as well," Ruth added.

"We know they communicate in Subax too," Mary added, glowing with her own pregnancy. Her baby was due in less than a month. It would be the last born.

"May I say something?" Phillip Margolin asked.

"Of course," Ruth answered. She too had the magic aura of motherhood about her. The daughter she carried continued to grow and remain still. Ruth sensed birth was imminent.

"Alicia and I have been talking. This may be way out of line and maybe none of our business, but if you're not sure about how cocooning or space travel will affect the children, why do it?"

"What other suggestion do you have?" Bernie Lewis asked.

"Stay here," Philip Margolin answered.

Bernie laughed. "I'm sorry. It's just that the memory of that gung ho mindless colonel is still a fresh memory. Look, part of this government means to hold us against our will. Defense Secretary Mersky knows a lot about us. Alma Finley told me he can block, and he is on the verge of understanding how to telepath. You know that, Phil. You know how dangerous that can be."

"All I'm saying," Margolin continued, "is that we might explore some alternatives."

"Such as?"

"Such as staying here." Alicia answered. "Staying on Earth in a safe place. The President isn't like Mersky. He would understand." The room was silent for several seconds as they all considered the idea carefully. "

"He's a politician," Bernie finally said.

"He's a good man," Phillip countered.

"Good men come and go. Governments change. The Mothership is on the way," Bernie remarked.

"The children don't want to leave," Rose announced. That shocked everyone.

"They told you that?" Ruth asked cautiously.

"No. I sense it. I think it would be a mistake to take them from here."

Beam had listened patiently. She decided it was now time for her to speak as Amos had instructed. "The custom of bearing young on home-planet is very old. Most of the traveling races like our own and like you would become always try to avoid the uncertainties of alien environments for the newborn. Until the young mature, no one can know what they are, what they can be. On home-planet, the genes are safe. Later, it will become clear who among them are space travelers, as they are possibly a new race of Earth-humans."

"And what about the mixed-mated babies?" Ruth asked the Antarean medical officer, knowing that though addressing Beam, she was speaking to Amos Bright as well.

"They are special. The Master mixes many kinds in the galaxy. Each is the beginning of new life, new possibilities. We will have to see what these are, and how they must be nurtured. So far, we know that Tern, the Penditan woman, has a child that can live on this planet. Ellie-Mae's Betchian baby cannot. It must be taken to where it can survive naturally. But the Earth-human babies can live here on Earth for now."

"And if we, the Brigade, stay," Rose asked. "What will become of us?"

"If you mean do I know if you will grow old and pass on," Beam answered, "I do not. The processing we did was to prepare you for space travel, to be like us, to move through the void as universal particles. The other change—this ability to reproduce again, to be free of disease... we have no idea what that status might be after returning to Earth."

"So we are faced with the same challenge as five years ago," Mary Green said softly. "Do we stay or leave?"

"Not exactly, Mary dear," Rose answered. "Who says that all of us must remain? It is only the children who may need to stay... who I sense really want to stay."

Alicia and Phillip had the same thought at the same time. "We could care for them, teach them and protect them." The commanders and Beam read their strong thoughts instantly. They all knew of the love the two scientists had for each other. It was also apparent they shared a deep mutual love for the Brigade children. And the children responded to them in kind.

Maybe it was the children who put the thought in the minds of those in that meeting. Perhaps it was worth considering that these babies knew something about their own future that their parents did not.

CHAPTER FORTY-SEVEN
THE BLUE BABY

Dr. Chollup stayed at the NASA hospital until Ruth Charnofsky gave birth to her Subaxian daughter. There was no doubt that it would be a cesarean section. She went into labor on the day of the Autumnal Equinox. That had no significance other than the child was named Autumn, although Skye would have been more appropriate. She was pale blue when born and appeared to have blonde or silver hair covering most of her long, muscular body. When the nurses had cleaned the infant and dried it, it became apparent that the hair was actually soft, downy fur. Autumn's features were human, but her body was Subaxian.

Panatoy viewed his daughter's birth on a closed circuit television hookup in the environmentally controlled apartment he shared with Ruth.

The baby was healthy and vital. Mary Green, now nearly three months pregnant, was relieved since Ruth was the first commander to deliver a child. Mary sent the word out to the other commanders, now light years away and being transported by their Parman guides toward Antares. Those commanders in turn sent forth the good news to Antares, where Ruth was an honored citizen, and beyond to the rest of the Geriatric Brigade scattered across the galaxy.

Ruth recovered rapidly from surgery. Her healing powers, common to the commanders, were phenomenal. Within a few hours she asked Beam to bring Autumn to her. Dr. Chollup was concerned. He had a proprietary interest in the beautiful blue downy infant. Something was wrong. The child's active demeanor at birth had slowly changed.

She was quiet. Listless. Her eyes, originally dark and clear like her mother's, were now glassy. Her temperature was normal. The blood tests were normal, similar to all the Earth-human babies. Dr. Chollup kept the baby in intensive care while he stayed by her side, monitoring and pondering what appeared to be Autumn's slowly deteriorating condition. When Beam came for the baby he immediately brought the infant to her. Ruth held the listless girl to her breast, but the baby would not nurse. Beam reached over and touched the infant's forehead.

"It is warm," she said to Ruth.

"Normal temperature," Dr. Chollup said.

"What does Panatoy say?" Ruth asked.

"He has not held the baby yet," Beam answered.

"Then take her to him. Quickly." Ruth's voice was firm. Dr. Chollup stopped Beam as she reached to take the child from her mother's arms.

"You can't put that child in such a frigid environment. It will kill her."

Beam hesitated. "We will wrap her in blankets."

"Hurry," Ruth begged. Her fear was apparent. Beam rushed out of the room with the baby. Dr. Chollup and two pediatric nurses followed close behind.

Panatoy held the child in his strong blue arms. He bent his face close to his daughter, parting the layers of blankets to see her face. His room was ice cold. In deference to the baby he had lowered the ultraviolet light necessary to his survival to the minimum level he could tolerate. Beam and Dr. Chollup, both dressed in heavy fur-lined Air Force parkas with hoods, stood nearby and watched with great interest. The Subax spoke to Beam in his language, which she understood and spoke.

"The child is ill. Do you know what is wrong?"

"No, Panatoy," Beam answered. "She was functioning normally at birth."

"How long has she been like this?"

"Nearly three hours. I am concerned."

The Subax stood. His height and deep blue coloring made him an impressive figure. Dr. Chollup stepped back a little.

"Is this the medical officer who helped Ruth while she carried my daughter?" he asked Beam.

"Yes. He is a very skilled doctor who has my respect."

"He is ignorant about the Subax. You, an Antarean traveler, should know better." Panatoy began to remove the blankets and clothing that had been put on the baby in intensive care. He threw the warm, bulky coverings aside, scattering them like a stripper in high-speed motion.

"He'll kill that baby!" Dr. Chollup shouted, moving to take the newborn from its father. Panatoy turned and faced the doctor as a lioness might confront a hunter who'd come between her and her cub.

"Tell him to stay away," Panatoy warned Beam. But she didn't have to tell the arrogant surgeon. Panatoy's glare and offensive body language were universal. A translation was not necessary.

Panatoy, stripped little Autumn naked. He turned up the ultraviolet light source to maximum and held his daughter close to the source of the light. Steam began to rise from her body as it cooled to the below-freezing Subaxian temperature.

"Oh, my God. He'll kill her," Dr. Chollup moaned. The baby was his patient.

Then the improbable happened. Once the baby's body stopped steaming, she began to move and howl with delight. She wriggled in its father's arms, reaching for the deep purple light source. Then she laughed. Not a small chuckle, but a gurgling of joy. Panatoy brought the naked baby down to his face and kissed her. The child grabbed at her father's face and thick long white hair.

"She is hungry," Panatoy told Beam. "Can you bring Ruth to us?"

In all his days in medicine, Dr. Chollup would never forget the sight of a woman over ninety, wearing protective eyeglasses, nursing her naked, blue, furry newborn in subzero temperature, dressed in a parka with special holes cut into it in order to expose her nipples to the baby's hungry mouth. Panatoy remained close to his family, as proud as any new father had ever been.

As her daughter nursed, Ruth Charnofsky's thoughts went out to Ellie-Mae Boyd, who was also nursing her new baby in the environmentally altered duplex next door. Ellie had to wear breathing apparatus since her mate, Dr. Manterid, and infant required an oxygen-free, nitrogen-rich atmosphere.

Both women knew their babies could never live naturally on Earth. Both would have to be returned to their father's home-planets, Subax and Betch.

CHAPTER FORTY-EIGHT
ALTERNATE PLANS

The NASA security people and the Secret Service detail assigned to the hospital by Benton Fuller performed efficiently. There had been no breaches of security since the Brigade arrived. When the Army colonel from Fort Campbell arrived and presented his authorization papers, personally signed by the Secretary of Defense, they were checked, double-checked and certified. He was allowed access to the first and second floors. Only special visitors, always with armed escorts, were allowed on the critical top floor.

Bernie Lewis was on his way to meet with Alicia Sanchez and Phil Margolin when he perceived a familiar presence in the hallway. He ducked into the doorway of the kitchen staff quarters. Colonel James "Jimmy" Smith was reconnoitering the hospital, making mental notes on various doorways and facilities. He was especially interested, as Bernie Lewis learned reading the intruder's mind, in the location of the security people, their number, posts and quarters. Bernie called up to Rose, who was in the main nursery on the second floor. He alerted her to close the floor visitors.

"Use any pretense. We don't want him near the children," Bernie told Rose.

The commanders met again, this time in Lewis's apartment. Sanchez and Margolin were there.

"That SOB Mersky has the arrogance to send his puppet soldier into our midst. We can't afford to wait any longer." Bernie was adamant. He wanted to confront the Secretary of Defense now.

Ruth had been confident that the attempt to detain the Brigade and their babies wouldn't be made until the last birth had occurred. But now that she was a mother, and in spite of her wisdom and abilities, she reacted protectively as any mother might.

"I think you're correct Bernard. But before we confront this problem, we'd better have a solution to the larger question. What are we going to do about the children?"

The night before, just for a change of pace and scenery, Sanchez and Margolin had gone into Houston for a first-class seafood dinner at Christie's and some laughs at the Comedy Workshop. On the spur of the moment they decided to take a hotel room for the night, winding up with a posh suite high above the glittering ribbon of nighttime traffic on the Southwest Freeway. The suite had a huge four-poster bed. The bath was a pink marble tub with gold fixtures. As they sat side by side in the warm scented water, sipping wine, relaxed and satiated, Phillip asked Alicia if she would marry him. She didn't say yes—she said, "Of course! What took you so long?"

At the meeting with the commanders, the young couple announced their intentions. Everyone was delighted. "We didn't tell you this just to garner some good wishes," Phillip told them.

"No," Alicia continued, "we've been giving the problem of the babies in space serious thought. We have an idea... sort of a plan..."

"But it can work," Phillip interrupted. "It can be the answer to all your concerns."

The meeting lasted for hours as the commanders listened carefully to the plan the two young scientists proposed. They questioned every detail of the proposal. Then, after they were sure Colonel Smith had left the premises, they went to look at the computer models Alicia had prepared.

"By God, I think it can work," Bernie said with a grin, "but it will require exquisite timing."

"It does answer the concerns we have about taking the babies into space," Rose added.

Ben and Mary Green weren't that positive. Their baby had not been born yet. "It will have to be put to a vote," Ben suggested.

Ruth was recovered from her operation and enjoying motherhood.

She knew her daughter would have to travel to Subax and that she would go too.

"A vote may not be the proper way," she finally said. "That is to say, *our* vote. The children have a voice too. Rose speaks with them."

"And with us," Phillip Margolin added.

"Yes. We know. The plan you two young people have devised is brilliant. But this is not an easy decision. We need more facts. And we need the births to be complete."

"That's only three to four weeks away," Bernie Lewis reminded her.

"Yes," the chief commander responded. "The Mothership is coming. We are here for it. We should develop two plans—one to leave and another to stay. Part of our decision will depend on what Bernard finds when he confronts Gideon Mersky in front of the President."

"You know that the children will want to have a voice in the decision," Rose reminded everyone.

"Of course," Ruth said. "But for now we must proceed on the basis that we are all prepared to leave with the Mothership. Bernard will go to Washington. I'd like you to accompany him, Ben," she asked the remaining father-to-be. "But if you want to stay here with Mary, I'll understand."

"The docs say we have three weeks to go," Ben answered. "I know Bernie can be a little long winded," he joked, "but even he can't talk for that long."

"All I need is a few minutes with that sleaze Mersky. I won't waste any breath," Bernie said, not finding humor in Ben's remark.

"Good," Ruth said. "Make your appointments in Washington for next week. I'll ask Jack Fischer to pay us a visit to get things moving on the other plan."

After the commanders had left, Alicia and Phillip went back to the model for their plan.

"Now that we've sold it, are you sure it can be done?" Phillip asked his new fiancée.

"Theoretically, yes. But until we try it for real… well… stuff can happen. But yes, it can work!" There was confidence in her voice.

He took her in his arms. "I love you," he whispered softly. "I want to have many children."

"Me too," she responded, caressing the back of his head. "And perhaps they'll have more playmates than they'll know what to do with…"

CHAPTER FORTY-NINE
AWAITING BIRTHS AND DECISIONS

It was mid-September. There were only six Earth-human couples and one mixed couple awaiting the arrival of their babies. The staff had been cut back and only one delivery room and intensive care team was on call. Everyone was confident that the births would continue to go smoothly. In the next two days two women went into labor and delivered healthy baby boys. They were moved without incident to the main nursery, which had become the busy center of the hospital. There were now twenty-two babies, ranging in age from four and a half months to four days, in the nursery. Three others were with their parents in the off-planet environmentally altered duplexes.

If the staff were able to hear the communication Rose Lewis monitored and joined between the babies, they would have been shocked. The children were learning at a rapid rate from observing their caretakers, from Sanchez and Margolin, from Rose Lewis and each other. The older ones, those born on the Watership as it came to Earth, were now absorbing and passing information from beyond the facility. Using Rose Lewis as a conduit, they reached out to the commanders on the Watership.

The Erhardt twins and Melody Messina were also telepathing with Amos Bright and Beam. It was apparent to the Antareans that these children were a special race of Earth-humans, created in part by what their space processing equipment had done to their parent's genetic makeup. It was possible that they were destined to be important instruments in the service of the Master.

The Watership approached Antares as the Mothership neared Earth's solar system. Decisions would have to be made about the future of the children and the Brigade. Amos communicated his thoughts in the Antarean language to all the commanders and Ruth Charnofsky.

"Our race has traveled the galaxy for millennia. As you know, we have chosen to reproduce our race with genetic improvement using science over time. Most of the traveling races tend to do that. But you Earth-humans are sudden travelers, thrust out into the galaxy with most abilities of Antareans—even of commanders. Your offspring appear to be unique. In the cosmos there are a myriad of beliefs regarding the existence of life, its purpose and its future. Many of the races keep to their own kind, as we Antareans have. Many others mix and interbreed, forming new races, new possibilities. They are in the majority. They believe that the grand plan, life, will mix and blend until there is one that encompasses all. There are many who believe we are all one now… that we come from one common universal seed placed among the stars by the Master, whatever he or that power might be. The one you Earth-humans call God. Who is to say what it means? The great civilizations, the laws, written and unwritten, the overwhelming respect for life—these great truths have been given to us by the mixed races, by the blending of the common DNA and genetic matter within the universal spark of life itself. These children are a new race. They are to be protected. I will confer with the Antarean council as soon as we arrive and pass along their opinion as to a plan of action."

Under instructions for Chief Commander Charnofsky, Jack Fischer had met with Mr. DePalmer at the Coral Gables Bank and located several promising situations that fit the alternative plan Sanchez and Margolin had developed. The final decision would be made after Amos Bright presented it to the Antarean Council, and after Bernie Lewis and Ben Green completed their mission to Washington.

A baby girl was born to a couple from New Orleans. It was the only child that had been conceived on Parma Quad 2. When the Parman guides on the Watership learned of the event they asked the flight crew to request that the child be granted citizenship on their planet. Amos sent the message and the parents accepted with gratitude. The girl was named Parmabelle.

That left only four Brigade mothers waiting to give birth.

CHAPTER FIFTY
CONFRONTATION

Bernie and Ben flew to Washington a week after requesting a meeting with the President and the Secretary of Defense. As they crossed the Key Bridge in a taxi, Ben looked back at Arlington National Cemetery. His only son, Scott, killed in Pleiku during the Tet Offensive, lay buried under one of the thousands of snowy white marble markers that covered the rolling Virginia hillside. Some minutes later, as they drove past the somber black marble Viet Nam Veteran's Memorial, upon which Scott Green's name joined fifty thousand others, Ben's thoughts went out to Mary with a silent prayer that their new baby would be a son.

Bernie understood his friend's emotions. He'd been a soldier too. He'd seen his friends die in foxholes next to him. He remembered the mass graves and still warm, corpse-filled ovens at Buchenwald. Both men understood they were about to confront a man who was planning to use military force to control their lives and the destinies of their children. Passing by these monuments to dead heroes, which also symbolized the senselessness of war and oppression, gave strength of purpose to both Geriatric Brigade Commanders.

"It's going to be all right," Bernie said to Ben as they approached the White House reception gate.

"Yes. And this time, I believe, life is going to be the winner!"

"Amen!"

Bernie Lewis and Ben Green had requested that in addition to President Teller and Secretary Mersky, Caleb Harris, the NBC Washington News Bureau Chief, Captain Thomas Walkly, the Navy

Undersecretary, and Doctor Khawaja also be present at the White House meeting. They all were gathered informally in the Oval Office, the place where President Malcolm Teller first learned about the Geriatric Brigade from Alma Finley. Only Gideon Mersky was not yet there. He had been unexpectedly detained by the crash of a Huey helicopter on a training mission at Fort Dix, New Jersey. Nine soldiers, there for advanced training, had been killed along with the pilot and co-pilot.

"Mrs. Finley sends her greetings, Mr. President," Bernie began after hello's were exchanged and they were seated in the middle of the room on two sofas and four matching arm chairs. "She is now aboard the Watership rapidly approaching Antares."

"She never called to say good-bye," Caleb Harris said wistfully.

"There was little time, and a great deal to accomplish," Ben told Caleb. "The Antareans are eternally grateful to all of you for your efforts that enabled them to bring their cocoons home after five thousand years."

"They are entirely welcome," President Teller said. "And please let them know they are always welcome in America." A momentary uncomfortable silence gathered in the room. Tension filled the air. Bernie and Ben knew it was something else. Gideon Mersky was nearby.

Ben let his mind open while Bernie blocked his. Mersky entered the room as his mind probed Ben's consciousness. *So he's learned to do it, Ben thought to himself,* masking the revelation as he sensed the Defense Secretary groping to make contact. Mersky gave his apologies, greeted everyone and sat down. He then continued to look into Ben's mind, but he was blocked.

"That's enough." Bernie Lewis's abrupt thought cut into Mersky's and the President's minds.

"What's enough?" the President asked, unaware that he had not heard the words said aloud.

"Our stay here on Earth," Bernie answered. "The time grows near when we must also depart."

Malcolm Teller was clearly surprised and disappointed. He glanced at Mersky with a questioning expression. "I thought you were going to stay," the President said. "Didn't you tell Secretary Mersky's people that the babies were too delicate to travel and that you were going to keep them here on Earth for a while until they were stronger?"

Ben Green now riveted his concentration on Mersky as he spoke to the President.

"No, sir," Mersky answered. "That was just a suggestion your medical staff made. It was never a firm decision. Dr. Khawaja can confirm that."

"That is true," the Undersecretary of Health told the President. "We believe it is dangerous for the infants to be subjected to the rigors of space travel as it was described to us by the Antarean medical officer, Beam. The children would have to be put into a state of suspended animation. The Antareans believe that such a procedure with ones so young might be very unwise."

"Nevertheless," Bernie Lewis said, "we've made the decision to leave. There is an Antarean Mothership scheduled to arrive shortly. We have begun our preparations for departure."

"I'm sorely disappointed," the President remarked. "Secretary Mersky was confident you'd stay. He's had a special living area, a secure compound, prepared for you out west somewhere. In Arizona, I believe."

"That's correct." Mersky spoke for the first time.

"I'm sure he has," Ben Green said sarcastically. "But it's time to end the games. The lives of our children are at stake." Ben's belligerent tone of voice confused everyone except Bernie Lewis and Gideon Mersky.

Before the President could assess that there was a problem, Gideon Mersky stood. As he did, both Brigade Commanders sensed that Colonel Smith was outside the Oval Office and he was armed.

"Mr. President," Mersky began, his tone of voice even and measured, "you will recall several months ago, when these senior citizens returned from their adventures in space, I took the position that they were obligated as Americans to share their knowledge and special talents with the rest of their countrymen. The woman, Mrs. Finley, insisted otherwise, and, in my opinion, used her extrasensory powers to persuade... no to actually force you to give them everything they needed to secretly have their babies and get those cocoons out of our territorial waters."

At any moment it was possible for either Bernie or Ben to stop Mersky, but they chose to let him continue. Mersky's voice grew stronger now as he came to his conclusion.

"At your insistence I put military facilities, manpower and equipment at the disposal of these people. Undersecretary Walkly informs me the Navy budget alone was more than three million dollars. I imagine the NASA figures might be twenty times that. We have spent taxpayer's money. We have been party to a conspiracy to perform secret activity within the borders of our own country with aliens. Now we are being told thanks and good-bye. For me, as a government official and as an American, that is just not good enough. Deny it or not, these people here and in Houston are Americans. The others, the aliens that travel with them, are in this country without a visa. They all come under United States law. I believe the time for accountability has arrived. I believe they are manipulating us. I believe they have subtly forced and coerced us into supplying and fulfilling all their needs without once offering anything in return."

"What do you want?" Bernie Lewis asked calmly.

"The list is long," Mersky replied immediately. "To begin with, this talk about leaving in a few weeks has got to end. Your country has need of the technology you and these Antareans possess. We want to learn how to use telepathy as you use it. We want…"

"That's enough," Ben Green said aloud, cutting Mersky off. "Mr. President, it was explained to you months ago that we no longer consider ourselves Americans. We are human beings from planet Earth. We are galactic travelers. We have come home to bear our children. That is now our natural way of things…"

"You're back in America!" Mersky cut in. "We have our own way here!"

"BE SILENT!" Bernie Lewis commanded. His authoritarian voice stilled the room. At the same time, Bernie sent and unheard emotional shock through Gideon Mersky's mind that stunned the Defense Secretary.

"Now just a minute…" President Teller began.

"We're sorry. There are no more minutes, Mr. President," Ben said quickly. "Outside your office door right now, an armed American Army colonel is prepared to harm Mr. Lewis and myself."

"What?" The President was visibly shaken.

"He's only there if these two don't listen to reason, Malcolm," Mersky said, having recovered from the jolt Bernie sent through him.

"There'll be no gunplay here!" The President was incensed. "Just who the hell do you think you are, Gideon? This is the office of the President of the United States, not some back alley for kidnapping." He stood and went to his desk. He rang his reception secretary. "Midge? Is there an Army colonel out there?"

"Yes, sir," was the reply on the speaker phone.

"Please send him in here immediately."

"Yes, sir." A moment later, Colonel James Smith entered the Oval Office. He started to walk toward the end of the office where everyone was seated.

"That's far enough, Colonel," the President said. Smith stopped and stood stiffly at attention. He saluted.

"Yes, sir."

The President approached him. "Colonel Smith, what were you doing in my outer office?" Smith glanced over at Mersky. "I'm asking you a direct question, Colonel, and as Commander in Chief I'm ordering you to answer me. Now!"

"Yes, sir. I was ordered there by Secretary Mersky."

"For what purpose?"

"This is difficult, sir."

"Answer me, Colonel, or you'll answer a General Courts Marshal." Mersky stood up. "Answer the President, Jimmy."

Malcolm Teller spun around and pointed his finger at Mersky. "You sit down. This officer is under my command, not yours." He turned back to Colonel Smith, who had turned pale. "I'm waiting, Colonel."

"Yes, sir. I was there under orders from Secretary Mersky to be prepared to take those two gentlemen into custody." He pointed toward Ben and Bernie.

"How?"

"By force if necessary."

"If they resisted?"

"I was to shoot to maim and subdue them."

"I see," President Teller said softly. "Is there anything else you want to say?"

"Well, sir... yes, sir. My command, the 1159th Light Infantry Brigade, is under orders to take charge of that wing of the Space Medicine Center at 0230 hours tomorrow morning." The colonel looked down at the rich blue carpeting that bore the Great Seal of the President of the United States.

"Surrender your sidearm," Malcolm Teller told the officer. "I am now ordering you to place yourself in the custody of the chief of my Secret Service detail. He is in his office adjacent to my secretary. Good-bye, Colonel."

Smith unsnapped his holster and placed his silver-plated .45 on the coffee table. He then saluted the President and left the office. President Teller turned to Captain Walkly. "Tom, please get on the horn and notify the base commander... where would that be, Gideon?"

"Fort Campbell," Mersky said quietly.

"Of course. Notify General Packlaw of the 101st Airborne that I'm ordering the 1159th confined to barracks until further notice." Walkly left the room to issue the President order immediately.

"Now," the President continued, "let's get a few things straightened out here..." He proceeded to explain to Gideon Mersky that he, Malcolm Teller, was the President, that the Geriatric Brigade, the Antareans, the other off-planet parents were his guests and guests of the United States under his executive protection. He made it clear that their space vehicles, Operation Earthmother, and the removal of the cocoons using military personnel and equipment were done as a direct order from the President. "No one forced me, Gideon. No one got into my mind. No one coerced me. I know what these people are capable of doing. But not once did they resort to violence or coercion. But you were ready to do violence, weren't you? These people are correct when they say we still live in caves. I am ashamed. I want your apology for what you've attempted, and I want it now."

"I apologize," Mersky said unhesitatingly. "I only thought I was doing what was best for the country."

"That, thank God, is my job." The President then ordered Mersky to cooperate with Bernie and Ben. "If you cannot, then I'll have your resignation."

"They will have my complete cooperation, Sir," Mersky answered. "And you can have my resignation whenever you wish." Ben and Bernie knew Mersky sincere and beaten.

"Good. Now let's help these folks get to wherever they have to go. Dr. Khawaja, is there anything we can do to help them protect those babies in space?"

"We don't have that kind of technology, Mr. President."

"The Mothership will arrive soon. We are in communication with our commanders on the Watership and Antares." Bernie said. "We are confident we will have an answer to that problem. Now, what we'd like to discuss is the plan Mr. Margolin and Dr. Sanchez have devised to bring us all up to the Mothership."

Caleb Harris, who had quietly watched the events in the Oval Office, had a thought. "You know, Mr. Green, this visit... everything that has happened... well, it won't remain a secret forever."

"Yes," Ben responded. "We understood that from the moment we knew how many people would be involved in Operation Earthmother. We have begun to release staff from Houston and take over the care of the children ourselves. Some of the medical data, videotapes of the births and of our off-planet guests are missing or have been copied. We expected that. Perhaps it is time that the human race knew they are not alone in the universe."

"May we tell them?" Caleb asked.

"After we are gone, we expected you to do that," Ben said. "How much you tell, we suggest be done slowly and thoughtfully. You will be revealing things that will be at odds with many beliefs and myths. It will change the world... for the better we hope, but we urge caution.

"But for now," Bernie Lewis interjected, "it is critical that you keep a lid on it until we are gone."

"Of course," the President agreed.

After they had revealed and set up coordination of the departure plan, and finalized areas of responsibility, the meeting was over. Mersky had been quiet during most of it, answering only when asked a question or if he saw a flaw in the plan. There were few such times. Sanchez and Margolin had done their homework. The President had a few more questions to ask Ben and Bernie before they adjourned. "You are sure that there is no way we could convince some of you to remain behind for a while?" Malcolm Teller asked.

"I'm afraid not," Bernie answered.

"What if Secretary Mersky's plan had worked?"

"You mean if you had taken us prisoner?" Ben asked.

"Yes. Would you have fought the soldiers?"

"We would not. Neither would the Antareans or the other off-planet beings. I think they would respect our wishes."

"But what if we threatened to separate you from the babies?" Caleb asked.

"I'm seventy-eight," Bernie said. "Most of us are pretty old by Earth standards. If you tried to hold us here against our will, then I believe we would die. We know what it is to grow old here, and we know what it is to face the prospect of a very much longer life out there among the stars. The advanced beings we've met have evolved to know that no one can own another being; no one can enslave another being or imprison one. Threatening a life, imprisoning a body, making war, hating those who are different... at the moment, all of that is the way of this planet. I have not been away that long to have forgotten what we Earth-humans have done to one another. I was one of those GI's who liberated Buchenwald concentration camp." Bernie sighed and took a moment. "But," he then continued, "we have learned, out there among the stars of our Milky Way, that when you threaten another, when you kill senselessly out of petty hatred or greed or fear, then you are no longer part of life. You have only succeeded in destroying yourself."

"I understand," the President said. "But you didn't answer Mr. Harris about the babies."

That is true," Ben said. "Bernie was speaking for the Brigade. The babies can only speak for themselves. Perhaps someday they will answer that question for us. But if you want my opinion, if the soldiers, if anyone tried to imprison us, or them, the infants would protect themselves."

"How could they do that?" Caleb asked.

"I wouldn't even venture a guess," Ben answered.

"And I wouldn't want to be around to find out," Bernie stated flatly.

CHAPTER FIFTY-ONE
DEPARTURE APPROACHES

On the first of October, Tommachkikla, "Tom," the farmer from Destero, held his son proudly above his head, spinning and dancing with happiness. His wife, Karen Morano, formerly of Mill Valley, California, delighted in his joy. Their living quarters were divided into a hot, oxygen-rich room for Tom to match conditions on Destero, and a normal tropical Earth atmosphere room for her. The infant was comfortable in both environments, but seemed to prefer his father's more. The baby boy was the last of the mixed matings

Nine light years from Antares, drawn along in the solar orbit of the first-magnitude star Vega, a Mothership dwarfed the Watership, with its three storage tanks in tow, rendezvoused and linked.   A team of scientists and medical officers from Antares onboard the Mothership that was on its way to a giant red star in the Perseus arm of the galaxy transferred to the Watership to inspect the cocoons and travel back to Antares with them. A huge celebration was being planned for the homecoming with special accolades for Amos Bright. Also aboard were cocooning experts who studied the data available on the human and mixed babies back on Earth. It was decided that the risk was not as great as Beam had feared. The infants were growing physically and developing mentally at an astounding rate. Most of the experts concluded that they would survive the journey to the oxygen-water planet in Quad 2 that had been graciously set aside for them by the Parman civilization. The Antarean crafts then detached, and each went on its separate journey with the blessing of the Antarean council.

One more Brigade woman gave birth to a son. Three days later another boy was born, leaving Mary and Ben Green as the only occupants of the top floor left to become new parents.

During his years on Parma Quad 2 Bernie and Rose Lewis had been translators and lived with the Parman guides. Because they were to be used aboard the Antarean spacecraft, Bernie had to learn everything he could about the various Antarean space vehicles. He could pilot any of them.

Bernie Lewis spent most of his time in early October teaching Jack Fischer, Phil Doyle and Madman Mazuski to pilot the Probeship. They made several practice trips under and above the ocean, barely skimming the surface, from Galveston Bay where the Probeship was secreted, to a small cove called Sea Feather Bay on the British Crown Colony of Cayman Brac in the Caribbean.

Jack, with the aid of Mr. DePalmer, had purchased a defunct hotel and forty acres including the sequestered cove on Cayman Brac. The hotel was in disrepair, but sat high on a bluff that commanded a view of the whole island and surrounding crystal-clear waters. With local workmen cleaning up and making necessary repairs, and some paint, Jack estimated the place would be livable in two weeks.

By this time, all of the Brigade parents who went out to visit their families had returned to Houston. Most of the medical staff was gone, instructed to maintain secrecy. President Teller had signed an order making it a class A felony to do otherwise. The care of the infants was in the hands of the Brigade parents, Beam and two of her Antarean medical team. Mary Green knew she would not have time to see her family again, but hoped that the baby would come in time for Ben to make a fast trip to Scarsdale. Because he was so busy, he hadn't had a chance to visit.

Alicia Sanchez and Phillip Margolin were married by a Catholic Priest and Reform Rabbi in the multidenominational chapel at NASA. Then, after one final meeting with NASA and the Defense Department staff to coordinate the movement of the Brigade to the Mothership, the young married couple said their farewells and left on their honeymoon. They were honored guests of Jack Fischer at his refurbished hotel on Cayman Brac.

The Brigade anticipated their departure. On instructions from special medical team on the Mothership, which was fast approaching our solar system, the babies were prepared for spaceflight. Their food intake was reduced. They were kept in a cool environment that lowered their body temperature. But even with the assurances from the Antarean Council and Amos Bright, Drs. Yee and Khawaja were worried about the children going into space.

On October ninth, Mary Green went into labor. With her husband at her side, Dr. Yee and Beam delivered a beautiful baby boy and placed him on her chest. She and Ben tearfully named him Scott in honor of their first son, who was born and died on Earth. Their tears were of joy and remembrance. "The soul never dies," Beam reminded them as she took little Scott Green and left with him for the intensive care nursery.

President Teller came to Houston for his last visit. He was optimistic about the safety of the children and about seeing the Brigade people again. Bernie Lewis spoke for all of them.

"We have contacted the others in the Brigade and told them about the babies. They now know they can safely start new families if they wish and will be welcome on their own home-planet, Earth."

"Will we see any of you again?" Teller asked.

"From our travels in the galaxy," Mary Green answered as she held her newborn son, "we have learned that anything and everything is possible."

"Keep in mind that governments change," the President said. And if the world learns of your existence, the Antareans... the life you have found in our galaxy... well, who knows what that knowledge might mean.

"We can hope it will be a positive," Ben Green said. The others agreed.

Gideon Mersky, who accompanied the chief executive on this trip, had never been to the hospital. He had never seen the babies. "At our last meeting in the Oval Office," he said to Bernie Lewis, "I apologized for my actions. I am truly sorry. Now that I see these children, I know how special they are to all of us. I can feel their strength and the power of their future."

For reasons known only to Bernie Lewis, later that day he took Gideon Mersky aside and asked the Defense Secretary if, when he'd grown old enough, he might contemplate joining the Geriatric Brigade.

"At a moment's notice," was the enthusiastic reply.

"That is good to know," Bernie said, ending the conversation but making no promises.

When Ruth Charnofsky asked why he'd done that, Bernie replied, "Just planting seeds that might bear important fruit one day."

The next day Ben Green made a fast trip to New York and spent five happy hours with his family in Scarsdale. Their farewell was teary. But the knowledge that Mary and he could reach out to them from across the galaxy with thoughts of love tempered the sadness of the parting.

On October fourteenth, the Mothership entered our solar system, disengaged her Parman guides and decelerated along a trajectory plotted to intercept Earth's orbit in eleven hours. They would then anchor and wait on the dark side of the moon.

That night, under the blanket of darkness, the hospital was abandoned. They divided into three groups. The first and largest consisted of the Brigade parents, led by commanders Mary and Ben Green.

Next a smaller group traveled in special steel cargo containers with the required controlled atmospheric environments for Panatoy and his daughter, Dr. Manterid and his son and Tommachkikla and his son. Their human spouses led by chief commander Ruth Charnofsky traveled with them. Beam and her two Antareans, also traveled with this group.

The last group was the babies. Each was encapsulated in a plastic container with life-support systems attached. They were an adaptation of the intensive care incubators Dr. Yee had originally designed and supplied when the Watership first landed months ago in the Atlantic. Traveling with the babies were Peter Martindale, Tern and Bess Lewis.

Bernie Lewis traveled alone to the secret anchorage of the Probeship. At the proper time, according to the plan designed by Sanchez and Margolin, he would join the others.

The three groups boarded separate military aircraft and flew off to their designated locations.

In the early morning hours, President Teller's Press Secretary, Margo McNeil, called the television networks and requested a White House hookup for a special announcement. Just before dawn, Eastern Standard Time, President Teller waited to inform the American public and the world that shortly, in an exercise designed to insure the future of space exploration, there would be three separate and consecutive launchings of the American space shuttles *Liberty*, *Freedom* and *Brotherhood*.

CHAPTER FIFTY-TWO
LAUNCH

The first launching was from Wallops Island, Virginia. The space shuttle *Liberty*, with the Brigade parents, lifted off just as the sun rose on the horizon to the east. The passengers onboard nestled comfortably in the cargo bay aboard a specially sealed and life-supported container that could be released intact into space. It was painted a deep red color.

At the same time President Teller stood at a podium in the Lincoln Room and smiled out at an audience of bleary-eyed reporters. He read from a prepared statement.

"The United States," he began, "is about to take a first step in the development of a long-range deep space exploration program..." He went on to detail that there would be three shuttles launched within a few hours of each other. The first, from Wallops Island, was on its way. The three would eventually rendezvous in a high orbit and deposit the initial materials required for the construction of a huge space platform from which future space exploration would evolve.

There was nothing new in the plan or program. The surprise was that it had begun suddenly, without announcement or press coverage of the launches. An irate media fired questions about the secrecy at Malcolm Teller.

"The reasons for our decision to launch and commence platform construction will be made public at a later date. At this time I can only say that they are compelling reasons and I am certain that the American public will concur with my decision."

Angry reporters, who had become used to the game of embarrassing, baiting or badgering American presidents at press conferences, began to fire questions that bordered on arrogance and disrespect for Malcolm Teller. He responded in the calm, measured manner of a man who knows he has all the cards in his hand.

Later that day the opposition party would call for Congressional investigations. The President just smiled, stating, "That has always been the right of Congress. Investigation and honest discussion is what makes our democracy work."

In a few weeks the fantastic visit of the Brigade parents and their friends would be known. The world would have proof that Earth was not the center of the universe, that a myriad of life existed beyond our troubled, polluted, rather backward planet, and that if we ever had hopes of joining the rest of God's living creatures, we'd best clean our own house and put it in order.

Freedom, the second shuttle, lifted off from a previously unused NASA backup launch facility on Padre Island, Texas. It was an hour after *Liberty's* launch, just as dawn reached the south Texas coast. On board, nestled in the cargo bay in specially sealed life-support containers, were the Antareans and three of the four mixed couples. Peter Martindale, Tern and their infant son were aboard the third shuttle.

Bernie Lewis guided the Probeship out of Galveston Bay as *Freedom* separated from its booster rocket tanks high above. He kept the sleek craft submerged for several miles until he'd cleared the last of the offshore oil-drilling platforms that dotted that part of the Gulf of Mexico. Surfacing, he slowly rose into the air at subsonic speed. Climbing to a commercial airline altitude of thirty-thousand feet, he circled his craft back toward the Texas coast. The sun was rising. He began to climb and gather speed over the west Texas desert. Then, as *Liberty* reached orbit and *Freedom* was well on its way to joining her sister shuttle, Bernie fired the ion drive and rocketed the Probeship into a parallel trajectory with *Freedom.*

The third shuttle, *Brotherhood,* had its launch from Vandenberg AFB in California delayed fifteen minutes. There was a suspected leaky gasket in the special white cargo container that housed the babies, Rose Lewis, Peter Martindale, Tern and their infant son. The gasket was removed and replaced. The lift-off took place without any problems. The babies were all safely nestled in their containers that would absorb the stress of lift-off. Rose, seated among them, listened to their excited chatter. They knew they were leaving Earth. They also knew the plan.

The purple to deep blue California dawn sky lit up as the powerful main rockets lifted *Brotherhood*'s precious cargo into an orbit that would eventually coincide with those of *Liberty* and *Freedom*.

The Antarean Mothership slipped out from behind the moon and drifted toward the planet Earth, glittering as a bright morning star in the sky. On the flight deck the Antareans monitored the progress of the three shuttles as they closed on one another in a orbit more than twenty-thousand miles above the blue planet.

Bernie Lewis shadowed *Freedom* and communicated with the commanders on board the shuttles as well as the Mothership.

Five hours after the launch of *Brotherhood*, the three shuttles converged at the apogee of their polar orbit. They presented a large radar target. The world was watching. The Mothership aligned with Earth, keeping the shuttles between it and the magnetic north pole. It closed in on the shuttles as they orbited in formation, emitting powerful radar blocking of the Mothership.

Bernie Lewis departed from the trio and flew up to the fast-approaching Mothership. He entered the huge craft through a cargo membrane and parked. He then proceeded to the flight deck where he greeted and embraced many old friends.

At the predetermined point, *Liberty* opened its cargo bay doors and released its red cargo container into space. Moments later *Freedom* did the same. Its blue container floated in a tumbling orbit, slowly drawing away from the shuttle formation. Finally, with what was the most precious cargo of all, *Brotherhood* released the children in their white container. For the first time in months the members of the Geriatric Brigade and their offspring were free of home-planet Earth's gravity.

The Mothership descended rapidly toward the floating, tumbling cargo containers and gently plucked each from the void into the Mothership through its cargo membrane. Within a few minutes, the containers were safely aboard.

Speaking from the flight deck, Bernie Lewis thanked the American shuttle crews for their excellent work. Then the Antarean Mothership slowly turned away from the trio of shuttles. The Parman guides were set in place above the flight deck. The membranes were sealed, and the Mothership sped away toward deep space, leaving the empty shuttles behind like a huge bumblebee deserting flowers from which it has drunk all the nectar.

Those back on Earth, aware of what was happening, felt a deep sense of loss. Yet they knew they had experienced something truly wonderful. They had met beings from other worlds, and had, for a brief moment, a glimpse of what their own race might someday become.

EPILOGUE

The shuttles remained in orbit for three more hours, then separated and commenced their individual descents to Earth.

As *Liberty*, the first shuttle, approached its landing strip at the Kennedy Space Center on Cape Canaveral, the Mothership slowed down and eventually came to a dead stop in the orbit of Venus. The cargo membrane opened and the Probeship, piloted by Bernie Lewis, sped out and away from the huge host vessel.

As *Freedom* glided safely onto the runway at the White Sands Space Harbor in New Mexico, something that appeared to be a meteor streaked across the darkening Caribbean skies. Bernie Lewis, with Bess in the co-pilot seat, guided the Probeship through the Earth's atmospheric enveloped in a fiery descent.

As *Brotherhood*, the last of the shuttles launched that morning, came to halt on the five-mile runway in the dry, hot desert of Edwards AFB in California, the Antarean Probeship plunged into the water of the Caribbean Sea, five hundred miles south of Miami.

A few hours before dawn, the powdery white sands of Cayman Brac glistened like silver ribbons below Jack Fischer's renovated hotel. On the balcony overlooking Sea Feather Bay, the newlyweds, Alicia Sanchez and Phillip Margolin, held hands and breathed in the sweet predawn air. Peter Martindale and Tern joined them as the sky to the east lightened.

In the lush rain forest below the hotel, Jack Fischer, Phil Doyle and Madman Mazuski carefully covered the Probeship with camouflage netting as the sun rose in a clear pink and blue sky.

On the top floor of the hotel, now renamed Butterfly House, Bess and Bernie Lewis tucked the last of the Brigade infants into their cribs. The Lewises, Martindales, Margolins, Jack Fischer and his two friends would all share in the care and upbringing of these very special Geriatric Brigade children on their mother's home-planet. Through the commanders, their education would be universal in scope while their secret home on Earth nurtured and protected them. Time would tell what they would become.

The children lay quietly with their eyes open toward the heavens above. They all heard the same message beamed from the Mothership as it left our solar system in Quad 3 of the Milky Way Galaxy.

"Serve the Master as we do.

"We are joined to you forever.

"Grow in peace.

"We love you."

Acknowledgments

Roger Challop, MD—Director, Washington Heights Pediatric Group; New York Associate Clinical Professor of Pediatrics, Columbia University, College of Physicians and Surgeons

John Driscoll, MD—Director, Neonatal Intensive Care Unit Babies Hospital; Professor of Clinical Pediatrics, Columbia University, College of Physicians and Surgeons

Ming-Neng Yeh, MD—Consultant in Ultrasound, Department of Obstetrics and Gynecology, Columbia University, College of Physicians and Surgeons

Captain Dick Pleasantdon—Boynton Beach, Florida

Captain Joe Klein—Boynton Beach, Florida

Capt. Alan L. Bean, Ret. U.S. Navy—Astronaut—Retired from NASA June 1981

Mr. Robert T. "Terry" White—Public Affairs Specialist, NASA

Mr. Douglas K. Ward—Deputy Director of Public Affairs, NASA

Mr. John E. Riley—Chief of Media Services Branch, NASA

Ms. Susan Allison—my original "out of this world" editor

Ms. Susan Schulman—who did it again

John Silbersack and Rachel Mosner—who brought me into the e-book world

Jason Katzman—my editor at Talos Press

John Jay Moore—whose designs speak volumes

Alexandra Rutsch—whose art captures all

Ellen Saperstein—my primo editor and life-long support

Elizabeth Saperstein—my eagle-eyed copy editor

Ivan Saperstein—the best son and intellectual property attorney ever